ONE L
ENCORE

THE PETE PETERSON TAPES PART III

Des Tong

APS Books
Yorkshire

APS Books,
The Stables Field Lane,
Aberford,
West Yorkshire,
LS25 3AE

APS Books is a subsidiary of the APS Publications imprint

www.andrewsparke.com

First published worldwide by APS Books in 2024

A catalogue record for this book is available from the British Library

ONE LAST ENCORE

CHAPTER ONE

The darkness threatened to engulf her as she desperately fought against it. She was underwater, and her lungs were bursting as she tried to swim back up to the surface. The harder she tried to use her legs and arms, the more she felt herself being drawn into the abyss.

What was it they said about your life flashing before you as you were about to die?

Suddenly she was back in Ballykobh sitting on a park bench with her sister. Her dad was taking their picture with his new camera. She was telling him she didn't like the bow her mum had insisted she wear in her hair, but he couldn't hear her because he had become Gerry Fortuna, and he was down on one knee asking her to marry him. She reached out to say yes, but now he was lying in her arms with a knife sticking out of his chest. She cried out, but no one could hear her because she was surrounded by young girls screaming. They were trying to reach Pete Peterson, but he was being held back by Mandy Velasquez who put a gun in her mouth and pulled the trigger. The noise was so loud it frightened Janine and she found herself falling down a never-ending flight of wooden steps. The pain in her stomach was terrible as she hit each one, and then she was back in the water. It was cold and inky black. She couldn't hold her breath any longer and was about to give up, when a pair of arms encircled her, pulling her upwards.

She slowly opened her eyes. She had no idea where she was, but there were lots of tubes attached to her body, and she was lying in a bed with crisp white sheets. She blinked as her eyes adjusted to the light and saw people standing around her who she thought she recognised. Then a man in a white coat was talking to her, and she felt a small prick in her arm. She was instantly tired and closed her eyes again. This time she wasn't underwater, and she fell into a deep sleep.

Janine Law had been in a coma for two days and almost died when her heart stopped. Fortunately, the quick reactions of the doctor and nurses had saved her. Now she was lying in a hospital bed, recovering from the tragic miscarriage she'd suffered while escaping the violent events at Benny Mulligan's villa on Coconut Grove in Miami. She'd been rushed straight into the operating room, suffering from severe internal bleeding from her fall down the steps leading to the jetty. Then she'd almost

1

drowned until she was rescued and resuscitated by Shanice, Benny's Filipino maid.

Her husband Ray, Pete Peterson, Pete's journalist girlfriend Carly Jones and Don Rosario, Pete's tour manager had kept a bedside vigil and were now celebrating her recovery. The doctor had warned them she wasn't out of the woods just yet, but the early signs were encouraging.

The following day after a long sleep she felt better. She was allowed to eat, and they removed the tubes from her body. She could now recognise the friends at her bedside who all said how worried they'd been. Thankfully the doctor had told them she was much better and that he expected her to make a full recovery. He'd stressed they shouldn't stay too long and make her tired. Ray had kissed her and said how relieved he was that she was getting better. Then apologised because he had to get back to LA to finish his album. She had been disappointed when he left, but Pete, Carly and Don had remained which had been comforting. Eventually the nurse had asked them to leave to enable Janine to get some rest.

Now they'd all gone she had time to reflect on what had happened to her. She clearly remembered leaving the Super Bowl in a limousine, and smelling a distinctive fragrance as she drank the glass of champagne the chauffeur had already opened for her. Then when she awoke, she was being held captive by Benny Mulligan. She recalled talking to his maid who through sign language explained she couldn't speak, and Ray and Don were coming to rescue her. They were all in Benny's lounge when he shot Don and she stabbed him with her comb, which she remembered vividly. After that it all became a blur.

But there was something Benny had said to taunt her that was driving her to distraction. It was about her husband Ray, and she remembered what he'd said word for word.

"Well now he's finished screwing his backing singer." *Screwing his backing singer.* It stuck in her mind going round and round. Why didn't she know about it?

Carly had been up to the studio where Ray was recording on a couple of occasions, to write an article about him. But she hadn't mentioned anything even though Janine had quizzed her about the visits. She'd thought Don Rosario, Pete's tour manager had seemed strange with him; there was definitely an atmosphere between them, although she'd put that down to the fact Don had been shot and could still have been in pain. It was unusual that Ray hadn't stayed down in Miami for very long. He said he had to get back to the studio, but that was only after he knew she was going to be OK, and there was nothing else he could do.

So why was she so concerned?

She was turning all this over in her mind when Manny Oberstein, head of Westoria Records burst into her room with a huge bunch of flowers, a bottle of Bollinger, her favourite champagne and a cassette of Ray's album. They'd sat in her private lounge and listened to the recording together from start to finish. After the last track ended Janine looked at Manny and waited for him to speak.

"Well, I have to admit it's not my cup of tea, but it has something don't you think?"

She always knew when he wasn't being honest with her and removed the cassette from the portable player he'd brought with him. She dropped the tape on the bed.

"Don't bullshit me, Manny! Something's happened between when he first sang Pete's songs and now. I don't think it's the material or the production. It's Ray. He's lost the soul he had. It's like he's not really there; like his head's somewhere else."

Manny nodded, reluctantly agreeing.

Janine took a deep breath. "Who's this backing singer that Benny Mulligan told me about? He said Ray had been screwing her."

Manny was silent, trying to avoid her questioning gaze.

"Come on Manny, you can tell me. I think we've known each other long enough."

Manny finally answered her. "Look Janine, I've only heard rumours so I don't know for sure, but there was talk of a tape of Ray and a singer called Josie Thomas. I spoke to Curtis and he told me he'd dealt with it. That's all I know, I swear."

Janine picked up the cassette turning it over and over in her hand. "So what's the next move with this?"

"Well as it's down to Curtis, I can't really say. It's his call, so I suggest we get a meeting with him as soon as you're well enough. At the same time I think it would be wise for you and Ray to get together and sort things out. But hey, that's none of my business." He leaned over and gave Janine a kiss. "You know where I am. Call me any time!"

He stood up and left the room, and as the door slowly shut behind him Janine lay back and closed her eyes as the tears began to roll down her cheeks. It was the first time she'd ever had any real doubts about Ray since they'd met, and she didn't know what to do. What if it were true? How would she cope? Her mind was racing when she heard a noise and became aware she was not alone. She opened her eyes expecting to see one of the nurses waiting to take her blood pressure or temperature. Instead she was surprised to find Don Rosario standing at the bottom of her bed holding a small bunch of flowers and looking embarrassed. She quickly brushed away her tears and sat up with a smile.

Don shifted nervously from side to side.

"Hey Janine. I'm sorry if I disturbed you. I just thought I'd see how you were before we left."

"Ah Don, that is so sweet," she said smelling the fragrant blooms he handed to her. There was a silence and she didn't know what to say. "Did you see Manny?"

"Yeah, we had a quick chat in the corridor before he left," Don seemed flustered.

Janine knew there was something on his mind. "Look Don, if there's something you want to get off your chest then let's hear it. I'm a grown woman, I can take it. What's Pete been up to now? I'm beginning to think nothing he does would surprise me anymore."

She watched as he pulled up one of the chairs to the side of the bed and sat down.

"It's not Pete, Janine. It's Ray. There's something I think you should know."

She felt the blood drain from her face. "Go on."

"The day you were kidnapped from the Super Bowl I felt terrible. It was my fault for not checking the limo driver before he drove off and I was panicking. I rang the studio to tell Ray what had happened, maybe get some advice. Except he wasn't there. In fact nobody was there. It was closed because of Super Bowl weekend."

Janine interrupted him. "Hang on, I asked him to come down to the game with me but he said he was recording vocals and couldn't get away."

4

Don carried on. "So I got hold of Curtis the producer. At first he said he had no idea where he was, but when I explained what had happened he gave me the number of the hotel he thought he was staying in."

Janine was gripping her bedsheet so hard her knuckles were white.

"He was there with the singer wasn't he? He was there with her!"

Don nodded. "She answered the phone, but I demanded to speak to him. I won't tell you what I said, but he met me and the guys in Fort Lauderdale the next day. And, well you know the rest."

Janine was silent staring straight ahead. She finally looked at Don.

"Thanks Don. It seems everybody knew what was going on, but you're the only one man enough to tell me the truth."

"I did it because I like you Janine, and you don't deserve to be treated like this. Don't blame the others; they were pretty embarrassed like me, but I'll tell you something. You need to sort him out, because if you don't, I will. And don't forget, if you ever need someone for support, I'm always here."

He stood up to leave and Janine reached out to him. For a split second their eyes met and something more than friendship flashed between them. He bent down and kissed her lips gently and fleetingly he felt his stomach flutter before he stood up and left the room.

After saying goodbye to Janine at the hospital, Ray had gone straight to Miami International Airport and caught a flight to LA While he was waiting to board, he'd called Josie Thomas and told her to book a room at the hotel in Van Nuys where they were staying before. Josie was already waiting for him in the room when he arrived, lying on the bed, naked except for the black velvet choker he'd bought for her. Her long legs were crossed at the ankles and she shifted slightly, leaning on her elbow, watching him undress. Ray was visibly excited as he climbed on the bed and kissed her. She pushed him onto his back and still kissing his mouth stretched her leg across his body and slowly began to ride him. She realised that so far they hadn't spoken a word since he'd walked in, but she didn't care. She could hear him groaning as she worked her pelvis like a piston and knew she had him completely under control. But she wasn't prepared for what he did next.

Grabbing her waist, he lifted her off him and slid behind her in one move. With his hands on her shoulders he held her tight while he rhythmically pushed himself deep inside her until she screamed that he was hurting her, begging him to stop. It was then he noticed the blood stains on the sheets. Josie was still kneeling on the bed sobbing as he stood up and went into the bathroom. He stood in the shower and let the hot needles of water scour his skin and watched the water stained red as it ran away from his body. By the time he dried himself and came out Josie had gone. He pulled the sheets off the bed leaving them in a pile and dressed slowly, pouring himself a large glass of brandy from the bottle he'd bought at the airport. He took a mouthful and felt the burn as he swallowed it. He finished it with his next gulp and topped the glass up again. It didn't matter to him that it wasn't a crystal glass, or the fact that it was Remy Martin. He just needed to feel the hit of the alcohol.

CHAPTER TWO

Pete and the band, along with Don and Carly had decided, belatedly, to celebrate the end of the tour. There had been so much going on during and after the last gig, it had almost been an anti-climax. They'd booked a tiki boat and spent a whole day eating, drinking and slowly cruising around Miami seeing the sights. An impromptu version of 'In Flames' sung by Pete, raised everyone's spirits as they passed by the smouldering remains of Benny Mulligan's villa in Biscayne Bay. Then later, back in their hotel bar they gave a toast to Janine, "Absent Friends!" as they finished off with a night cap. Don swallowed his drink and wondered to himself whether it had been a good idea to reveal his true feelings, but it was too late to worry about that now. Tomorrow they were flying back to LA and then work was due to begin on the next Peterson album. Pete and Dave Sanchez had written half of the songs which were already sounding fantastic, and Don was hoping while they were in the studio he could get some free time. After all that had happened he was physically shattered, and although his shoulder was healing well he needed to rest.

Perhaps he could hook up with the actress he'd met at Kathy Blake's party, provided of course that she still remembered him. Although he felt he'd left a pretty good impression the last night they were together. But then there was Janine…He stopped himself from going any further with that train of thought. *Don't be a fool. She's married. And to a guy, who until recently you called your friend.* But was that still the case? He'd gone to bed confused and very drunk.

Carly and Pete were still enjoying each other's company, and their nightly sexual adventures were amazing, although just recently Carly's interest in autoeroticism was beginning to worry him. She'd told him how she was researching it for a new article she was thinking of writing. She'd tried on a couple of occasions to persuade him to experiment saying it would be the biggest rush he'd ever experience, but he'd refused point blank. Her article, 'Pete Peterson, The Man Live' had received critical acclaim, with particular praise for the way she'd managed to get inside Pete's mind and his attitude towards 'the gigs, the girls and the good times'. Her editor had thought she could be up for a Pulitzer Prize judging from the response they'd received. However, she was slightly apprehensive about how her other piece, 'Ray Law, The New Face Of

Soul' would be received, especially by the soul scene, which was renowned for being less than enthusiastic about anything written by someone not of the preferred gender or creed.

Pete had managed to get hold of a rough mix of Ray's album and they had been disappointed, but as he pointed out it could all change once it was remixed and mastered. Secretly Pete had been surprised by how Ray's voice had changed so much from when he first heard him sing back in Birmingham. Then, it had been fresh and exciting, but now it was just…flat, as if he had his mind on something else. Or if the rumours were true, someone else. He was sure Janine could handle him once she was back, and when he and Carly had dropped in to see her before they left, he was pleased to see her looking a lot better. She'd told them the doctor had said he was hopeful she could go home next week which was great news, and Janine had said she would call Carly to arrange another lunch date as soon as she was back.

They'd left to catch their flight and Janine was settling down to have a sleep when there was a knock on the door of her room. She couldn't think who it could be because none of the doctors or nurses ever knocked and everybody had been to see her. She called out.

"Come in."

The door opened and to her surprise in walked Shanice, Benny Mulligan's maid, with her four-year-old son. They had a bunch of flowers which the child gave to Janine and holding out her arms to Shanice they tearfully embraced.

Janine remembered that Shanice couldn't talk but could hear, and began to thank her but Shanice stopped her by putting up her hand and smiled.

"It's OK," she said taking Janine by surprise. "After I dived in the water and rescued you, it took the shock of seeing you lying on the jetty needing help to make me shout out, and suddenly I found I could."

Janine was amazed. "Oh my God, that's incredible! So what's happened to you, where are you staying?"

She pulled her son to her side. "The police chief has been fantastic since the night of the fire. He knew we'd lost everything, but he's found us a wonderful family who were looking for a maid, and we're settled in another property in the same area on Biscayne Bay. We have a fantastic place all of our own in the grounds, and I thank the Lord everything is fine now. I'm so happy to see you looking well again, but you look tired and I think it is time we must go."

She leaned over and kissed Janine on both cheeks and left the room holding her son's hand. Janine lay back and smiled as she closed her eyes and immediately fell asleep.

CHAPTER THREE

Janine was released from hospital the following week, and flew back to Los Angeles by private jet where Ray was waiting to meet her. He had a huge bunch of flowers in his arms as she walked into the arrivals hall, and had arranged for a limousine to take them back to their house on the Strand in Hermosa Beach. He seemed genuinely excited to see her, and fussed over her every move until she told him to calm down and leave her to do things herself. There was a strange atmosphere between them; whilst nothing had been said, it was there all the same.

As a surprise Ray had booked a table at their favourite restaurant that evening, and although she felt more like going to bed, Janine made the effort to shower and put on a loose-fitting white cotton dress and fresh make-up. The taxi arrived and they were leaving the apartment when Janine heard the phone ringing, and although Ray told her to let it ring she went back in to answer it. She knew there was someone on the other end, but at the sound of her voice whoever it was had then rung off. She replaced the receiver as Ray came back in to see where she was.

"Are you ready, babe? The taxi's waiting."

Janine was shaking. "Does she have this number?"

Ray looked puzzled. "Does who have this number?"

"You know damn well who! Josie Thomas!" Janine was shouting. "Does she have this number?"

Ray tried to change the subject and calm things down. "Look the taxi's waiting and the table's booked, come on let's go babe."

"Fuck the taxi and the table," she said through gritted teeth.

"I asked you, Does. She. Have. This. Number?"

Ray was flustered. "No. I don't know, maybe. Look it was all a big mistake; I can explain."

She threw her bag down on the table. "You don't have to explain Ray. What I do want to know though is how many other times?"

He slammed the door and looked at her defiantly standing his ground and putting his hands on his hips.

"The same number of times as you, I suppose."

She was taken aback, and looked surprised at his reply tilting her head slightly.

He carried on. "So having sex with Mandy here in our bed doesn't count then? Oh and your little trip up to San Francisco together? How do you think I felt? I mean I called you a couple of times from England, once in the middle of the night to your hotel room, and some strange woman answers the phone. What was I supposed to think?"

It was Janine's turn to be flustered.

"I told you about it when you came back. I said it didn't mean anything."

"Ha, really! That's not exactly how you explained it at the time. Look Janine, I admit I was wrong doing what I did and I'm sorry. I promise it won't happen again, but don't play the martyr. We've both done things we now regret, but I still love you."

He walked over and kissed her.

"I love you too," she replied as he wrapped his arms around her.

They held each other tight until he broke away.

"Now I'm starving and we still have time to get our table." He held out his hand and Janine took it. "Let's call that cab again."

They sat down at their reserved table in the restaurant and studied the menus presented to them by their friend the maître d'. Janine ordered her favourite - shrimps in a spicy tomato sauce served with linguini - and Ray a medium-rare New York Strip, but when their orders came he was so preoccupied reflecting on the lucky escape he'd just had, he hardly touched his food and asked to take it home in a doggy bag. For once Janine decided she was too tired to comment, and when they got back she left him sitting on the balcony drinking a brandy as she climbed into bed and closed her eyes.

The meeting with Ray and Janine in Manny Oberstein's office was not going well. The reviews for his album had been mixed, with the main recurring comment being that it lacked feel and energy. Curtis Jackson was sitting uncomfortably as Manny read them out one by one, frowning. The one good piece of news was that it had been relatively well received in the UK, and although the British market was nothing compared to the US in sales of units, it was always regarded as highly prestigious to have a hit there. Were that to be the case with Ray's album, it could save a career which was threatening to stall before it had even started.

Both Manny and Janine were of the same opinion about the album, but before they had chance to say how they felt, Ray took them all by surprise.

"I was always uncomfortable with the set up. If you remember at our first meeting I said I wanted to work with Pete, but was overruled. So instead of creating a fuss I went along with it."

Curtis suddenly stood up and glared at Ray. "Fuck you, you devious bastard!" he exclaimed. "The reason the album is shit is because of you, and you know why!" He stood and walked out of the office slamming the door.

"So how do we proceed?" Janine asked, trying to remain positive.

"Well looking on the bright side, your friendly journalist Carly Jones has written a really good article about Ray, and so far there's not been much negativity from the soul scene. So let's keep our fingers crossed and hope it stays that way. And on a positive note, I've heard some of the new stuff coming out of Whitland that Pete's recording and it's sounding awesome."

Ray suddenly spoke. "So why can't I work with Pete on a single from my album? There's at least two great songs on it, and I'm sure if Pete were to produce me, we could come up with something special. We did it before just playing live in the studio and you all loved it."

"Wouldn't that be a problem with the producer and Curtis though?" Janine asked.

"Not necessarily," Manny replied thoughtfully. "We own the tapes and everyone's been paid. It's all down to whether Pete has the time, or if he wants to do it."

"He'll do it," Janine said under her breath, but loud enough that everyone heard. She glanced at Ray who had a smug grin on his face.

'Let's hope for your sake this comes off,' she thought.

Amazingly it did come off and proved an absolute master stroke. When Janine and Ray met with Pete and Dave Sanchez to explain Ray's idea they loved it, and chose one of the strongest songs on the album to work on, along with the original tune Pete and Dave had written which had got everyone so excited in the first place. The studio at Whitland was already set up from working with Peterson and within days they had two fantastic songs recorded. Pete and Dave had skilfully mixed their song to sound the same as the others on the album and after hearing the new versions Manny commissioned them to re-record Ray's vocals on the whole album. Just over a week later they were all sat in Manny's office listening to the finished product with smiles on everyone's faces.

The new re-recorded and remixed single 'The Love Game' had been sent out to the top radio stations and was already receiving heavy airplay. Far from being a problem as Curtis had originally suggested, the name of Pete Peterson attached to the single had given it a massive boost and it was already climbing the charts both in the US and UK.

Janine now had the envious task of managing two hit artists on both sides of the Atlantic in two completely different genres of music.

CHAPTER FOUR

While Janine was working hard on planning the promotion for Pete's new album 'The Dawning', Ray was sitting in a small smoky office off Sunset and Vine with Eddy James and Charles T. Brown, the two men behind SoulTown Promotions who had made him an offer to sign to them. In return they were promising to promote a string of club dates down the West Coast, and then a place on the bill with Motown stars Jimmy Ruffin and Edwin Starr on their UK tour. It sounded too good to be true, but snowed under with organising Pete, Janine hadn't put up any objections to him signing with guys who seemed like they knew what they were doing. Now with a hit record, plans were underway for a string of promotional club appearances. The drummer and bass guitarist who played on the album had been recruited, along with a young guitar player and keyboard player and rehearsals had started in Whitland Studios a week before the first gig, the opening of a new disco in Santa Monica.

Pete and Dave had been in the studio next door occasionally dropping in to see how the show was progressing, and everything was going fine until Ray announced he wanted to bring in the three backing singers who had performed on the original versions, including Josie Thomas. Pete had taken him to one side in the corridor outside the studio. "Are you out of your fucking mind!"

Ray had an annoying way of standing in front of people but not listening to what they were saying, and this had the effect of winding Pete up.

"Ray, man! You're risking destroying everything we've just created. There are hundreds of great girl singers in LA. Why her? She's not that good! Does Janine know?"

Ray shrugged his shoulders. "I don't see what it's got to do with her. I just wanted the same sound as on the record."

Pete laughed. "Fuck off Ray. You know exactly why you want her on it. I mean, you do know Janine will go mad don't you?"

"Listen Pete, maybe Janine should stick to what she's good at. Let's face it, you've got a new album and tour coming up, and she's concentrating on that. Eddy and Charles are getting me some cool club dates and then a tour over in the UK alongside some big Motown names, Edwin Starr and Jimmy Ruffin."

"Well it all sounds great on paper, but what's their background? Don't forget Janine is well linked in with Manny and the label. You don't want to jeopardise that. And what about your relationship? Doesn't that mean anything?"

Ray suddenly turned on Pete. "You want to keep your nose out of our business, man. Just because you and Janine had a scene once before. You still holding a candle or what?"

Pete was shocked at his outburst. "Screw you, Ray. I care for Janine. It's because of her I'm where I am today. And as a matter of fact it's because of me you're where you are today, and don't forget it. Look I'm too busy for all this shit, but let me give you a friendly word of advice. You carry on drinking like you do and you're gonna fuck your voice, and there won't always be me around to cover it up!"

"Ha, don't give me all that self-righteous shit. Clean up your own act before you start preaching to others. What about your child back in the UK? Ever think about him?"

Ray turned on his heel and walked off leaving Pete to contemplate what he'd just said. Maybe he had a point. Here he was living the life of a rock star and back home Judy was bringing up his son. He had to admit he hadn't given them much thought recently. Perhaps it was about time he did.

Josie Thomas was cool towards Ray when she turned up at the rehearsal. She'd been professional and gone through the routines with the other two girls without making too much eye contact with him. After two days the show was starting to come together, and by the end of the week it was tight. Everyone was grooving and they decided to go for a drink to chill out, but instead of staying in the studio bar, Ray decided they should all go to a place he knew which was a short drive away. As they left he found himself in the back of a cab sitting next to Josie. He'd started to apologise but before he had chance to speak she pulled him to her kissing him. Her hands were at the belt on his jeans and she lowered her head in the darkness as she unzipped him. Her mouth found him and he almost passed out as she pleasured him to the point of no return. Then just as he was about to lose control she calmly sat back up.

"Have you missed me?" she whispered in his ear still holding him tight.

The taxi arrived outside the bar and Ray hurriedly zipped himself up before stumbling out. They joined the others and Ray ordered drinks for everyone, while at the same time never losing sight of where Josie was. Numerous rounds of drinks later, the group had started to drift apart, some going home and others to find another bar leaving Ray and Josie alone together in a darkened booth at the back. By now Ray had drunk the best part of a bottle of brandy and was feeling quite relaxed, when he realised Josie had slipped down under the table and was on her knees between his legs undoing his jeans again. He closed his eyes and leaned his head back as she worked on him until he could hold back no longer. He was just thinking she was the most outrageously sexual woman he'd ever met when his thoughts were rudely interrupted by a loud voice.

"Sir! I'm arresting you for gross indecency in a public place. I need you and your friend to come with me now."

Ray opened his eyes and sat bolt upright as he was confronted by a police officer and the barman standing at the table. Josie was sitting on the floor looking shocked.

"Officer, please allow me to explain." Ray was desperately trying to think his way out of the situation. "It's all a big mistake."

"I don't think so!" The barman had his arms folded in front of him. "I saw what was going on. You wanna have sex, go get a room."

The white, middle-aged policeman pointed his night stick at Josie. "What he pay you for the trick, honey?"

She jumped up and pushed him. "I'm not a hooker you dirty-minded bastard."

"Committing a sex act in public and assaulting an officer! Looks like you two are in deep shit to me."

By now Ray had regained his senses and tried to calm things down.

"Look officer, we're really sorry and deeply regret causing any problems. We had a few too many to drink and things kind of got out of hand."

The policeman looked at Ray. "Say that's not a local accent, where you from son?"

"I'm from the UK, sir," Ray answered desperately turning on his diplomatic charm.

"Whereabouts in the UK you from? My sister lives over there."

He sensed the officer was loosening up. "Liverpool, sir."

"Hey that's where the Beatles come from ain't it? She lives in Birmingham? You know it?"

"Know it? I used to work there. I was a DCI in the West Midlands Police."

"Damn one of us. So what you doin' over here?"

Ray sensed he could swing this. The barman turned away shrugging his shoulders and returned to the bar. "I'm a singer, sir. I have a record in the charts and we were out celebrating and like I said, we went a bit too far."

"You don't say; a hit record. What's your name?"

"Ray Law, sir, and the record's called The Love Game."

"Hey I've heard that on the radio. My wife loves it. She's always singing it. And you say that's you? Well I'll be!" He thought for a moment. "Listen Mr. Law, I'm willing to forget about this little misdemeanour on one condition."

Ray was holding his breath. The officer reached into his pocket and pulled out his notebook. "Would you sign this to my wife, Edith?"

Ray's hands were shaking as he took the book and pen. "To Edith, love and best wishes, Ray Law. 'The Love Game' There you go." He drew a small heart next to his name.

The officer looked at the page and carefully closed the notebook. "She'll love that. Now I suggest you and your friend get yourselves out of here before I change my mind."

Ray and Josie quickly left the bar waving down a cab, and fell into the back laughing as it pulled away.

"Shit, that has to be the craziest blow job ever," she said pulling him close to kiss him. He kissed her back but thought to himself that a situation like that could never happen again. 'This girl is dangerous and perhaps Pete might have a point.'

* To see and hear 'The Love Game' use your smartphone to scan the QR code below

CHAPTER FIVE

Judy Watson had taken to motherhood like a fish to water. She had felt bad at how the meeting with Pete and Rick had gone at The Lexxicon but since then she'd taken everything in her stride. He was a wonderful child and watching him grow up was a daily pleasure. He had the looks of Pete and he loved to listen to music. Judy had the radio on constantly and every time one of Pete's songs was played he would instantly react. She'd decided Rick was a nice name which seemed to suit him and had taken to calling him that. He was past the baby stage and had developed into a little character walking and talking, slowly turning into a real little boy. Her one regret was that Pete was missing all of this, but she'd bought herself a cine-camera and made sure at every possible occasion she took film footage of him growing up. Pete hadn't completely neglected them, and each birthday and Christmas there would be a parcel from America full of gifts.

The club and agency were now really successful and Judy had slowly increased the number of staff to enable her to have more time with Rick. Her original assistant George was now office manager at FAM and had blossomed into an extremely shrewd agent, and alongside Judy they had become one of the best teams in the business.

The Lexxicon was regarded as one of the top clubs in the UK and virtually every band added a night there to their tour. It still amazed Judy that they could have a rock band on one night, followed by a soul band the next and still the club was full. She was flicking through her post one day when she saw a contract for a soul show that had been booked in starring two Motown stars, Jimmy Ruffin and Edwin Starr plus new UK soul star Ray Law. She looked again at the enclosed flyer and there was a picture of Janine's husband. She'd heard the song 'The Love Game' on the radio but never connected the name. She couldn't wait to speak to Janine and called her number in LA. It was just coming up to 4.30 pm in the UK so it was 8.30 am in Hermosa Beach and hopefully Janine would be just having breakfast. She heard the ring tone and then Janine's voice.

"Hello?"

"Hey Janine, it's Judy over in the UK."

Janine sounded surprised. "Hey Judy, how are you? How's the baby?"

"Everything's great. I haven't woken you have I?"

"Ha-ha, no I was just about to leave for the studio. So what's happening over there?" Janine asked biting a piece of toast.

"Well I was just going through some contracts for The Lexxicon and spotted a soul tour booked in featuring a couple of Motown stars and Ray Law. I mean I've been listening to the record on the radio but didn't realise it was your Ray. Isn't it fantastic? You must be really pleased."

There was a long pause before Janine replied. "Well just to put you in the picture. The phrase 'your Ray' isn't quite correct at the moment. There's a few things right now that, erm," she paused again and Judy sensed there was a problem.

"Hey Janine, is this a bad time? I mean I can call you back later if you want?"

"No, look I need to talk about it so just bear with me." Janine coughed. "I'm sorry, this is stupid. So Ray is now with another management company specialising in black artists who got him the tour. Which is cool. In fact it's a relief for me as trying to handle both him and Pete was a nightmare. But the main problem is he was having a scene with one of his backing singers behind my back. It happened when he was recording his album and he promised it was over and all a big mistake, but now he's out touring and she's in the band."

"Oh my god, I didn't know!" Judy exclaimed.

"No well you wouldn't; it's not public knowledge."

"So what are you doing about it?"

"Well for once in my life I don't know what to do. I'm up to my eyes in Pete's new album and tour which is keeping me busy, but when I get home it's terrible. I want to kill him, but at the same time I still love him. The worst thing is I just can't trust him anymore."

Janine stopped for a moment and took a drink of coffee.

"But look how are you and the baby? It's been ages since we spoke. And I never got round to apologising for what I said at the club."

Judy laughed. "Don't be silly; you don't have to apologise. Anyway he's no longer a baby. He's an incredible little boy who looks just like his dad."

"It's times like this I wish I wasn't so far away," Janine said. "Hey but we're working on Pete's new tour dates and I'm sure there will be one in Birmingham. Maybe I'll fix it so I can come over."

"That would be lovely," Judy replied.

"Look I have to go. It's been great to talk, and I mean that. Let's not leave it so long next time. Love you."

"Love you too," Judy said as the line went dead. She sat quietly for a moment thinking. 'Hmmm, Ray Law. Didn't see that one coming'.

Dave Sanchez was a world-class keyboard player and loved what he did. He and Pete Peterson had formed a great songwriting partnership and were having lots of success. The latest Peterson album was nearing completion and sounding fantastic and plans were in progress for a new world tour as well as which he and Pete had written a song for Janine Law's husband Ray and produced his new single which was racing up the charts. On the face of it, everything was perfect except for one thing. Dave was gay and it was becoming more difficult to keep it secret. He knew the guys in the band understood, but being gay in a rock band was not as yet widely accepted; which made it all the more frustrating because he never got chance to talk to any of the young guys who were at the shows. Even though he knew some of them were gay too, but were afraid to reveal it.

Regularly groups of young girls would invade the dressing room to see Pete and would start talking to him in a suggestive manner, which he found really annoying. He felt like shouting at them to leave him alone, but knew by doing so he would reveal himself.

The most worrying thing though was the homophobic organisations that were appearing in some states, and who were becoming a threat to his freedom. He was finding more and more he had to be ultra-careful how he behaved especially in strange bars when they were on tour. One wrong move and he could find himself in big trouble.

He'd recently been introduced to a small group of like-minded people in LA who felt under threat. They met at confidential locations where they could relax in each other's company and talk freely about their lifestyle. However, since the advent of Woodstock and the new radical ideas circulating, the original reason behind the group was slowly being eroded. He found himself being swept along by the tide of unrest with his own attitudes changing and hardening, swallowed up in anti-political agendas and overshadowed by hate. He no longer spent all his spare time practising and working on new songs; instead more and more he would be attending meetings discussing ways to protest against a new law or finding new causes to support.

Pete had noticed the change in Dave. He'd never had an issue with his sexuality and was always very protective towards him, but recently he'd sensed his increasingly militant and hostile opinions. Their writing was becoming more fragmented and when he had them, Dave's lyric ideas always had a contentious theme, which didn't sit too well with Peterson's style.

They'd just finished the new album 'The Dawning', which had a progressive, 'concept' feel with certain tracks merging with others and longer instrumental breaks allowing Dave and Pete to showcase their individual talents. It had been a bold step by Pete to take this new direction, and he knew he was risking alienating a certain commercial, pop-loving section of his fans; but he'd never been frightened to take risks before and he felt confident they would come with him, and judging on early feedback from the radio stations it appeared he would be proved right.

The first gig to promote the new album was at a huge free festival in Northern California. Peterson were the main band and were scheduled to play at 10.00 pm on the Saturday night. Wary of trouble at previous festivals, the promoters had ensured security was tight and the capacity crowd had enjoyed a whole day of music from a varied selection of bands playing soul, reggae, blues and rock, and by the time nightfall came the atmosphere was electric with anticipation.

In LA at Whitland Studios the day hadn't started out well for the band. Dave had arrived late and was complaining one of his keyboards had developed a fault. Unfortunately because of the tight time schedule they were forced to leave without resolving the problem which put Dave in a foul mood. On board the bus, Don was doing his best to placate him but wasn't being helped by the others, mainly Randy and Marshall, who having already consumed various substances, constantly saw the funny side of the situation. This riled Dave all the more and by the time they arrived at the festival site an impasse between them had developed. Pete had been powerless to stop the relentless barrage of jokes from the two rhythm players and had given up trying, but now they had arrived he decided something had to be done before they went on stage.

It was a clear night with no clouds and the stars were shining brightly with the constellations of Leo, Cancer and Virgo clearly visible. The aroma of cannabis drifting over from the audience was strong as he walked around the backstage area, but he resisted the temptation. He knew the guys had some cocaine and once he had sorted out the problem with Dave, he'd make sure he had a sample before they went on.

He spotted Dave coming out of the dressing room with Randy laughing and joking and breathed a sigh of relief. At least that was one problem solved. Now all he had to concentrate on was the new songs they were playing for the first time tonight.

Don was waiting for him as he entered the dressing room, which was in fact one of three converted shipping containers all luxuriously fitted out for the bands. He had read Pete's mind and presented him with a ready-made line of coke which he snorted down in one long go. The hit was immediate and he took a deep breath feeling the grade A drug working. Marshall the drummer was over in the corner getting himself ready, hitting a rubber practice pad with his sticks as Pete changed into his stage gear, the black leather trousers and white shirt with his trademark neckerchief.

They both made their way to the back of the stage where Randy and Dave were waiting for them. They could feel the tension as the MC introduced them and were greeted by an almighty roar as they walked on stage. Pete had taken the bold decision to start with one of the songs from the new album which contained a long solo by Dave and they immediately launched into it, but halfway through he was beginning to doubt hisown wisdom as the audience seemed to be getting restless. He looked round at Dave to give him a sign to cut his solo short when there were two loud bangs like gunshots which came from the crowd somewhere in front of the stage. He felt his guitar shudder strangely and there was massed panic with women screaming and people running everywhere desperately trying to escape from the area. Don had immediately rushed on and grabbed Pete, pulling him off the stage while at the same time ushering the rest of the guys away from the front. The MC had found a microphone and was trying his best to tell the crowd to stay calm, but he was fighting a losing battle. Pete and the guys made their way back to the dressing room and slumped down depressed, but Randy the bass player looked up and said, "Well at least that did us a favour and saved the first song." One by one they all started to laugh.

Don walked in moments later with a serious expression on his face carrying Pete's guitar. "The gods must have been smiling on you today," he said showing Pete his Les Paul. There was a .22 bullet wedged in the thick body of the guitar. "Six inches either way and you would have been another rock and roll casualty!"

The blood drained from Pete's face as he realised what Don had just said.

Dave sat quietly and said nothing. There had been two shots fired and he knew where the other bullet was; lodged in the back of his Hammond Organ. Was it by chance or could it be to do with one of the factions he'd joined? A warning perhaps.

CHAPTER SIX

Ray's first gig with his band was going well. The opening night of 'Kaleidoscope', a brand new disco in Santa Monica was packed. The band were playing great and the audience were loving it. There was an abundance of beautiful young women standing at the front of the stage watching and smiling at Ray as he sang. He decided it would be good to have a bit of audience participation, and invited one of them to get up on stage and dance with him during the next number. A slow ballad. She was a sexy-looking girl with short black hair cut in a fashionable bob and a sparkling top was barely keeping her large breasts under control. She didn't need a second invitation to leap up beside Ray, and when he asked she told him her name was Laura. She moved in close when the band started to play and he pushed his leg between hers as they swayed together. The audience were lapping it up and everyone was enjoying it except for one person.

Josie Thomas was not amused by what she was watching. She had already given Ray a disgusted look which he'd noticed out of the corner of his eye but chose to ignore. The girl was laughing and reacting to her friends' encouragement by suggestively rubbing herself into Ray's crotch as they moved to the slow groove from the band. Suddenly all hell broke loose. Josie picked up her microphone stand, swung it above her head and crashed it down onto Ray's shoulder. The microphone had shot out, landing on the stage with a loud bang which then became a squeal of feed-back. She grabbed the girl by her top and tried to pull her away from Ray, but in doing so ripped it open and her breasts tumbled out for all to see. Josie was screaming at Ray and made the mistake of taking her eyes off the girl, who decided to take matters into her own hands and lifted her off her feet with an uppercut of which Mohammed Ali would have been proud. By this time the band had stopped playing, and the scene on stage resembled a surreal female boxing match with a topless pugilist, her opponent prone on the floor and Ray with a microphone stand bent at a ridiculous angle over his shoulder.

Later describing the events to Eddy and Charles who unfortunately were in the manager's office at the time, the drummer said he would pay good money to see a repeat contest. It turned out that besides being a very attractive and well-endowed young lady, Ray's dance partner was also a self-defence expert who was on a night out with her fellow club members. She'd apologised profusely to Ray who found the whole thing highly amusing, apart from the huge bruise on his shoulder. He had managed to get her phone number though and suggested they take the opportunity to finish the dance somewhere more private. The kiss goodbye she gave him as she left seemed to indicate she would enjoy that.

Josie had recovered and was sitting in the dressing room as Ray, followed by Eddy and Charles walked in. She started to say she was sorry and it would never happen again when Ray stopped her.

"Damn right it won't. There's no way I can work with you. We'll pay you for the next two gigs but you leave tonight."

She sat silent for a moment before standing up and suddenly swinging her hand to slap him but Ray was too fast and caught her arm before she connected and twisted it behind her back.

"Bastard, you're hurting me," she shouted as he pushed her out of the dressing room.

"Be thankful I'm not suing you," he said and slammed the door.

It was late when he arrived home and Janine had already gone to bed, but she woke up when he came in the bedroom. "How'd it go?" she yawned as he slipped into bed beside her.

"Yeah, it was great. The club was packed." He flinched as she touched his shoulder turning on her side to look at him.

"What the hell happened?" The bruise was vivid and his arm was swollen.

"Ah it was nothing, just a bit of trouble and I got hit by a stray mic stand, but it was all sorted."

"That doesn't look like nothing to me. You need to get that checked out, you could have broken something."

He didn't want to go into any detail in case Josie's name came up. "I'll see how it is in the morning, but I've got another gig tomorrow night up in Sacramento and we're leaving early. How did Pete's gig go?" He asked, changing the subject.

"Don called me; it was a bit of a disaster. They were halfway through the first song when someone in the crowd fired two shots at them. One bullet hit Pete's guitar. It could've been much worse."

"Shit!" Ray sat up. "Did Don say if they got the guy who did it?"

"No, whoever it was got away in the panic afterwards."

"But why would someone do that? Maybe I should give Don a call."

"He seemed to think it was some random nut job trying to make a name for himself. That's the problem with big festivals. They were supposed to tighten up security. Anyway they're off to the East Coast next week."

"They're not doing Boston are they? That's got to have bad vibes for Pete."

"He's OK with it." She paused. "So when were you going to tell me Josie Thomas was in your band?"

Her change of subject surprised himbut he covered it well enough. "It was Eddy and Charles' idea. They wanted the sound to be like the record."

"I didn't ask whose idea it was, even though I don't believe you. I asked when were you going to tell me?"

"I'm assuming Pete told you. He and I need to have words."

"Pete never told me. You don't think I can't find out these things for myself? So I'll ask you again. When were you going to tell me?"

"Well for your information, she's no longer in my band as of tonight. I sacked her."

Janine laughed. "And that's alright then is it? You've been with her every day for the past week or so and partying on at least one night so I'm led to believe. What's going on Ray? What's happened to us?"

He laid back down and put his arm around her, feeling her tense as he did.

"Nothing's happened to us, babe. I'm here aren't I? I still love you, I've just been doing my job. I've got a new career and finally stand a chance of stepping out on my own instead of relying on you all the time. Don't you understand what that's like? Ever since we came here it's been all about you and Pete bloody Peterson, and I've stood in the background being the dutiful husband; ever ready when needed. Well finally for once it's about me, Ray Law, and d'you know what? I love it, and I kind of thought you would love it too."

"Hey hang on, there's no one appreciates what you've done more than I do, and if you remember it was me who encouraged you to sing when you weren't sure. So don't throw that one at me. All I want to know is do we have a future? 'Cos right now I just don't know anymore."

"I love you Janine, nothing's changed. Now if you don't mind I'm going to close my eyes. I'll see you in the morning."

He leaned over and kissed her then lay back and within minutes was snoring.

Janine lay in the darkness her thoughts confused by what he'd said. She knew she still loved him and desperately wanted him just as much as ever, but could she still trust him? And more to the point could she still trust herself?

Dave had called the leaders of the group as soon as he got back and arranged to meet them the next night. He'd been shaken by the incident of the gun shots at the festival and wanted to address his concerns with the others. There were five of them; Jorge and Rudy owned 'Taco Taco' a Mexican Cantina in Studio City, Jacob was a leading gay rights campaigner, Alice a militant Animal Rights activist and Claus was a brilliant organiser who protested about anything and everything.

A diverse bunch of individuals, they met in Jacob's apartment in a new large condo development in Glendale. He worked as an interior designer during the day, and as a result lived in an ultra-modern space full of trendy furniture and art. His clothes sense bordered on the outrageous but with taste, tonight's ensemble consisting of a cyclamen pink shirt, pale blue trousers and a lemon-yellow cravat, the the opposite to Alice who resembled an urban guerilla direct from a Rambo film, dressed head to toe in camouflage fatigues with a black headband holding her streaked blonde mullet in place.

Jorge and Rudy had arrived still wearing their matching blue uniforms with the company logo on the shoulder after closing the restaurant early, and Claus had chosen a mundane brown checked sports jacket and cream slacks. With his short flat-top haircut he resembled a baseball commentator.

Dave surveyed his fellow protesters and wondered how he'd ever got involved with such an eccentric bunch but then who was he to comment with his long brown wavy hair hanging down past his shoulders and a tie-dye T-shirt and jeans.

Once they had finished greeting each other, Dave started to speak. They listened as he related what had happened the previous night but couldn't associate it with anything they'd been involved with recently. No one thought protesting about tax increases or the building of a new road in Santa Monica warranted being shot at.

The next item was a lot more serious though. They had recently discovered there was a company called Maltrocorp based on the outskirts of Anaheim developing a new kind of drug reputedly to cure cancer, a good cause except that live monkeys were being used to test the serum and they were planning on raiding the site to set them free.

Claus addressed the group with details of how they were going to do it. He'd already been down to the site and checked it out and as far as he could tell, the security wasn't too tight at weekends when none of the scientists were working. His plan involved Jorge and Rudy, along with a group of volunteers, staging a demonstration at the main gates to keep the guards occupied, while Alice and Dave cut through the perimeter fence and slipped in through the back. The shed containing the monkeys was only a few yards from where they would enter and it would be a simple job to break in and release them. As soon as the monkeys were free the saboteurs would make good their escape with Jacob, who would be waiting outside the enclosure in his truck. Once back in LA an anonymous message would be sent to all the news channels and newspapers in the morning giving the reason for their action.

After Claus had finished he allowed them time to think before asking if there were any questions.

"Where do the protesters come from?" Peter asked.

Jorge spoke up. "We have friends and family down in Santa Ana and they can easily get a group together. That shouldn't be a problem."

He and Rudy would leave immediately after they closed the restaurant and would meet up with the group of friends. At the same time, Dave, Alice and Jacob would drive to the back of the site. The demonstration outside the front would start at midnight occupying the security guards and five minutes later Alice and Dave would enter through the fence. They would break into the shed and free the animals and be away at the latest by quarter past. Claus was very exact in his timings and expected everyone to report back to Jacob's apartment by two o'clock.

Dave was constantly impressed with the way Claus worked and wondered if he had been a commando in the war carrying out dangerous raids behind enemy lines. His plans were always reliant on military-like precision with nothing left to chance.

They were all about to leave when Claus called them all back. "One more thing. No guns. Do you hear me Alice? There will be no need for violence. The minute any kind of force is used we lose all support for our cause."

Alice shrugged and left the apartment followed by the others.

CHAPTER SEVEN

Janine, Pete and Don had met at Manny's office to discuss the events of the weekend. The promoters of the festival were apologising profusely for the obvious breach of security. They swore that they had employed adequate staff and the searches at the entrances had been thorough, but still someone had been able to smuggle a pistol in and take two shots at Pete.

Don was pacing the floor looking concerned and not listening to what the others were saying. He finally spoke. "Something's not right."

They looked at him questioningly.

"The local police chief up in North California was in touch with my old boss in LA and he's puzzled about what happened. It was either a very lucky shot that hit Pete's guitar or a very accurate one, and if so that says professional. And then there's the other shot. Where did the bullet end up? The police searched the stage but couldn't find it. I'm worried there's more to this than just some crazy fan trying to make trouble."

"Have you spoken to the other guys?" Manny asked.

"No, not really. It was all so confused afterwards. The police did a quick interview before we left but they were more interested in trying to speak to some of the fans down at the front, and by the time we got back home it was late." He paused and looked at Pete. "How does Dave seem to you? Have you noticed any change in him recently?"

"Funny you should ask," Pete replied. "I was only thinking the other day how he seems to have become withdrawn and serious all the time. I know it must be hard for him being gay, but we've never made an issue of it. He doesn't talk about it much although he did once mention he had joined some kind of club of what he called 'like-minded people' whatever that means."

"Hmmm, I might have a quiet word with him," Don said thoughtfully.

"Well after the disaster of the opening number we're having another run through before we leave for the next gig so maybe then would be a good time. It was a blessing in disguise. We're gonna have to rethink the start completely; the audience was getting restless halfway through Dave's solo."

"Well early sales figures are looking good," Janine said. "Maybe you just need to introduce the new stuff slowly."

"How's Ray? Looks like his single is doing well," Pete asked.

"OK I suppose, and thanks for telling me about Josie Thomas by the way."

"Yeah, he and I had words about her the last time I saw him down at Whitland studios."

"Well it appears she's no longer with the band according to Ray. I don't know what happened but something went down at the gig in Santa Monica and he sacked her."

"I honestly don't know why he wanted three singers in the first place. The guys in the band all sing and it's more mouths to feed. Those two managers of his must be pulling good money to afford a band that big."

"Yeah well it's a bit of a sore point at the minute, so let's just concentrate on getting your stuff together shall we."

Eddy James and Charles T Brown, owners of Soul Town promotions and Ray's managers, had called him into their office for a meeting. After the chaos of the first gig, Sacramento's show had gone to plan along with the next one in San Diego and they were receiving good reports back from the club owners. Since Josie Thomas had left, the question of backing singers had been raised and they were now deciding whether to use the guys in the band and get rid of the girls altogether. Financially it was an easy decision but they wanted to make sure Ray was happy before they went ahead.

"I don't have a problem," he said. "To be honest they're a distraction, and the women at the front aren't interested in a couple of girls. The focus should be on me. The part where I get a pretty lady up to dance with me is going down great."

"Yeah we heard," Charles remarked. "I believe you and one of them were getting it on backstage after the gig the other night. Is that right?"

Ray laughed. "Just giving the lady what she wanted. Hey man, a satisfied customer is a happy customer. Am I right?"

"Yeah well just so long as there's no comeback. We don't need any more trouble with jealous women, and we've heard your wife can be pretty tough when she wants," Eddy added.

"You just leave Janine to me," Ray replied. "So we're decided on the lineup now. Can we get a couple of hours in the studio with the guys before the next gig?"

"Well it just so happens there was a cancellation tomorrow and you can have two hours in the afternoon. I believe Pete Peterson's in as well."

"Great!" The look on Ray's face said it all.

Don had called his ex-boss in LAPD again and told him he would be having a conversation with the guys in Pete's band, although he wasn't holding out much hope. Once the spotlights were on it was a limited view of the audience from the stage, but it was worth a try. The local police had searched the area again thoroughly but still hadn't found the other bullet, which Don thought was strange. Considering the first shot had accurately hit Pete's guitar he was sure the second would be somewhere nearby. And the minute he walked into the rehearsal room he saw it.

"Hey Dave, d'you mind if I look at your organ?"

There was a laugh from across the room but the look on his face meant he wasn't joking around.

Dave was immediately defensive. "What for?"

"Well I don't remember there being a hole in the back of the Hammond the last time I looked, and that's suspiciously like a .22 slug stuck in the wooden casing."

"Holy shit!" Randy the bass player exclaimed as he and Marshall came over to look. "I was standing right at the side of you, man."

Don was watching Dave and once again thought there might be more to this than met the eye, but not wanting to cause any further disruption he arranged to meet him after they finished.

As he left the studio he noticed Ray sitting in the café area on his own. He hadn't spoken to him since the hospital in Miami and went over. "Hey man, how's things? I hear the show's going well."

"Hey Don, how's the shoulder?"

Don had forgotten about the gunshot wound he received the night at Benny Mulligan's. "Yeah, ya know, it aches a bit but I'm cool. So how's life as a soul star?"

Ray laughed but seemed uncomfortable. "It's early days. We're having a few personnel problems which is why I'm here today, but otherwise it's going great."

"And how's Janine?"

"She's good, won't take things easy like she's been told, but you know Janine; always knows best."

Ray's band came in as they were talking and he was happy to use them as an excuse to finish the conversation.

Don watched him walking away and thought to himself that things definitely weren't right between him and Janine and he knew the reason why, but was it his place to interfere? He remembered looking into her emerald, green eyes in Miami and being spellbound, but this was not the right time to be getting involved in someone else's problems. On top of which he was about to set off on tour with Pete which would take him halfway across the world and back by which time everything could be back to normal.

Don spotting the bullet hole in the wooden case had thrown Dave and he knew the way he handled his question had been bad. Now the rehearsal had finished he felt more relaxed and ready to answer anything Don asked him. He was sitting waiting for him in the café.

"It's hard to believe you didn't feel the bullet hit the organ," Don said.

"In the heat of the moment I don't feel anything. I was into my solo and in the zone. It's difficult to explain."

"No, I get that. So did you hear the two shots?"

"Yeah, kind of. Where I am everything's so loud though. I thought it could have been Marshall's snare drum."

Don was writing notes down as he talked. "Is everything OK at the moment? Pete and I have noticed you've changed a lot recently."

"Well apart from what usually bothers me, as you well know, I'm fine. How do you mean changed?"

"It's maybe nothing, but Pete was saying you've become a lot more serious, almost militant, lately."

Dave bristled slightly. "Well not that it's any of your business, but there are a few issues I don't agree with. There's nothing for you and Pete to be concerned about though. So, is that all?"

Don put away his notebook. "That's cool, and I'm sorry if I offended you. Obviously having two shots fired at the band is a serious thing and we want to make sure everyone's alright."

Ray and his band had set off for a two-night gig at a soul festival in Fresno. It was a four-hour journey and they were staying over in a local motel on the Saturday night. Janine had considered asking if she could go but decided it would cause too much trouble the way things were at the moment, and so she was sitting at home wondering what to do. She'd already drunk a couple of glasses of champagne when she suddenly decided she fancied going out. But where? Then she remembered the bar in Santa Monica where she first went with Mandy. It was an exclusive place and seemed safe enough to go on her own, so she searched through her wardrobe and found an outfit she'd bought recently but hadn't had a chance to wear. The silver voile top was a little revealing, but with the tight-fitting black trousers and high-heeled black suede shoes, she entered the bar feeling good. She'd let her long red hair hang loose and noticed receiving quite a few glances as she walked up to the bar. Sitting down on an empty stool she ordered a glass of champagne from the barman and lit a cigarette as he poured it for her.

She blew the smoke out and was just about to take a sip when a female voice on her right spoke to her. "That's a beautiful outfit if you don't mind me saying so."

Janine turned to look into the sparkling blue eyes of an attractive woman with shiny black hair pulled back into a loose ponytail who she thought she recognised but couldn't immediately place. She appeared to be on her own and eager to make conversation.

"I haven't seen you in here before. Is this your first time?"

"Actually I came on the opening night," Janine replied.

"Really? I was here that night too. I'm surprised I never met you; you're such a beautiful woman. I'm Claudia by the way."

Janine took her hand and as she did so realised why she recognized her. It was Senator Claudia Inestes. She thought it seemed strange that such an important person would be out on her own without any security, but Claudia didn't seem too concerned.

"Can I get you another drink…?" Claudia left the question hanging, hinting she wanted to know her name.

"Oh sorry, I'm Janine and yes please."

"That's an unusual accent Janine. Where are you from?"

Claudia caught the barman's attention and pointed to Janine's glass.

"Oh I'm from a town called Ballykobh in Southern Ireland." Janine accepted her glass of champagne from the barman and crushed her cigarette out in the ashtray.

"How interesting. I don't think I've ever met anyone from there before." Claudia was becoming more friendly and let her fingers rest on Janine's hand.

Janine was enjoying the attention but still a little wary.

"I'm surprised you don't have any security," she said looking round the bar.

"They tend to stand out in a place like this," Claudia replied nodding her head slightly, acknowledging the fact Janine knew who she was. "But I like to go out on my own occasionally and have a little fun. Do you like to have fun, Janine?" Claudia ran her fingers down Janine's spine which made her body shiver.

Janine took a mouthful of champagne and for a moment wondered what the hell she was doing. As she turned to answer her, Claudia pulled her close and kissed her mouth softly but with a passion that made Janine tingle.

When their lips parted, Janine smiled at her.

"Oh yes Claudia, I love to have fun."

CHAPTER EIGHT

In Fresno the club was packed with women who were pressed up to the front of the stage waiting for Ray to come on. His single was in the top ten with a bullet and the DJ was whipping the crowd up creating the atmosphere ready for the show. The band started the opening number, and accompanied by screams Ray walked out dressed in a tight-fitting white jump suit which left nothing to the imagination and began gyrating to the groove. Taking the microphone from the stand he slowly moved across the front of the stage scanning the audience, making his choice of who he would choose to invite up on stage with him to perform the slow ballad later. He spotted a tall raven-haired woman in the second row who was making eye contact. She was very attractive and he wondered for a moment if she would be coming back to the motel with him after the show, then put it to the back of his mind as the chord sequence to the first song brought him back to the present.

Dave and Alice were sitting in Jacob's pickup parked around the back of Maltrocorp. There was an almost full moon which lit up the area, and they were waiting for Jorge and Rudy to start their demonstration at the front gates. Alice was dressed in her usual camouflage gear while Dave was wearing all black. He'd bought a black ski mask especially, although Alice had laughed when he put it on. "Ooh! Don't we look like Special Forces!"

Suddenly the noise from around the front signalled the beginning of the demonstration and they prepared themselves to begin. Alice removed a large pair of wire cutters from a canvas holdall she'd brought with her, and within a couple of minutes she'd cut a hole large enough for her and Dave to slip through. The disturbance at the main gate was obviously working as they hadn't seen any security guards and they silently made their way across the open ground to the shed where the monkeys were kept.

Dave checked his watch and so far they were ahead of Claus' schedule. Alice set to work on the shed door easily snapping the lock off and carefully turning the handle. However, the moment she pulled the door open there was a deafening wailing sound from an alarm inside the shed which set all the monkeys in their cages screaming and panicking. This hadn't been in Claus' plans and momentarily they were taken by surprise.

Pulling himself together Dave turned to Alice and shouted. "The cages! Quick, open the cages then let's get out of here!"

The monkeys were still frantically jumping up and down as Alice wrenched opened the cage doors. Two of them immediately understood what was happening and leaped out on to the floor as she was making her way down the row encouraging them to escape. Dave had been standing just inside the door watching, and noticed one monkey in particular was reluctant to leave his cage. He reached inside to encourage it, but before he had chance to react the monkey leapt up and bit his hand. Fortunately he'd had the foresight to wear a pair of gloves, but even so he felt the animal's teeth penetrate the material and scratch the skin. He pulled his hand back and shouted to Alice that they should leave.

By now the monkeys were pouring out of the shed and the two of them ran out just as a pair of security guards came round the corner.

Dave dived through the hole in the fence first and was running towards Jacob's pickup. He glanced over his shoulder to see Alice climbing through the gap just as one of the guards pulled out a gun and fired. The bullet hit her in the leg and she collapsed on the floor with a squeal. Dave turned round to go back but she shouted for him to leave her, as she produced a pistol from the holdall and shot the first guard between the eyes as he ran towards her. He collapsed on the grass as she twisted her body to aim at the second guard who had stopped running; but he was too quick for her, and crouching down fired a burst from his gun hitting her in the chest, killing her instantly. Dave had been riveted to the spot watching in horror what had just happened, but Jacob was yelling at him to get in the truck and he slammed it into gear as Dave threw himself onto the back seat, driving off with a squeal of tyres.

They had been hurtling down the highway for ages before anyone spoke. "What the fuck happened?" Jacob's voice was shaking.

Dave had taken his ski-mask and gloves off and was examining his hand. "There was an alarm in the shed. Claus never mentioned an alarm."

"They shot Alice. What are we gonna do, man?" Jacob was becoming frantic and Dave noticed they were doing well over the speed limit. The last thing they needed was to be stopped by the police.

"Slow down and pull over to the side." Dave was trying to remain calm.

Jacob was shaking as he finally stopped at the side of the road. He opened the driver's door and threw up.

"It's OK man, just calm down. Let me drive back." Dave helped him out of the driving seat.

They eventually arrived at Jacob's apartment at almost three o'clock to find Claus on his own panicking. "Shit, shit, shit," he shouted as they explained what had happened. "I said no guns! I specifically told her no guns!"

"They were armed. They fired first," Dave replied.

"But she didn't have to kill the guy," Claus was distraught.

"Where are Jorge and Rudy?" Jacob asked.

"They managed to escape when the shooting started," Claus said.

Dave was rubbing his hand. "I think we're OK. I don't think the other guard got a chance to see the truck's licence plates. He was too busy with Alice."

Claus noticed Dave's hand. "What's the matter with your hand?"

"It's nothing. One of the monkeys bit me, but I had gloves on."

"You need to get that checked out."

"Oh yeah? So I just wander into an Emergency Room and announce I've been bitten by a fucking mad monkey. That's gonna go down great. Look it's alright, it didn't draw blood. It's just a scratch, I'll be fine."

But in the back of his mind there was something telling him it was more than just a scratch.

CHAPTER NINE

Janine was lying in a king-sized bed in Claudia Inestes' bedroom. She was taking in the sensational uninterrupted view across Los Angeles afforded by the fact that the rear of the four-bedroomed timber house was supported by a huge slab of rock protruding from the side of Laurel Canyon and one complete wall was floor-to-ceiling glass.

Claudia wafted into the room wearing a sheer gown over her toned naked body which Janine couldn't help but admire. She watched as her host carried a tray with two crystal champagne flutes and a bottle of Louis Roederer Cristal champagne in an elegant ice bucket. Putting it down on the mirrored console table she poured them both a glass and letting her gown slide off her shoulders she joined Janine under the black satin sheets. They both sipped the elegant liquid taking in its refined apricot and hazelnut flavours. Janine had always thought Bollinger couldn't be beaten, but this was just sublime.

Claudia smiled as she slowly pulled the sheet from their bodies and saw Janine's silk knickers. "Oh my, why so shy?" Claudia slowly slid down the bed, hooking her fingers under the seams. Janine felt her warm breath between her legs and her tongue probing her, teasing her, making her groan as she was played with. Claudia was highly skilled and the way she controlled Janine frightened her. She seemed to know just where to touch to send a shock wave through her body and then seconds later she would use her mouth to lick and suck her most private parts that she was powerless to stop.

Why did she like this so much? Was this a part of her she didn't know existed. She'd always loved sex with men, but just recently with Mandy and now Claudia, they were introducing her to feelings she'd never experienced before and she was loving it. Claudia's fingers were stroking her and she was arching her back to meet them, her breaths coming faster as her whole being suddenly exploded.

She lay back on the bed gasping as Claudia kissed her mouth, then sat up reaching for her glass and swallowing it down in one go. "Jeesus, that's given me a hell of a thirst!" Claudia watched horrified as she swilled her best champagne like soda.

Claudia was about to pour them another glass of Cristal when the phone rang. She slammed the bottle back in the bucket and draping her gown around her shoulders stormed out of the bedroom into her office next door. Janine stretched out and gazed at the view through the panoramic windows but couldn't help overhearing the conversation through the open door.

"How many times have I told you not to bother me at home." She listened.

"No, I'm entertaining. Wait a minute."

There was a click and a television came on. Janine could hear a reporter talking about a shooting in Anaheim and the name Maltrocorp. Claudia spoke again.

"Fuck! How the hell did that happen?" She listened again.

"Well there's nothing I can do now, you'll just have to deal with it.... Yes, whatever..... I don't care just do it! Look, I've got to go, I'll call you tomorrow."

She put the phone down and switched off the TV. Moments later she strolled back into the bedroom with a smile as if nothing had happened. Janine watched her as she poured them another glass of champagne and noticed she wasn't as relaxed as she was making out and wondered why the shooting in Anaheim had bothered her so much.

It was eight o'clock on a Saturday night and Don Rosario was sitting on a stool in his local bar alone. His relationship with the actress friend of Kathy Blake had been short lived. Understandable really as he'd been on tour with Pete and the band for ages and he'd hardly kept in touch. And in a week's time he would be off again for months on end travelling the world, which sounded exciting but in actual fact could be as lonely as sitting here on his own nursing a half empty bottle of beer. He'd often thought about settling down, but what would he do?

The LAPD had been his life until the shooting and then all he'd known since was travelling on the road with a succession of bands. He had to admit Pete and the guys were by far the best and he loved it, but maybe he should start thinking about the future. Then his mind drifted back to the kiss he'd shared with Janine in Miami. Was it his imagination or had she responded. She certainly hadn't reacted badly or pushed him away. He knew she was married to Ray and until recently he'd been a good friend, a brother in arms, but he'd treated her so badly Don no longer had any respect for him. And from what he'd heard on the grapevine he was rapidly gaining a reputation as a womaniser at his shows with no regard for Janine whatsoever.

Don finished his beer and made his way to his car. There was something he had to do and it couldn't wait. He stopped at a liquor store just around the corner from the bar and chose a bottle of Bollinger champagne from the chiller cabinet and set off to Hermosa Beach.

The atmosphere had noticeably changed in Claudia's bedroom since the phone call and she visibly breathed a sigh of relief when Janine said she thought maybe it was time for her to leave, and after promising to meet up again at the bar in Santa Monica Janine climbed into her taxi. It had been an interesting evening and her body ached from their lovemaking, but she had to admit she was looking forward to having a chilled glass of her own champagne on her balcony overlooking the ocean.

Don had arrived at Janine's house on The Strand in Hermosa Beach five minutes earlier and found it in darkness. He thought maybe she had gone up to Fresno with Ray or was out with Pete, and was making his way back to his car when he saw her taxi pull up. He met her as she climbed out.

"Hey Don, what's up?"

"Hi Janine, listen I just thought you might be on your own and I've got this bottle of champagne I know you like and thought maybe we could share it?" He knew he was waffling and sounded embarrassed.

"That is so nice," she said giving him a kiss on the cheek. "Come on in, I'll get us some glasses."

She flicked the lights on and quickly found a couple of champagne flutes which they took out onto the balcony along with Don's bottle. It was nicely chilled and he poured them a couple of glasses. She admired the way he opened the bottle recalling how Gerry had first shown her the correct way to do it in Georgie's so long ago. They clinked glasses and savoured the biscuity taste. 'I was wrong, this is much nicer than Cristal' Janine thought to herself.

"Hey it's really nice up here," Don said relaxing back and admiring the view.

"Sometimes at night the waves have a mysterious glow to them," she said glancing at him, realising that he actually was a good-looking man. He was built like a boxer but had a gentle manner that she really liked. She remembered when she first met him in Manny's office and how she'd thought at the time they would get on.

"So where's Ray tonight?" Don asked.

"He's up in Fresno doing two nights at some club there."

"Those two guys he's signed to are certainly working him hard."

"Yeah, his single's in the top ten this week with a bullet. I have to admit it's taken the pressure off me trying to deal with him and Pete at the same time. And to be honest I don't know anything about the soul scene so it's a good thing really."

"And if you don't mind me asking, how are things between you now?"

She took a long swallow of champagne and filled up her empty glass again.

"Truthfully Don, I don't know. He comes home after his gigs smelling of a different perfume every night and tells me he's tired. We say hello in the morning and then he's off again to the next gig. Don't get me wrong, I can't complain because this is what he's always wanted to do ever since he was a young guy in Liverpool, but he seems to have become a different person. Someone I don't know anymore." She stopped. "Oh look I'm sorry for going on, here let me top you up."

She picked up the bottle to fill Don's glass and as he held it up he noticed she was crying. He stood up and enveloped her in his huge arms and held her as she quietly sobbed into his shoulder. Finally he let her go and she smiled at him with teary eyes. "Thank you, I needed that."

He put his finger under her chin and kissed her lips gently. He felt her respond and push herself against him tensing as she felt how excited he was.

"I'm not sure this is a good idea," she said. "I mean I really like you and I know you like me, but if we went to bed together I would be afraid we'd destroy what we have and I don't want to lose it."

Don looked at her, "Hey, I understand. One day the time will be right and I'll be here waiting."

She kissed him again. "Thank you Don, I know you will."

CHAPTER TEN

Ray had chosen the woman with the raven hair to join him on stage for the slow ballad. She'd made it quite obvious during the show watching his every move and giving him smiles whenever their eyes met. She told him she was called Gina when he invited her up to dance and had a slim, lithe body which she seductively rubbed against him as they moved to the groove of the band. At the end of the song Ray gave her a kiss and as she left the stage whispered he would like to see her later. He was sitting in his dressing room after the show having a glass of brandy when there was a knock at the door. He opened it to find Gina standing there, waiting for him to invite her in.

"Hey listen we're all heading back to our motel for a party; do you want to come? It should be fun."

"Sounds great," she said. "Give me a minute and I'll tell my friends I'm going back with you. Where are you staying?"

"We're at the Night Owl Motel just down the road about a mile," he replied packing his bag.

Gina went out and returned moments later. "That's cool, I told them I'd be back late; I mean if that's OK with you." She walked over to Ray and kissed him putting her arms around his neck.

"Yeah that's OK with me," he said running his hands down her back and cupping the cheeks of her bottom as he pulled her close to kiss her again.

She slipped her hand down to his crotch and stroked him. "Mmmmm. Hope you got some protection for that thing, I don't want you gettin' me into trouble, you know what I'm sayin?"

"Don't worry baby, I'm cool," Ray said leading her out of the club.

She looked over her shoulder as she climbed on the tour bus and saw a car flash it's lights.

Once back at the motel the party was soon in full swing with the band keeping the night receptionist busy behind the bar. After a few minutes Ray whispered to Gina to follow him. He took her hand and they left the reception heading down the corridor as two men wearing overcoats and carrying small cases came in unnoticed. They watched Ray and Gina leaving, making a note of where they went. Ray opened his door and Gina followed him in glancing back to make sure her two accomplices had seen them.

Ray poured two glasses of brandy passing one to her and sat down on the bed patting the mattress at his side for Gina to join him. He put his arm around her shoulder as she sat next to him and kissed her neck smelling her perfume.

"You smell nice," he said nuzzling in close. She reached down and felt the growing bulge in his trousers, undoing his belt and slowly lowering his zip. Pushing him back on the bed she pulled his trousers down to his ankles and flipped his erection out of his shorts. He lay back as she teased him with her hand.

"Stay there baby, I want to blindfold you and play with you."

Ray leaned forward but she pushed him back. "Relax." She pulled a scarf from her bag and tied it around his eyes as she kissed him. "Stay just like that," she whispered in his ear, "This is gonna blow your mind."

She climbed off the bed and silently opened the door. The two men from reception were waiting outside and slipped into the room. Gina climbed back on the bed and started to use her mouth on Ray keeping him occupied as the men put their cases down on the floor. Ray was making noises on the bed as Gina teased him, and was unaware of the preparations going on around him. He was becoming more excited telling Gina not to stop when he felt a sharp prick in his arm and jerked up pulling at his blindfold. The last thing he remembered seeing as he ripped the scarf from his eyes was two men standing watching as Gina still held onto his slowly diminishing manhood.

He didn't know how long he'd been unconscious but as he opened his eyes he realised he couldn't move. He'd been trussed up with his wrists tied tightly to his ankles and a rope around his neck forcing him to arch his back, his legs held apart by a bar between his knees. He was naked and in a kneeling position on the bed with a rubber ball in his mouth held in position by a gag, forcing him to breathe through his nose. He was facing towards the wall and even though he could move his head a little he couldn't see behind him. Suddenly he felt a horrendous pain as something large was pushed inside him from behind. He shouted into the gag but only a muffled sound could be heard. The pain came again and again as he was forcibly penetrated and his legs started to shake as the man behind drove into him. There was a brief respite as the men changed places with the second man taking over with something which felt like it was ripping him apart. He was screaming into the gag when Gina came into his vision holding an enormous black phallus and smiling. He watched as she strapped it to herself and then replaced the second man mercilessly fucking him.

He was on the point of passing out when she stopped, and appeared again unstrapping the giant dildo which was covered in blood. She dangled it in front of Ray's face and dropped it onto the bed in front of him. She put her mouth close to his ear and whispered. "Josie Thomas sends her love."

He was mumbling a reply into the gag when one of the men appeared and blew him a kiss. Then he felt another prick in his arm and passed out.

The two men tidied up, picked up their cases and left the room followed by Gina who pulled the door closed hanging the 'Do Not Disturb' notice on the handle. They walked through reception where there was still a couple of musicians in the bar, by now too drunk to notice them, and drove off in their car.

The next morning Ray awoke with a thumping headache. He opened his eyes and looked around the room but everything appeared normal and he was lying in bed naked. He began to think it must have been a bad dream and went to sit up but was hit by a pain like he'd never experienced before. He tried to move his legs but that made the pain worse. He pulled the cover back and saw a giant blood stain on the sheet beneath him and the horror of the previous night's events came crashing back. He closed his eyes and saw Gina's face and remembered her words, "Josie Thomas sends her love." He managed to crawl out of bed into the bathroom and threw up into the toilet on his hands and knees.

He checked the time and saw it was just before eleven o'clock which gave him plenty of time before that night's show to sort himself out. He would have to get some painkillers and something to stop the bleeding but he didn't want any of the band to know what had happened. He could barely stand, but struggled into the shower and cleaned himself up. He cautiously dressed and taking his time walked over to the drugstore across the road where he bought a bottle of the strongest painkillers they sold and a pack of disposable nappies, which he found were called diapers in the States. Slowly making his way back to his room he met one of the band in reception who looked as bad as he felt. Mercifully he wasn't interested in having a conversation and Ray guessed it was probably self-inflicted, judging by the amount of empty bottles and glasses on the bar. He finally reached the comfort of his room and swallowing a handful of tablets washed down with a large glass of brandy he carefully pressed the diaper in place and lay back on his bed closing his eyes.

Pete had recently decided it was time to move on from his apartment to somewhere more spacious, and had found an amazing Art Deco styled property on Mulholland Drive called The Red House. So called because not surprisingly it had been painted bright red. The realtor had told him he had an eclectic selection of neighbours including film producers and actors, although most of them were pretty reclusive. Having been used to the non-stop party atmosphere of Venice Beach it had been a bit of a culture shock to Pete and he found himself feeling cut off at times. He'd thrown a couple of parties inviting the guys from the band, but rattling around in the huge mansion was beginning to get him down. Lying by the side of his pool or watching films in his own private cinema soon became boring especially as he was unattached again. He and Carly had parted ways, amicably, but her sexual deviances had begun to concern him and he'd decided it was time to move on. He'd called Janine to see if she fancied coming out for a drink but got no reply. The same with Don, so finally he'd driven down to Santa Monica to see if there was any action.

He parked his car on a side street and was walking down towards the pier when he spotted Janine across the road getting out of a taxi and was just about to call out when she disappeared into a bar called 'Renée's'.

His first reaction was to follow her, but then he remembered being told it was a renowned gay bar. Not that it was any of his business, but why would Janine be going into somewhere like that? His curiosity got the better of him, and he strolled over to look in through the window and spotted her sitting at the bar. He watched as she ordered a drink and lit a cigarette, then the woman next to her turned and they struck up a conversation. Pete began to feel like a Private Investigator spying on her. He thought he should leave when he recognised the other woman. It was Senator Claudia Inestes. Now he was intrigued and couldn't believe his eyes as the senator's hand seductively stroked Janine's spine and she leaned across and kissed her. Pete was so shocked he was rooted to the spot and only just managed to turn away before they both came out of the bar, climbed into Claudia's car and drove off.

'Well, well, well, I'd never have believed it if I hadn't seen it with my own eyes,' he thought to himself as he wandered down to a bar he knew by the pier.

CHAPTER ELEVEN

The experience at Maltrocorp had scared Dave. Luckily both he and Peter had managed to get away without being seen, but it was too close for comfort. He had been watching the News bulletins but so far there had only been a short mention of the incident which he found strange considering there had been two people killed. He decided to do a bit of digging to see if he could find out more about Maltrocorp. It was a tricky job as details were pretty much non-existent and everyone he asked knew little or nothing about who they were or what they did.

He eventually discovered the company was listed as a pharmaceutical development facility, but he had his suspicions. His main concern was the fact the security guards had been prepared to shoot intruders; which said there was something more serious going on there than they first thought, and they weren't afraid to use force to protect it. As he considered the little he had found out, he automatically rubbed his hand where the monkey had bitten him. Luckily the glove seemed to have saved him and apart from a slight ache the mark had disappeared. He decided it was time to come clean before anything else happened and called Don to arrange a meeting as soon as possible.

Manny Oberstein, Don Rosario, Pete Peterson and Janine Law were in Manny's office when Dave arrived. He sat down and thanked them for coming.

"As you all know being gay in a rock band is not the easiest of things and up until now I've managed to deal with it. A while ago I found a group of people in LA and went to their meetings on a regular basis. It started out as fun. I met some cool people and we talked about our problems. Unfortunately as our group grew, more outside influences joined and I'll admit, I got sucked into supporting causes that in hindsight maybe I shouldn't. One of those was the Animal Rights group which was run by a woman called Alice."

Pete interrupted. "Is this the Alice who was shot last week in Anaheim?"

"Yes it was," Dave replied. "I was there."

"Shit, man why didn't you tell me?" Don exclaimed.

"Well it was kind of scary what happened. Look, all we planned to do was release some monkeys who were being used for experiments. But things went wrong and the next thing I know there's a gun fight between two guards and Alice. One opened fire and shot her in the leg so she shoots him. Bang, right between the eyes and then the other one killed her. It was horrendous."

"They fired first? Are you sure about that?" Don asked.

"Yeah, there was an alarm went off as we were going in the monkey house. She opened all the cages and we were just getting out when these two guards came round the corner and all hell broke loose."

"Did anyone see you?" Manny asked.

"I don't think so. I was wearing a mask and managed to get in the truck as we escaped."

Janine had been quietly listening. "Where did you say the place was you broke into?"

"Anaheim" Dave replied.

Her mind went back to Saturday night in Claudia Inestes' bedroom listening to the phone conversation with someone about the incident in Anaheim. She wasn't going to say anything now, but maybe she would have a conversation with Don separately.

"Thing is, I'm really nervous about staying on my own," Dave said. "I mean I think we got away without being seen, but I can't be sure."

"Look why don't you come up and stay at my place until we leave," Pete said. "It's not like I don't have enough rooms."

Ray had arrived home late from the second gig in Fresno. Janine was asleep and he slipped into bed being careful not to wake her. The last thing he wanted was a conversation about how the shows had gone. He was still in pain although thankfully the bleeding had stopped and he'd been able to discard the diapers.

The second show had been awful, mainly because he'd had to stand still to sing instead of dancing like he usually did. A couple of the musicians had commented, but he'd made an excuse he had a bad stomach and didn't want to risk having an accident on stage. Fortunately, he had a few days off to recover before the next run of gigs. He lay staring at the ceiling in the dark thinking. If one thing the other night had taught him, was to be a lot more careful about inviting women back after the show. It was tricky dealing with a jealous boyfriend or husband, but a woman scorned was something far more dangerous. So he'd chosen a real 'plain Jane' last night and made no effort to invite her backstage afterwards.

Janine met up with Don the next day and they sat in the cafe area at Whitland Studios to talk.

"What do you know about Maltrocorp?"

"Not a lot. They appear on the surface to be an ordinary pharmaceutical company working on Cancer cures, but it does seem strange to have armed guards patrolling the place who are prepared to shoot."

"If I were to tell you that Senator Claudia Inestes has an interest in the company what would you think?

Don looked at Janine. "I'd think how the hell do you know that?"

Janine smiled. "For the moment let's just say I found out by mistake. But she wasn't happy about what happened on Saturday night."

"Hmmm, I'm intrigued. But that is interesting. Considering she's standing for Mayor she has to have a squeaky clean image and any kind of scandal would put paid to her ambitions."

"Yeah, that's what I thought."

"Maybe I'll have an off-the-record chat with my ex-boss at LAPD to see if he knows anything. For now you be careful."

But her interest had been piqued after talking with Don and she decided to go against his wishes and carry out a bit of detective work herself.

CHAPTER TWELVE

Senator Claudia Inestes had called a meeting in her Downtown Los Angeles office. She was sitting at the head of a polished olive wood table smoking a thin black cigarillo.

She studied the faces of the men around her.

"What the fuck happened at Maltrocorp?"

The man on her right answered. "There was this bunch of idiots at the front gate making a load of noise and we had it totally under control, then suddenly the alarm goes off in the monkey shed and Tomaš and I go round to check what's going on and there's this crazy woman dressed up like Rambo making a run for the fence. Tomaš shoots her in the leg but she pops him right between the eyes and was about to do the same to me when I took her out."

"Was she on her own?"

"No there was a guy with her who'd got through the fence and a driver waiting with a truck. They took off before I had chance to deal with them."

"Did you get the plate of the truck?"

"Yeah, it's being dealt with."

"What about the accomplice?"

"Nothing so far, I didn't see his face because he had a mask on. But we're keeping our eyes and ears open. He'll turn up sooner or later don't worry."

She crushed her cigarillo out and stared at him. "But I do worry, and I don't like loose ends. I expect you to deal with it."

Dave had been calling Jacob since he'd moved into Pete's house but hadn't been able to contact him. The interior designers where he worked hadn't heard from him either and he was starting to get worried. He was watching TV when he saw a news report about a head-on collision between a large semi-trailer and a pick-up truck. As the camera focussed on the mangled remains, Dave spotted the licence plate and realised with horror that it was Jacob's truck. The reporter was saying that eyewitnesses heard a loud bang like a gunshot before the pick-up veered sharply to the left in front of the oncoming traffic. A black sedan also believed to have been involved left the scene without stopping. Pete had been in the kitchen fixing a drink and returned to see his friend sitting staring at the screen shaking uncontrollably.

When he finally managed to calm down and explain what the problem was, Pete called Don who said he would be right over. When he opened the door an hour later it was to Don and another man he thought he'd met before.

Don introduced his friend. "Dave, this is my ex-boss Captain Lewis from the LAPD who I'm sure you remember, Pete. I had an off-the-record chat with him after our meeting the other day and I thought it would be useful to have him here."

Dave looked worried, but Captain Lewis reassured him he was there to help. "So what you're saying is, the victim in the report you saw on the news was your friend, Jacob?" Dave nodded.

"You're sure?"

"I recognised the licence plate on the truck. It was definitely Jacob's, and I haven't been able to contact him."

"So it would appear you were seen after all," Don said. "It sounds like Maltrocorp has more to hide than just a shed full of monkeys."

"What do we know about Maltrocorp?" Captain Lewis asked.

"Well all I discovered was it's listed as a pharmaceutical research company working on Cancer cures but nothing else," Dave answered.

"Hmm, I might just get a couple of my guys to look into it. It would be interesting to find out who's behind it. It's good that you're off on tour. I suggest you keep your head down. And for now I'm going to pretend I didn't hear anything you told me tonight." Captain Lewis turned to

Don. "You were right to call me. There's a bad smell about Maltrocorp and I aim to find out what it is."

As Pete let Don and Captain Lewis out he wondered what the hell his friend had got himself into.

Senator Claudia Inestes had just dismissed the men from her office and was packing up ready to leave when the phone rang. Normally her secretary would have dealt with it, but she'd left early so Claudia answered it herself and immediately recognised the accent of the woman calling her.

"Hey, Janine. How are you? You're lucky to catch me, I was just leaving."

"I was wondering if you're free tonight. Maybe we could get a few drinks at Renée's?"

"That sounds great." Claudia decided she would reschedule her meeting with a local charity organiser. "I'll meet you there at eight o'clock."

Janine put the phone down and wondered whether she was doing the right thing especially after what Don had said, but she was only going for a couple of drinks so what harm could it do.

Ray had gone out earlier for a meeting with Eddy and Charles and she didn't fancy a night in on her own. She climbed out of the shower and, towel-drying her hair, flicked through her wardrobe and found a new top she'd bought from her favourite boutique in Hermosa Bay which fitted her in all the right places. Not too provocative but she thought it would serve its purpose. She pulled on a tight pair of blue jeans, a pair of red pumps and she was ready. As she walked into the bar with her long red hair flowing across her shoulders she felt numerous pairs of eyes on her and enjoyed the attention as she spotted Claudia sitting at a table in the corner. She was talking to a man who stood up and left as soon as Janine arrived.

"My security decided to accompany me tonight," she said standing up giving Janine a peck on the cheek.

'Slightly more reserved tonight' Janine thought.

"I ordered champagne, I hope you don't mind," she said as Janine sat down.

"Wonderful, just what I need," Janine lit a cigarette.

Claudia took a pack of cigarillos from her handbag and lit one, drawing deeply and slowly exhaling. "It was a surprise to hear from you," she said looking Janine in the eyes.

Janine felt like she was being studied and decided she needed to be cautious. "Well the other night ended so abruptly I hoped everything was alright. You seemed upset after your phone call. Was it about your campaign to be mayor?"

Claudia was studying her again. "No, just one of my staff. I constantly tell them not to bother me at home unless it's urgent but they never listen. But enough about me, how are you? You look sensational tonight."

Janine tilted her head acknowledging the compliment. "Thank you. Hey, I've been reading your manifesto pledges. Very strong, you'll definitely get my vote," she replied trying to change the conversation back. "Your support of charities is so commendable. That was such a terrible thing that those awful Animal Welfare protesters should try and disrupt the good work companies like that place in Anaheim do, don't you think? Terrible!"

Claudia was watching her again. "I'm not sure I saw that, I've been so busy recently, I don't get the chance to watch TV. I am however speaking at a rally this weekend in aid of cancer research here in LA. You should come along." She paused. "Say, you never told me what brought you to our wonderful city." Another subtle change of subject.

"After my husband died he left me extremely well off and I decided to come over here to start anew. Los Angeles was a place I always wanted to visit so I rented a house here and I love it."

As they were talking Janine could see Claudia's security man hovering nearby, finally coming over when he noticed a lull in their conversation. "I'm sorry Senator, I've just been informed you're required at your office."

She gave him a look which couldn't disguise the fact it was pre-arranged. "Can't it wait?"

"No, I'm sorry, it appears to be urgent."

"Damn! Janine I'm so sorry. Maybe we could do dinner, my treat." She stood up and gave Janine another kiss on the cheek. 'Definitely cold this time.' "I'll call you," she said as she left accompanied by her minder.

Janine leaned back and finished her drink, crushing her cigarette out. It hadn't gone as well as she'd hoped and she doubted she'd be seeing Senator Inestes again because unless she was psychic, Janine hadn't given her a phone number.

The Senator climbed into the back of the limousine waiting outside and lit another cigarillo, crossing her stockinged legs as she relaxed back into the soft leather seat. "I think we're going to have to be careful with her," she said to the driver as he pulled away. "She asks far too many questions." She caught his eye as he glanced at her in his rear-view mirror. "I hope you've not got any plans for later."

Janine waited until Claudia had left then called Don from the public call box on the wall by the bar. He'd just arrived back home when his phone rang.

"Hey Janine, what's goin' on? Where are you, I can hear music in the background?"

She told him where she was.

"Renée's in Santa Monica? That's the expensive gay bar. What the hell are you doing there, Janine? Hey look forget I asked, I don't want to know."

She explained what had just happened with Claudia.

"I thought I told you to be careful. We don't know what we're dealing with here!"

"There's definitely something not right about Senator Inestes," she said ignoring his comment. "Why did she say that she didn't know about the

Maltrocorp incident when I heard her switch the TV on and watch it at her place?"

"Well I won't ask what you were doing there, but yeah, it does sound suspicious. I'll call Captain Lewis and tell him what you just said. I've just been up to Pete's place and Dave came clean about everything he's been up to. You won't believe what he said, including what went on at Maltrocorp. Captain Lewis is going to put a couple of his men onto it so your info could be useful. Listen, you need to get back home; do you want me to come and pick you up?"

She said she didn't, so they said goodnight and she climbed into the waiting cab. She didn't see the car pull out behind as they left and tail her all the way home to Hermosa Beach making a note of her address.

Ray was in when she opened the door and welcomed her with a glass of champagne. It was the first time in ages they'd both been home and wide awake at the same time and after another glass of bubbly Janine was feeling relaxed and a little frisky as Ray kissed her and, taking her by the hand, led her into their bedroom. It had been so long since the last time they'd made love. She closed her eyes and held him tight wrapping her legs around him pulling him deep inside her. They were both on the verge of coming as she reached down and pushed her finger into his ass, intending only to excite him further but he let out an ear-piercing scream and rolled off her doubling up in pain by her side. She was so taken by surprise she froze not knowing what had happened, but when she looked at her finger she could see it was covered in blood and so were the sheets where Ray was lying. Her first instinct was to call for an ambulance but he said he would be fine, and crawling off the bed he opened the hold-all he took with him on his gigs and found a diaper which he held to his backside. She got off the bed and was trying to help him but he told her to leave him alone and everything would be alright in a few moments.

"What the hell just happened?" Janine pulled her dressing gown around herself staring at her husband as he gingerly stood up. If it hadn't been so frightening she would have laughed at the surreal sight of 'Soul Singer Ray Law' holding a child's nappy to his rear end.

"It's a long story and you really don't want to know."

"After what I've just seen, I really do want to know," she said pouring herself another glass of champagne.

"Could you get me a large brandy?" His mind was racing as he played for more time.

She fetched him a large cut-glass balloon half filled with Remy Martin and he took a long pull on it.

"It was all a crazy mistake. I've been doing this dance routine to one of the songs in the set and I started putting a few Northern Soul moves in. You know what I mean, spins and the splits. Anyway last weekend up in Fresno I went a bit too far. The lighting wasn't too good and instead of pulling off this great move I landed on my backside across the corner of the drum riser doing myself a bit of an injury. I thought it had healed up until you decided to stick your finger where the sun don't shine!"

"You fool, why didn't you tell me? Did you go to hospital?"

"Nah, it didn't seem too bad at the time and I got some pain killers and a pack of diapers and they seemed to do the trick. It'll teach me to watch where I'm dancing in future."

"Come here," she said and wrapped her arms around him. "I've missed you." She kissed him.

He rested his head on her shoulder and smiled at the way he'd just got himself out of a tight corner. "I've missed you too."

CHAPTER THIRTEEN

Pete had been a bystander as his friend and fellow band member Dave Sanchez revealed his secrets to Don Rosario and Captain Lewis of the LAPD. It had been a revelation to him what Dave had been up to, and the fact he'd had no idea about any of it surprised and shocked him. Listening to Dave relating stories about his recent exploits almost made Pete jealous. Looking around at the trappings of his stardom, the platinum disks on the wall, and the luxurious furniture in the designer house, all amazing, but he realised how insular he had become. Mulholland Drive was the cool place to live, but since he'd split with Carly he hadn't had a girlfriend. Maybe he wanted something more than just a temporary relationship, but all the while he was travelling around the world how could he ever contemplate anything more? Sure there would be plenty of one-night stands on tour, but had he come to a time in his life when he should think about settling down? Up to now it was a thought he'd always dismissed out of hand, but just recently he felt he'd changed. Was it down to the photos Judy had sent of his son Rick who was growing so fast he'd hardly recognised him? Dave had gone to bed after Don and Captain Lewis left leaving Pete on his own with a bottle of bourbon for company. He'd poured himself three fingers of liquor and rummaged through his writing desk to find the little handmade album Judy had sent him.

On the last page there was a photo of Judy and Rick sitting together laughing. He looked at it for ages and suddenly realised the bottle of Jack Daniels beside him was empty. He staggered as he stood up and made his way unsteadily to bed, leaving the book open on the floor where it had fallen.

Don Rosario was in Manny Oberstein's office going through the schedules for Peterson's upcoming tour. Manny had put a call in to Janine and she was on her way to discuss the expenses and everything else associated with making sure Pete and the guys had all they needed. Don would be driving them again on the first leg which took in most of the Eastern seaboard before they flew off to Japan and the Far East.

They would stop off in Europe for the last part before returning to the States and finishing with a string of dates on the West Coast.

Before she arrived Don was bringing Manny up to date with all the events that had been happening since they last met. Manny sat behind his desk listening as he told him about the Maltrocorp incident involving Dave Sanchez.

"This sounds like another fucking film script," he exclaimed.

"Not only do we have the kidnapping up in Boston and Janine's traumas down in Miami, now we've got saboteurs getting shot in LA. Please tell me that's all there is. I couldn't take any more excitement." He stopped a moment to stub his cigar out. "And before she gets here, how's things between Janine and Ray? Thank God she decided to offload him to those two cowboys down the road."

"To be honest Manny I try to keep out of their affairs. It seems Ray's doing alright now he's ditched that female singer. To be fair it was a master stroke getting Pete to produce his record. He's playing lots of discos and by all accounts doing well, and he was telling me he's got a tour of the UK with a couple of Motown stars."

"Well good luck to him with that. They're notorious for non-paying over there so I've been told. He'll need to have his wits about him."

They were just laughing as Janine came in.

"What's the joke?"

Manny got up to kiss her. "Don was telling me about Ray's UK tour. He's gonna have to watch them like a hawk. Tell him to make sure he picks up his money every night."

"I will, don't worry, but thankfully it's not my problem. Eddy and Charles seem to know what they're doing and so far so good."

"Is he playing The Lexxicon?" Don asked.

"I believe so. Judy called me a while back to say she'd had a contract. Turns out it's a bit of a coincidence because Pete's over in the UK at the same time."

"You should come over. You could visit your friend, see one of Pete's shows and catch Ray's as well. Surprise him."

Janine thought about what Don had just said. 'Surprise him. Yes. I might just do that!'

Pete and the band set out on their tour. They'd flown over to Chicago to pick up the new tour bus and, with Don at the wheel, pulled into the car park at the back of Wrigley Field, home of the Chicago Cubs baseball team. They were expecting a crowd of around 20,000 for the show, and the excitement was plain to see as everywhere they looked people were waiting to get into the stadium. Don couldn't help but smile as he noticed how many of Pete's female fans were wearing neckerchiefs, as well as T-shirts featuring the image from the front cover of 'The Dawning', the new album.

One particularly attractive young female fan wearing a leather jacket and tight jeans had managed to get a backstage pass. She excitedly told everyone her name was Elaine and that she was a huge fan. She disappeared with Pete, and eventually left happily clutching his neckerchief.

The rest of the East Coast tour thankfully went without any major incident. They played in Boston at the Red Sox stadium where, as they were leaving the bus to enter the stadium, a woman appeared carrying a small case. She seemed to know Marshall and Randy who greeted her with hugs and kisses, and along with Don followed Pete and Dave into the dressing rooms. The three guys were laughing with the woman who eventually introduced herself to Pete.

"Hi, my name's Cynthia Albritten and I've been dying to meet you for such a long time." Pete looked at Marshall and Randy still oblivious. "I'm sorry, maybe you know me by my other name, Cynthia Plaster-Caster," she said watching as the blood drained from Pete's face when he finally realised who she was. "Hey there's no need to worry," she said smiling and holding Pete's hand. "It's all quite painless."

Pete had to laugh, a chance to be immortalised in plaster. What would the guys back home think! He followed her down the corridor and half an hour later returned with a huge grin. His erect memento was safely packed away in her case to be added to her collection once it had hardened!

Later, the sad memories of the last time they were in the city were signified by a minute's silence to commemorate their keyboard player Richard Kaye, shot dead during the kidnapping of Pete.

They played Shea Stadium in New York where years ago The Beatles had performed. They broke the attendance record and were introduced on stage by legendary chat show host and now personal friend, Johnny Carlton. After the show he and Pete spent a couple of hours in their favourite bar, The Cloud Club on the 66th floor of the Chrysler Building, swapping stories and drinking bourbon.

The only negative was the night in Philadelphia when just as the band walked out on stage, a thunderstorm broke soaking the 30,000 fans in the Lincoln Field stadium. Undaunted they sang along to every song and by the time the show finished the rain had stopped and everyone went home happy.

Pete had noticed Dave rubbing his hand a lot lately. When he'd asked him if anything was wrong he'd passed it off saying it was strain due to the extra soloing he was doing on the new material, so Pete had let it pass. He had to admit whatever it was, it didn't interfere with his playing.

Don had stayed behind as the guys flew out for the Far East leg of the tour. He didn't speak the language and the crews over there were the best so he knew they would be in safe hands. He would fly over to London in two week's time and meet the guys when they landed after their flight back from Tokyo, to take charge of the British dates and then the final leg on the West Coast. Janine had flown over to New York to meet up with him and Pete to see the band off from JFK airport. She'd noticed Pete seemed a little distant as they were saying goodbye but put it down to tiredness after the last few gigs. The schedule never got any easier she thought, even though he was now a big star.

She sat in the limousine with Don heading back to their hotel in Manhattan. She was looking forward to a hot bath in her room, a few drinks in the bar and then dinner at Mama's, an old favourite of Don's in Little Italy. She'd packed a tight-fitting black dress and a sparkling black bolero jacket which teamed with high heeled shoes made her feel great, and as she walked into the bar to meet him she noticed every man in the room watched her. Don was actually wearing a suit, which she'd never seen him do before and he looked fantastic. He stood up and pulled out a bar stool for her and she slid onto it. He lit her cigarette and ordered an old-fashioned for himself and a glass of champagne for her.

Don didn't smoke as a rule, but enjoyed an occasional cigar and decided he would indulge tonight choosing a Cuban Havana for himself. The table was booked for later, so for now they relaxed and enjoyed the ambience of the busy bar. It had been a good idea to book a couple of rooms instead of flying straight back to LA. Janine had called Ray earlier but there had been no reply, so she assumed he had left to play a gig somewhere, but she'd lost track of his dates. The episode with his bottom still played on her mind and she wasn't sure whether to believe his story about falling on stage. It seemed a bit far-fetched, but short of asking one of his band there was nothing else she could do, so she put it to the back of her mind.

Don leaned over and touched her hand making her jump. "Penny for them?"

"Jesus, I'm so sorry, I was miles away." She sipped her champagne. "This is wonderful, and I can't wait for the restaurant, I'm starving."

"They do the best rib-eye in New York, and Mama is making a special Cioppino for you after I told her you liked shrimp. But you have to make sure you leave some room for her Tiramisu. It's sensational!"

Don had been eating at Mama's since discovering it on a visit to New York many years ago. He had been with a rock band who were playing at CBGBs and when they demanded Italian food after the gig they were recommended Mama's. He felt sure Janine would love it especially as Mama herself was cooking for them tonight. He wasn't disappointed. They had been welcomed by Mama with open arms and even serenaded by a singing waiter. The food was sublime, everything Don had said and better, and after coffees and large brandies they finally said goodbye to their wonderful host who had joined them for a nightcap.

Sitting in the taxi as it swept them back to the hotel Janine closed her eyes and felt a warm glow inside, something she hadn't experienced for a long time. They collected their keys from reception and they entered the lift, Don mesmerised by her emerald, green eyes as she turned to look at him. The doors opened on their floor and Janine reached out for his hand leading him to her room. He silently followed feeling his stomach churn as she opened the door.

Without speaking a word Janine stepped out of her dress and lay down on the bed watching as Don removed his jacket, his shirt, then his trousers, kicking off his shoes and socks. She reached out for him and he stood at the end of the bed, his huge frame towering over her. She slowly slipped his shorts down and held him. She pulled him onto the bed rolling him on his back and slipping off her silk panties climbed onto him. They both started to move together with Don holding her hips controlling their speed until she took over, moving faster and faster until they got to the point when neither both could hold back no longer. She felt him shudder as she drove down on him, holding him and feeling him as they both cried out in ecstasy. Her legs were shaking and she collapsed on top of him crying. It was if a dam broke and she couldn't stop it.

Don, taken by surprise, tried to comfort her, holding her tight. He wasn't sure what to say as she sobbed into his shoulder.

Finally she pulled away. "You know we can't do that again don't you?"

He looked at her, confused.

"No. No. Don't get me wrong, it was incredible and I wanted it so much, but I'm a married woman." She stopped him before he had chance to speak. "I know what you're going to say, but until I decide to do something about it I can't be seen to be as guilty as he is. Please be patient Don. The time will come, and when it does I want it to be right."

His eyes reflected the sadness he felt in his heart, but she leaned over and kissed him. "Jeesus, a woman could die of thirst here! See if you can rustle up a bottle of bubbly from room service will you, I need a pee!" He picked up the receiver on the bedside table and watched as she walked naked across to the bathroom, turning to smile and blow him a kiss before closing the door.

CHAPTER FOURTEEN

Ray didn't have a gig the night Janine flew off to New York but the last thing on his mind was staying in alone watching a movie. He'd made a phone call, then had a shower and put on his new white Piotr Pauli silk shirt. He'd recently found the latest hip designer and bought one of his bespoke creations. He slipped on a pair of beige chinos with tan Ralph Lauren penny loafers and pulling on a brown leather jacket he left the house and gave the taxi driver directions to the new disco he'd played down in Santa Monica, 'Kaleidoscope'.

The lady who packed one of the best right hooks he'd ever seen was waiting for him there, and if he was in luck he would be going more than a few rounds with her later. There was a long queue outside, but with his single still riding high in the charts he was immediately recognised by the doorman and allowed straight through. The club was packed and the music loud as he made his way to the bar, spotting Laura sitting at the end on her own. She was wearing a denim jacket and matching skirt and smiled as he walked up. He gave her a kiss on the cheek and noticed she was already drinking an exotic cocktail of some kind, so he ordered two large brandies for himself. When they arrived he poured one into the other glass and took a gulp. The liquor burned its way down his throat and he felt better as he turned to Laura.

"Where are your friends tonight?"

"I thought I'd come on my own. We do have that dance to finish; remember?"

Ray slid his hand down her back and pulled her close as he whispered in her ear. "So let's find somewhere quieter."

"My place is just down the road and my flatmate is away. We could go there," she said.

Ray swallowed the rest of his brandy down in one go and stood up. "What are we waiting for."

He leaned in to kiss her mouth but she pushed him away.

"Steady on, there'll be plenty of time for that later."

The four brandies he'd just had plus half a bottle before he'd left home suddenly kicked in, and he swayed as he followed her out to her car which was parked nearby.

She lived on the first floor of a block of apartments about five minutes' drive from the club, and as soon as they got inside she took off her jacket revealing a skimpy top, barely covering her ample breasts. Ray sat down on the sofa watching her pour them both a glass of brandy. He couldn't keep his eyes off her chest as she sat down next to him, and taking a mouthful of his drink slipped his hand beneath the loose material finding her nipple, which he began to squeeze gently between his fingers. Leaning back she closed her eyes as he lifted the top up and began to suck the now erect nipple, teasing it with his tongue. She was moaning softly as he pulled his trousers open to release his erection. He slid his hand under her skirt and started to pull her knickers down when she pushed his hand away.

"No, please, no!" She tried to sit up but he was pinning her down.

Her refusal came as a surprise to Ray who was used to always having his way and he tried again.

She managed to push herself up and knocked his hand away. "I said no!"

Ray gripped her wrist. "You bitch! Now I get it. You're just one of these silly little girls who gets her kicks from leading men on."

He tried to force her back down on the sofa but her self-defence training took over and she grabbed Ray's hair yanking him backwards. He almost lost his balance but he was bigger and stronger and wedged his knee between her legs. She lashed out with her fist catching Ray on the side of his head, and it was at that moment in his drunken stupor he lost control and punched her. It was only meant to stop her hitting him again, but he didn't realise his own strength and caught her on the throat as she frantically fought him. Suddenly she clasped her hands to her neck and stopped struggling, gasping for breath, and as he watched helplessly she went limp and lost consciousness. He jumped up off the sofa and desperately searched for a pulse, but it was too late, she was already dead; her trachea crushed from the blow he'd inflicted on her in a moment of rage.

He stood with his trousers still around his ankles and began to panic.

He'd actually just taken someone's life!

He, an ex-police officer, was a murderer!

He took a deep breath and told himself to calm down and think back to what he would have done when he was at a crime scene. What clues would he look for? Fingerprints! He picked up the glasses of brandy and poured the contents down the sink then wiped them clean with a cloth.

Had he touched anything else? Possibly the door handle when they came in, he couldn't remember but he wiped it clean anyway.

Had they been seen together? He thought back. They'd had a drink at the bar, but he could easily explain that. Had the doorman at 'Kaleidoscope' seen them leave? He didn't think so, he was busy at the time.

Did anyone see them enter her apartment? No, it was quiet and there was no concierge.

He began to relax. The only problem he had now was what to do with the body. He could leave it here, mess up the place so it looked like she'd been robbed and murdered, but that was too obvious. He would have to get rid of it.

She'd said her flat mate was away, so nothing would be discovered until she came back and eventually reported Laura missing. Her car was parked in the underground car park, so all he had to do was get her down there without being seen and then find somewhere to dump her.

He opened the apartment door and listened, but it was silent. He picked her lifeless body up and managed to half carry and half drag her down the corridor to the stairs leading down to the car park. He paused at the top listening but it was still all quiet. He picked her up again but swayed under her weight catching his knuckle on the wall as he carried her down to her car. Locking her in the trunk his mind went back to the trial of Bobby McGregor and how he and Gerry Fortuna had carelessly disposed of Alex Mitchell's body. Well, he'd make sure he didn't make the same mistake.

He started the car and carefully drove out of Santa Monica along the Pacific Coast Highway, making sure to keep within the speed limit. The last thing he wanted was to be pulled over for speeding with a dead body in the trunk.

There was a road on the way to Malibu that led to Topanga Canyon he remembered from when he and Don were investigating Surinam Chandra. There were several sharp bends with a dangerous drop which would be ideal for what he was thinking. He finally found the turn-off and flicking his headlights onto full beam drove up into the hills. About ten minutes later the road started to wind sharply and there was a sheer drop on his right-hand side. He came to a small lay-by on the left, and pulled off the road. He steered the car so it pointed towards the edge and switched off the lights. He slipped it into neutral and leaving the engine running got out.

He crossed the road and looking down into the darkness he could just make out the bottom by the light of the moon and decided this would suit his purpose perfectly. He went back to the car and manhandled the body out of the trunk and into the driving seat. His biggest problem now was how to get the car into the ravine and make it look like an accident. He couldn't find anything to use to jam down the accelerator so he finally decided he would have to risk doing it himself. By now he was stone cold sober and his adrenaline was pumping as he put it into drive, pressed down on the pedal and drove it towards the edge. He knew he had to get enough momentum otherwise it wouldn't be going fast enough, and held on until the last possible moment before jumping out just as the car went straight over. It somersaulted and smashed down into the depths of the valley ending upside down on the rocks at the bottom.

He rolled over and over, finally stopping inches away from joining it, and gingerly got to his feet brushing himself down. There was a loud *whoomph* from below as the petrol tank ignited and the car burst into flames. He watched for a few moments before turning away and walking back towards the lights of the coastal highway in the distance.

Pete and the band were playing to a sold out audience at the famous Budokan in Tokyo. Their treatment since landing in Japan had been nothing short of amazing, with everything they could possibly need supplied with a smile and a bow by one of the many pretty assistants working for their promoter, Saido Masakura. He'd arranged for them to visit all the usual tourist attractions which had been fun, and today he'd booked a reflexologist called Suki to come to the show and give them all a treatment. She explained that she could readjust the balance of their energy lines in order to correct the functions of their organs, while at the same time relaxing their body. It had all gone well until it was Dave's turn. Instead of going through her usual routine talking about his 'Qi' or universal energy, she stopped and immediately started to pack up to leave. Saido Masakura took her to one side and quietly asked her if there was a problem. At first she was reluctant to say anything, but eventually admitted she had found a serious imbalance within Dave's meridians and was unable to continue the treatment. When he asked her to explain more, she would only say he had a major problem that she could not solve, and bowing deeply, left.

Dave lay back on the treatment table and instinctively rubbed his hand, knowing that the monkey bite was the cause, but of what? He would wait until he was back in the States and book himself into a clinic he knew in LA to get some discreet tests done.

Pete had found himself struggling to maintain his concentration and commitment to the tour the longer it went on. The thoughts he'd had back in LA kept returning and the drugs, the women and the booze failed to have an effect anymore. He was focussing on the dates coming up in the UK, and in particular the one in Birmingham where he would get the chance to meet Judy and his son Rick. The last time he'd seen them had been a disaster and he aimed to make amends. They were playing the Town Hall this time which was a much bigger venue, but he intended to make time to go and visit them away from the distractions of the gig.

As a gift to celebrate the second sell-out night in Tokyo, Saido Masakura had arranged for a special Karaoke party at 'The Lotus Room' one of the city's famous Karaoke bars. Pete was reluctant to go, but gave in to pressure from the others who were all keen to enjoy the experience. It had been a fantastic gig and afterwards they were each whisked off to the venue in their own chauffeur-driven Rolls Royce. Basking in the luxury, they were escorted into a huge, lavishly decorated room by a string of scantily dressed hostesses and led to an enclosed VIP area.

Pete immediately sensed an atmosphere which made him feel uncomfortable, although Saido Masakura, Mitchell the drummer and bass player Randy were enjoying the attention being paid to them by the girls, drinking champagne and encouraging them to sit on their laps.

Dave sat on his own nursing an orange juice, looking bored. An attractive oriental girl wearing a skimpy costume approached Pete and in broken English asked if there was anything she could do for him. Hearing this, the others all laughed, egging Pete on with lewd suggestions. Ignoring his friends he politely thanked her but declined her kind offer and turned away, at which point the girl looked across at a crowd of men standing at the bar and said something in Japanese.

Out of the corner of his eye Pete saw one of the men walking across towards him shouting something he didn't understand. As he got closer he pulled out a knife and was about to attack Pete when Saido Masakura, who had watched what was happening jumped up and leaped across the table knocking both Pete and the other man flying. There were screams as more of the group joined in the fracas deliberately trying to pick out the members of the band, but fortunately the promoter had made sure his security men had accompanied them and within seconds they intervened.

The violence was over in a flash and Saido apologised profusely, explaining it was a local Yakuza, or gang, trying to make a name for itself by causing trouble with the famous band from USA. He said they should all relax, enjoy the ladies and have some fun, but Pete had had enough and wanted to go. The highlight of the evening ended up being the cheesy version of 'In Flames' from their last album played on the Karaoke machine as they were leaving.

Ray had walked for about half an hour before he reached the main Pacific Coast Highway again. He'd found a public phone box next to a diner and called a cab which took him home. Once through the door he poured himself a large brandy which he knocked back in one and followed it with another and by the time he drained the last of the bottle he was almost incapable of standing. He stumbled into the bedroom and stripped off his clothes, giving up trying to undo the buttons on his shirt and pulled it over his head, not noticing he was missing a button on his cuff. He dropped them all in the laundry basket and closed his eyes as the sun was just rising above the horizon.

Don and Janine had arrived back in LA having spent the rest of the night in bed together but resisting the temptation to do anything more than hold each other close. They parted ways outside the arrivals hall, Don making his way back to his apartment to contemplate what had happened, and Janine travelling back to Hermosa Beach wondering what her next move should be. She arrived home just as Ray was leaving, barely managed a kiss before climbing into a taxi. She let herself into the house, dumped her bag on the floor and poured herself a glass of chilled champagne. Walking out onto the sunlit balcony she took a long swallow and leaned on the rail taking in the view. She'd been contemplating moving to somewhere more central especially when she was pregnant, but now she couldn't imagine being anywhere else.

She wiped a tear from the corner of her eye when she thought back to the moment the surgeon told her she'd lost her son. Strangely, she remembered, Ray had hardly reacted at the news when they were in her hospital room in Miami and left shortly afterwards.

She sat down on one of the loungers with her mind in a spin. What on earth was she going to do next? Did she still love Ray or more to the point could she trust him? Being a hypocrite didn't help and she wished she hadn't slept with Don, but she had feelings for him and she knew deep down in her soul that one day they'd be together. The next few weeks would be interesting. Ray was leaving in a couple of days touring in the UK and so was Pete. She hadn't told either she would be going over so it remained to be seen what would happen, especially as Ray was playing at the Lexxicon for two nights. She could combine a night to see Pete, a visit to Judy and Rick and then she could watch Ray and the two Motown stars whose music she loved anyway.

She finished her drink and went into the bedroom to unpack her bag. The basket of laundry was in the corner, and as she tipped it out on the floor she noticed Ray hadn't undone the buttons on one of his shirts, a habit of his she hated. She was sorting the shirt out when she spotted one of the cuffs was missing a button. It occurred to her she'd need to put a message in for the cleaners to replace it when she sent it off later that day.

CHAPTER FIFTEEN

On the day he was leaving for the UK tour, Ray had joined the two Motown stars Jimmy Ruffin and Edwin Starr for a photo shoot at the airport. He'd met them briefly the week before at rehearsals, and they both seemed like good guys, congratulating him on his single and saying they were looking forward to the dates. Janine had accompanied him to the departure gate and they'd kissed and hugged each other briefly before Ray disappeared into the throng of passengers heading towards their flights. He waved as he turned round one last time. Then he was gone.

She stood alone on the concourse surrounded by passengers hurrying past her in different directions, trying to make up her mind whether she felt sad and lonely or happy and relieved. The days leading up to today had been fraught. Ray had been in a strange mood constantly snapping at her about the smallest things, resulting in her leaving him on his own most of the time watching the local television news channels. She'd arranged to drop by Manny's office at Westoria Records to catch up on Pete's tour and to plan her trip over to England. She gave the cab driver the company's address on Sunset Boulevard as she climbed in the back.

Detective Anna Delaney from LAPD had been assigned to the case of a twenty-five-year-old woman called Laura Weiss. She had been reported missing by Sylvia Svenson, the Swedish au pair who shared a flat with Laura. Sylvia had returned from a weekend skiing and found the flat empty, but when Laura's friends from her class called wondering where she was Sylvia became suspicious and called LAPD. Anna was a tough diminutive red head of Irish descent renowned in the department for her no-nonsense attitude and along with her rookie partner Sergeant Joe Budd had called round to their apartment to ask Sylvia some questions.

"Did she regularly go off on her own?" Anna asked.

"No. She might go out with her friends from her self-defence class but she'd always let me know where she was going, and I'd do the same. We looked out for each other."

"Did she drive a car?"

"Yes it's usually parked downstairs in the car park but it's not there."

"What's the licence plate?"

"179 ALA"

"Did she have a boyfriend? Maybe they could've gone off together?"

"No, she would have told me."

Anna raised her eyebrows towards her partner. "Well look Miss Svenson if anything changes or Laura turns up you let me know." Anna gave Sylvia one of her cards.

She and Joe got back in their squad car. "Where to now?" he asked.

"Pacific Palisades. I want to visit that class she belonged to; see if they can shed any light on our Miss Weiss."

The session was in full swing as Anna and Joe walked into the gym. It was full of women between the ages of twenty and forty. Anna went over to the one who appeared to be in charge and flashed her badge. "Sorry to interrupt , but we're investigating the disappearance of Laura Weiss. I wondered whether you could help?"

"Sure, we've all been really worried. It's not like Laura to just go off without telling anyone."

"So when was the last time you saw her?"

"It was here, last week. We'd all arranged to go bowling at the weekend but she pulled out at the last minute. Said she was meeting someone at 'Kaleidoscope,' the new disco in Santa Monica. We went there on the opening night and she got involved in a fight onstage with a singer. It was all a bit bizarre really."

"How do you mean bizarre?" Anna asked.

"Well there was this new soul singer called Ray Law performing, and he wanted someone to dance with him. So Laura, always game for a laugh jumps up on stage. Everybody was laughing and shouting out, and they did get a bit up close and personal, if you know what I mean; when all of a sudden, this girl backing singer picks up a microphone stand and whacks him with it and then grabs hold of Laura trying to pull her away. Rips her top and out they pop." She laughed cupping her hands in front of herself. "Laura's a very well-endowed girl! Anyway the next minute Laura plants a right hook smack on her chin and lays her out cold. It all stopped at that point."

"And you said the singer was called Ray Law?" Anna asked.

Joe was writing everything down in his notebook.

"Yeah, he's got a single in the charts, 'The Love Game.'"

"What about the other girl, did you get her name?"

"Josie something or other. We didn't see her again. He came over afterwards to apologise and got a kiss from Laura. Seemed like a nice guy, and then we all left."

Anna gave her a card in case she heard anything. They were sitting in their car when there was a code three call on the radio - an accident in the hills above Malibu on the way to Topanga Canyon. Joe responded and they set off with their siren blaring. They drove up the winding road and came to a black and white police car parked in a lay-by.

Two officers were standing cautiously peering over the edge down into the valley as Anna and Joe pulled up. "There's a burnt-out wreck down there," one of the officers said. "Reported by a couple of ramblers."

"Any identification?" Anna asked.

"Can't tell 'til we get someone down there. They said they thought there was a body in the car, pretty gruesome. There's a CSI team on the way from headquarters."

Anna looked round the area and then at Joe. "What do you notice?"

"No skid marks."

"Exactly! We need to get down there, come on." She climbed over the edge and found a narrow ledge which she started to shuffle along. Joe followed behind her looking nervous. She caught the look on his face. "Ah Jesus, don't tell me you're afraid of heights!"

He nodded but grimly held on as they slowly made their way down. Ten minutes later soaked in sweat they jumped the last few feet onto the valley bottom and made their way over to what was left of the car. There were definitely human remains in the driving seat but the intensity of the heat had destroyed most of the vehicle. Joe had wandered around the back poking around when he called out. "You might want to come and look at this."

The burnt remains of a licence plate were barely visible but they could just make out a number one and the letters L and A.

Anna looked at Joe. "I think our missing person just became a homicide!"

By the time they'd made their way back up to their car the medical examiner and a CSI team had arrived. Anna went up to them.

"I want you to treat this as a suspected homicide. We think we know the identity of the victim inside the car so if you can get the body back to the morgue ASAP I'd be grateful."

Anna and Joe left them preparing to make their way down to the wreckage.

"We need to get back to her apartment again."

Joe flicked on the siren and lights again as he drove back down towards Santa Monica.

Janine and Manny were going through the reviews from the Far East leg of Pete's tour and noticed the mention of a fracas at a Karaoke bar in Tokyo. According to Saido Masakura the promoter, it was an isolated incident involving some members of a local gang who were trying to make a name for themselves. Fortunately his own security team took care of it, and Pete and the guys were fine. He added that the tour had been a huge success. According to Manny's schedule they were on their flight back to Heathrow where Don, who had flown out that morning would join up with them in London ready to start their UK tour. Janine was looking at the itinerary for Peterson alongside the dates for the Motown tour trying to figure out when it was best for her to arrive. It would be great to be back in Britain again, she thought.

Ray had landed in London along with the rest of the tour members and they'd been driven down to the first show at the Top Rank in Croydon. The events of the last few days were now a distant memory as he concentrated on what he had to do. He was going to be the opening act every night with Edwin Starr and Jimmy Ruffin taking turns to finish the show, and very quickly learnt he would have to adapt his show from the one he'd been doing in the small clubs on the West Coast. Suddenly he was playing to two thousand people on much bigger stages which took some getting used to. Fortunately his hit record 'The Love Game' was popular over in the UK and lifted his show when he sang it, but he knew he had to up his game. The one venue he was really looking forward to playing was the Lexxicon in Birmingham. He'd been many times watching acts and now it was his turn to play there.

They'd already done shows at the Baileys clubs in Watford and Newcastle before they arrived in Birmingham for their two nights and Judy Watson had been there to welcome them. She gave Ray a special hug and said how happy she was to see him, although it was a shame Janine couldn't be there. He was pleasant enough to her but she sensed something was definitely not right and let the subject drop.

The large room, Lexx1, was packed, and the audience on the first night were eagerly awaiting the start of the show especially as it was a home-grown star on first. Ray was desperately trying to remain calm but the butterflies in his stomach had made him throw up while he was waiting. Edwin Starr had patted him on the back and reassured him it was no big deal. He said he was often sick himself before going on stage, but as soon as he heard the start of his first song he was fine.

Suddenly the band played Ray's intro and he was striding out to a huge cheer with all nerves gone. Every song went down great and then he came to the part in his show when he invited a young lady up to dance with him. There was no shortage of volunteers, and he chose an attractive blonde from the front row. As the sexy ballad began she leaned into his body and they moved together. He started to sing the verse guiding her with one hand while holding the microphone in the other and she rested her head on his shoulder. He looked over towards the tightly packed crowd and immediately recognised a face he could never forget.

She was staring straight at him; Julia Davies. He almost forgot his words, but managed to carry on to the end of the song and thanked his dance partner with a kiss on the cheek.

He finished his set and left the stage to a great ovation. Edwin had gone on next with Jimmy Ruffin finishing the show. They had both brought the house down with hit after hit and by the time Jimmy had done his two encores there was a long queue of ladies outside the dressing room waiting to meet the two Motown stars. On this night Ray had a few fans of his own who were desperate to get to see him. The security man was fighting a losing battle in his efforts to organise them and was trying to hold them all back when Ray heard a familiar voice and looking around the door spotted Julia trying to explain she was a personal friend of Ray Law. The guard was having nothing of it until Ray tapped his shoulder and said it was OK for her to come back. Finally she managed to squeeze her way through the throng and was standing in front of him. She looked stunning dressed all in black with tight leather trousers, a black t-shirt and a short black leather jacket with tassels, her hair wavy and loose down to her shoulders and her lips crimson.

"Well aren't you going to say hello?"

He pulled her to him and kissed her. "Hello."

Later that night as he opened the door to his room at the Crowne Plaza, she followed him in and slipped her hands around his waist undoing his trousers before they'd even reached the bed. As she pulled his shorts down and pushed him back on the bed she slipped out of her leather trousers and black silk knickers holding his excited manhood with one hand as she climbed across and lowered herself onto him.

"Ohhh God, you don't know how much I've missed this!" She pushed him back as he tried to sit up. "Don't you move until I tell you," she said riding him slowly.

Janine had arrived at Heathrow and spent the night at the Metropole Hotel in London. It was a place that still had lots of fond memories for her. She recalled the crazy days with Pete spent making love and drinking champagne. She was looking forward to his show tonight at the Dominion, and thought back to the night he collapsed there and how her quick thinking saved him. So much had happened since then. He was a superstar now and would be staying in one of the suites they had secretly shared, but on his own; unless he decided to bring one of his adoring fans back after the show. Their relationship was as strong as ever but on a purely professional basis. She knew he was desperate to see Judy and his son again and he'd told her he planned to spend some time with them. She would be gone by then as her trip was only long enough for her to catch his show here in London. She was travelling up to Birmingham early the next morning to make a surprise visit to see Ray at his hotel, before watching the Motown Tour at the Lexxicon that night and then catching the train back down the following morning to fly out later that day.

Pete's show had been amazing with tickets selling for astronomical prices from the touts outside. The fans had loved the new material, which by now had been trimmed down to a sensible length without too many overbearing solos, and the album was selling well on both sides of the Atlantic as well as the Far East. The band had been buzzing when they came off stage and the vibe continued back to the hotel where Pete and the rest of the guys seemed intent on drinking the bar dry. Midway through the proceedings Janine noticed a familiar blonde appear and watched as she and Pete disappeared into the lift on the way up to his room.

She could read Don's mind as they sat together in the bar, but reminded him they had agreed to be cautious, and when she decided it was time for bed his disappointment showed as he gave her a kiss on the cheek.

She was up at the crack of dawn the next morning and caught an early train which got her up to Birmingham in time for a late breakfast with Ray, and maybe something more to celebrate his appearance at the Lexxicon. It was only a short walk from the station and she was excited as she went up to reception to ask for his room number, introducing herself as his wife. The look the receptionist gave her should have been a clue, but she missed it and pressed the button to his floor in the vacant lift. It was ten thirty as she knocked on his door, and when he called out 'Who is it?' she decided to play a trick and replied 'Room Service'. Moments later, as he pulled on a gown and opened the door thinking he was sure he hadn't ordered Room Service, he got the shock of his life as Janine breezed into his room. She was about to give him a kiss when she noticed the naked woman sitting up in his bed. Her stomach dropped and she felt sick, realising her surprise had just turned into a nightmare. Doing her best to remain calm she steadied herself by holding on to the back of a chair.

Ray was desperately trying to make apologetic noises when she suddenly pointed at Julia. "I know who you are. You're that bitch who was in the lift with some idiot after our party. I never forget a face." She looked at Ray. "And you said you didn't know her, you lying bastard. The solicitor! Yes, now I remember."

She turned back to Julia who was trying to pull the bedsheets up to cover herself. "Well you'd better be a good one, because I'm about to divorce my shit of a husband, and if he thinks he's gonna get a penny of mine he can go fuck himself."

She turned around and walked towards the door, stopping to look at Ray with contempt. "Don't bother coming home. It's no longer yours."

With that she left, slamming the door behind her and stood in the lift shaking as it descended. She hurried through reception before bursting into tears outside. The liveried doorman came over looking concerned, but she waved him away pulling herself together and climbed into a waiting taxi telling the driver to take her to the station. By the time her train had arrived back in London she knew exactly what she was going to do, and sat back as her cockney taxi driver extolled the virtues of the sights of London while he drove her to Heathrow.

CHAPTER SIXTEEN

Detective Anna Delaney and Sergeant Joe Budd were back at the apartment Laura Weiss shared with her friend Sylvia Svenson. She had burst into tears when they told her their suspicions and Anna had sat her down to ask some more questions.

"Can you remember when you came home was there anything different? Anything unusual, or out of place?"

Sylvia thought for a long time looking around the apartment as she did.

"Well there was one thing. There was a bottle of brandy opened and two glasses on the side but they were both clean."

"Go on," Anna prompted her.

"Laura doesn't drink brandy. Oh, and the cushions on the sofa were messed up, and I'm always telling her to tidy up afterwards."

"Look. We're going to get a CSI team down here to check the place over, Miss Svenson. Do you have somewhere you could go for a couple of days?"

Sylvia said she had a friend who she could stay with and made a phone call. Anna asked her if she had a photograph of Laura, and she went into her bedroom and found one. A picture of the two of them at a bar smiling, looking happy. Then after throwing a few things into a bag she left, while Anna and Joe stayed behind to look around.

"So what do we know so far?" Anna asked Joe.

"OK, Laura Weiss is reported missing by her flat mate Sylvia Svenson. Says her car has gone too. Her friends at the self-defence class say she cancelled her night out with them to go to 'Kaleidoscope' to meet someone. They'd all been there the previous week to see a singer called Ray Law whose female backing singer, Josie something attacks her while she's dancing with him on stage. We find the wreckage of a car containing a body we think could be hers, in a valley on the Topanga Road. It had left the road but with no sign of skid marks to say whoever was driving had tried to stop."

"So, we need to go check out this 'Kaleidoscope' and see if they remember her going there."

They arrived just as the club was opening and were taken through to the manager by the doorman. He was about to leave the office when Anna showed him the photo of Laura asking if he'd seen her recently.

"Yeah, she was here on the Saturday. I remembered her from the fight on stage on the opening night when Ray Law was singing. He was here that night too."

Anna stopped him. "What on the Saturday?"

"That's right. He turned up and there was a long queue outside, but I let him through 'cos his record's in the charts."

"Did you see either of them leave?"

"No, I was too busy."

Anna thanked him and the manager for their time. She stopped just as they were leaving and asked if the manager knew how to contact Ray Law. He gave them a business card for SoulTown Promotions suggesting she should give them a call.

Ray was pacing around his room at the Crowne Plaza hotel while Julia Davies sat at the dressing table calmly applying her make-up.

"Shit, I need a drink!" He poured himself a large glass of brandy swallowing half down in one gulp. "I mean, who the fuck does she think she is making threats like that?"

Julia looked up from the mirror. "You need to take it easy with that stuff; it's not even lunch time yet."

"I'm fine, don't worry about me. Look, you're the solicitor here, can she do what she says?"

Julia thought for a moment. "Well she certainly was pretty steamed up about it. I've got a friend who's an attorney over in LA, I'll drop her a line. You need to calm down."

"Calm down! My wife just threatened to divorce me and you tell me to calm down!"

She leaned back and put her hand inside his robe. "Yes, and I know just how to do it."

Janine had managed to book herself on the next Pan-Am flight to Los Angeles and called Don at the Manchester Apollo to tell him what had happened. He listened as she let out her emotions and assured her he would help in any way once he arrived back. They had a few days off before the West Coast leg of the tour and he promised to see her then. In the meantime he suggested she do her best to relax on the flight home and not do anything rash.

She was sitting at the bar in the VIP lounge with a sad expression contemplating what to have to drink when a familiar voice suggested she might like to try a Martini. She turned to see Charles Morse the actor giving her one of his trademark smiles.

"I seem to always meet you when you've got a problem," he said catching the attention of the barman and ordering two Martinis.

Suddenly she was shedding tears into one of his handkerchiefs as he lit himself a cigarette. She dried her eyes and accepted one of his which he lit for her with his gold lighter.

"So don't tell me, the same thing as last time?"

"Yes, only much worse. I think this time it could be final."

She found herself once again in the company of one of the world's most famous actors pouring out her troubles, and him sitting listening offering sympathetic words of advice. When she finished he explained he was on his way to meet the director and producer of a new film in which he'd been offered the starring role and would once again be staying at the Beverly Hills Hotel where he insisted he buy her dinner. He would not take no for an answer and suggested she meet him there the following evening. She couldn't believe what an amazing gentleman he was, never once making any sort of pass at her, even though he was an attractive man and still most desirable for his age. The thought of a sexual encounter briefly entered her mind and she didn't dismiss it, but then her own situation took over and cancelled it out.

This time Ray had gone too far. She'd been prepared to forgive him for his dalliances as long as she didn't see them. Yes, she knew he'd been unfaithful, but, for the fact he came home back to her every night, she was prepared to forgive him. But to see him with that woman, especially as he'd lied to her that he didn't know her was the final straw. She would consult a lawyer as soon as she got back and start divorce proceedings immediately. She wanted him out of her life and the sooner the better.

Pete had arranged to travel to Birmingham as they had a day off before their Town Hall gig. He'd arrived at Judy's house full of nerves wondering how things were going to go. She'd met him with open arms and they'd held each other tight for ages. Finally she led him into her tiny kitchen and they sat talking and drinking tea. Their son Rick was at school and she left Pete at home while she went to pick him up. Suddenly the front door burst open and a ball of energy came rushing in taking Pete by surprise. It was like looking at a smaller version of himself and his eyes filled with tears as Judy introduced him to his dad. Within minutes he'd found the cheap guitar his Mum had bought him for his birthday and was playing one of Pete's songs singing along at the same time. Pete was speechless as his son went through his repertoire effortlessly while Judy proudly looked on.

That evening Pete took them all out for dinner in a posh restaurant and Rick was allowed to choose whatever he wanted for a special treat. His parents watched as he tucked into burger and chips followed by a double helping of ice cream. Then as he went off to bed he gave his dad a special hug and kiss before Judy tucked him in. The day had been everything Pete hoped for and when Judy asked if he would like to stay the night his heart missed a beat. They made love like the last time they were together, tenderly and caring.

The following morning as Rick was getting ready to leave for school Pete felt as if something inside had changed and that his life could never be the same again. He kissed his son goodbye and promised he would be back soon. And he meant it.

CHAPTER SEVENTEEN

Manny's advice to Ray about money had been correct.

The Motown tour had arrived at a huge club on the outskirts of Manchester called The Silver Dollar. With every ticket sold it was another incredible night starting off with Ray, who wowed all the women with his dancing and finishing with his hit 'The Love Game'. Jimmy Ruffin followed Ray and was his usual calm, cool self, singing hit after hit in his set, and finally the effervescent Edwin Starr brought the house down with his all-action style.

Ray was in his dressing room when he heard an argument outside in the corridor involving the two stars and seemingly the agent. As he listened it became obvious there was a problem with the money and both Jimmy and Edwin were not happy. The agent was trying his best to calm them down but neither was having any of it, demanding to see the takings for the night's performance. Tempers were becoming frayed so Ray decided to investigate and he opened his dressing room door to be confronted with an irate Jimmy Ruffin. He was brandishing what looked like a revolver and pointing it at the agent who by now was looking rather pale. Edwin Starr was standing behind his friend insisting it was in the agent's best interests that he brought them the money before anyone was hurt.

Ray in his previous guise as a police officer decided to try to diffuse the situation and suggested they all calm down before there was an accident, at which point he was told to "Get the fuck out of the way and mind your business," by the gun toting Motown star.

Eventually a young man appeared carrying a large bag containing a lot of money, which Edwin took and counted while his friend watched on. When the amount of cash they were looking for was finally in front of them they agreed it was time for them to leave and packed up the piles of notes. Later as they were on the bus driving to their hotel Ray sat down next to Jimmy and asked him where he got the gun from.

He laughed and pulled the pistol from his pocket. "What, you mean this thing! Hey man, it ain't real. But them thieving bastards don't know that, and there ain't one of em's brave enough to call my bluff."

Edwin leaned across the table. "That guy's well known for trying to rip off acts who play there. We just thought we'd teach him a lesson."

Janine was in her bedroom getting ready to meet Charles Morse for dinner when there was a knock on her door. She wasn't expecting any visitors so she pulled on her dressing gown and cautiously opened the door to find a woman and man standing on her doorstep showing her their LAPD badges.

"Detective Anna Delaney and Sergeant Joe Budd, LAPD. We're looking for a Mr. Ray Law."

Janine was surprised but invited them in explaining she was Mrs. Law, Ray's wife.

Anna apologised for intruding and explained that they wanted to talk to him about a homicide they were investigating involving a young woman who he'd met at one of his shows.

"Well that's going to be a problem," Janine explained. "He's currently on tour in the UK and won't be back for another week. But tell me, why do you want to speak to my husband?"

Anna explained that according to the young woman's friends she had danced with Ray on stage during his act at a disco in Santa Monica called 'Kaleidoscope' and had been involved in an incident with another female who was singing in Mr. Law's band - they were interested in talking to her as well.

"Her name's Josie Thomas, but she doesn't work with my husband anymore."

Anna said they'd spoken to SoulTown Promotions, who'd given them her details as well as Ray's."

"Do you happen to know where your husband was last Saturday, Mrs. Law?" Anna asked.

Janine thought for a second. That was when she was in New York with

Don. "I'm afraid I don't. I was away that weekend in New York on business."

"Well we won't bother you any further Mrs. Law. Thanks for your help." Anna apologised again for disturbing her and turned to leave then stopped.

"Say that's an Irish accent isn't it?"

Janine nodded. "Yes I was born in Ballykobh."

"My father is from the Emerald Isle; a town called Clongough," Anna said.

Janine smiled. "I know it well. It's a small world, detective!"

"Well thanks again, Mrs. Law," Anna said as the two officers let themselves out.

Janine stood for a moment wondering what kind of mess Ray had got himself into but then remembered that he would soon be none of her concern and went back into her room to finish dressing.

Charles was waiting in the bar of The Beverly Hills Hotel wearing a royal blue, double-breasted jacket, black trousers and black slip-on shoes, a pale blue shirt and cravat with a matching handkerchief in his top pocket. She had decided on a burgundy silk blouse, cream slacks and high suede burgundy stilettos taking into account Charles' height and knowing she wouldn't be taller than him. She had fashioned her hair in a loose plait pulled across one side of her neck and wore a cream shawl over her shoulders. Ever the gentleman he stood as Janine walked in giving her a polite kiss on the cheek. He ordered two martinis and offered her a cigarette as she sat down next to him at the bar. As their drinks arrived he lit her cigarette and she noticed a glint in his eyes she hadn't experienced before. Perhaps there was another side to Charles Morse she was about to experience.

After leaving Janine's, Anna and Joe's next stop was Josie Thomas's flat in West Hollywood where they caught her just as she was leaving the condo. She invited them in explaining she was on her way to a gig and couldn't stay long.

Anna explained why they were there and Josie described the events of the night at 'Kaleidoscope' as Joe took notes. She told them how her and Ray had been having a relationship, and when he blatantly made sexual advances towards a woman from the audience she lost her temper. She hit him with a microphone stand and attempted to pull the woman away. After that it was all a blur as the next minute she was knocked out cold. Then to add insult to injury she was sacked at the end of the night. She said she'd since heard Ray Law had a reputation for getting women to dance with him on stage and then having sex with them after the show. With that she apologised and drove off in her battered old VW Beetle.

Anna and Joe sat in their car analysing what they'd just been told. Strange that Mrs. Law hadn't made any mention of her husband's affair, but then why would she? It was definitely something for them to bear in mind, a thought cut short as their radio went off with a message for them to go to the morgue.

The condition of the body on the stainless-steel table wasn't as bad as they had thought it might be and the autopsy had revealed the female victim already been dead before the crash from a blow to the neck, possibly a punch, which had fractured bones and crushed her trachea. She had also been identified by her dental records as Laura Weiss.

Anna hated the morgue. It was the finality of it all. A young life brought to a premature end by an apparent act of violence. She went to talk to her partner but had to wait until he caught up with her after his hurried visit to the bathroom.

They drove in silence back to Laura Weiss' apartment.

The CSI unit had finished and were waiting for Anna and Joe when they arrived. Unfortunately there was not a lot to report in terms of evidence. No noticeable fingerprints apart from those of the flat mate Sylvia Svenson. They'd checked the bottle of brandy and the two glasses but they'd been wiped clean. The one area where they had been successful was the sofa. They'd removed the cushions and found a cornucopia of items obviously lost over time. Coins, hair clips, a discarded condom (unused) and a shirt button, which is where it became interesting. The rather distinctive button appeared to have come from a designer shirt. They bagged all their discoveries up and would examine them in more detail when they got back to their laboratory. Anna and Joe were just on their way down to the car park when she noticed a mark on the wall in the stairwell. It looked like blood although she couldn't be sure, so she scraped a section of the plaster off and put it in an evidence bag just in case.

The meal with Charles Morse at the Beverly Hills Hotel was exquisite. They both had Oysters Bonne Femme followed by a medium rare Filet Mignon for Charles while Janine chose pan-fried scallops and shrimp served on a bed of succotash which she'd never tried before but loved. During the meal she noticed Charles was becoming more relaxed than his usual reserved self and having downed two more martinis as well as most of a bottle of red wine was starting to make suggestive comments which were completely out of character. Janine thought back to the last time they had a meal together at the hotel and remembered they had met up with Charles' secretary and producer and at his suggestion she had booked a room to sleep off her hangover, all completely above board. Tonight however was a different scenario altogether with no sign of anyone else turning up, and Charles becoming more amorous by the minute; or by the martini!

It was strange how she had thought while they were in the VIP lounge back in London, that he was always the perfect gentleman, and even wondered about a sexual relationship, when here she was doing her best to fend off his wandering hands and planning on escaping as soon as possible before things became too embarrassing.

She desperately looked around for a knight in shining armour to come to her rescue, and right on cue into the bar walked Vince Boyd and his secretary. Vince instantly spotted Janine and came over to say hello, at the same time recognising she was *a damsel in distress*. Without hesitation he took her hand, gave her a kiss and a huge hug and escorted her away.

Poor Charles was left wondering what had happened and made a vain attempt to stand up but fell back down knocking over a table in the process.

The barman who had been watching, immediately came round and fussed over his famous client while Vince and Janine left the bar. It was a surreal moment for her as she realised her idol Vince Boyd had just appeared from nowhere and saved her.

It turned out he was in town to do an interview on the same TV show Pete had appeared on when he played at the Whisky A Go- Go and with the same host, Alan Brookstein. Vince was staying at the hotel but decided a change of venue would be a good idea and they jumped into a waiting taxi. Minutes later they arrived at a quiet bar that Vince knew just off Sunset Boulevard and they were shown to an empty booth at the back. Vince ordered a Cosmopolitan and Janine decided she'd have one too. He was as charming as ever and once again she found herself in the company of a world-famous star paying her attention when it was she who was star-struck. They laughed at what had just happened back at the hotel, and knew that Charles would be mortified when he awoke in the morning and remembered his actions from the previous night.

Two drinks later Janine was on her way home in a taxi with an invitation to Vince's show tomorrow to which she would definitely be going.

Pete and the band were on their way back to LA. The remainder of the shows in the UK had been great, ending with two sell-out performances in Scotland although the last night had been marred by an incident involving Dave Sanchez and the crew in charge of his equipment. Over the last few gigs Pete had noticed Dave becoming increasingly short tempered and constantly finding fault with everything the technicians did. This resulted in them pulling a bizarre prank involving flour bombing Dave as he was being introduced to the audience during the final tune. Understandably he was livid getting completely covered from head to toe, as well as his keyboards, in white powder. The fans thought it was part of the show and laughed and cheered loudly much to Dave's annoyance.

Dave was now relaxing in his seat watching a movie on the flight back home, although in the back of his mind was the strange thing that happened in Japan with Suki the reflexologist. Perhaps she had been mistaken, but in his heart he knew there was a problem which was all to do with the monkey bite from the incident at Maltrocorp. He'd made a call from his room in Scotland and booked an appointment with a doctor in LA as soon as he arrived back.

Elsewhere in the upstairs First-Class cabin Don Rosario was asleep while Marshall the drummer and the bassist, Randy, were sitting at the bar doing their best to get as much free alcohol as they could drink from the attractive stewardess. Ironically they were entitled to as many drinks as they wanted but they didn't seem to care.

Pete meanwhile was sitting at the back going over the visit to Judy and Rick in his mind and weighing up his options. It had been a beautiful day in Birmingham, one which he would cherish, but was he ready to dramatically change his life to include them?

CHAPTER EIGHTEEN

Janine had put her plan into action and contacted Vonda Statzler a well-known female attorney based in Santa Monica, renowned for her *take no prisoners* attitude in the divorce court. They'd arranged to meet in her office and Janine had arrived dressed in one of her favourite linen suits worn with low heels. Smart, relaxed but nothing too over the top.

The secretary rang through and showed her into the plush office. Vonda was on the phone and waved for Janine to take a seat in front of her desk. She sat down looking round and taking in the modern artwork on the walls spread around the room.

Vonda finished her call and stubbing out her cigarette stood up and walked round to shake hands. She was a tall, slim blonde wearing a Grateful Dead t-shirt and jeans tucked into a pair of well-worn brown leather cowgirl boots. Not the kind of outfit Janine expected for a top attorney.

"Hey Mrs. Law, or can I call you Janine. Thanks for coming in."

"Janine is fine, and thanks for seeing me."

Vonda waved her arm around the room. "You like modern art?"

"I'm not really sure I understand it."

"It's a passion of mine amongst other things." Vonda sat back behind her desk. "But let's get down to business. You're here because you want to divorce your husband, right?"

Janine took a deep breath before saying, "Yes, I do."

"OK. So why don't you tell me all about it."

Vonda listened to Janine relate what had happened in the hotel in Birmingham and the previous affair Ray had had with the singer Josie Thomas as well as the numerous one-night stands during his gigs whilst writing on a large leatherbound notepad.

She looked up when Janine paused. "That's some piece of work! How come it's taken you so long to decide?"

"I loved him. Well, I thought I did," Janine had tears in her eyes. "But there's only so much you can take, and the hotel in Birmingham was the last straw."

"And do you have any proof of these other affairs? I'm gonna need as much evidence as possible," Vonda said.

Janine told her there was supposedly a tape of Ray having sex with Josie Thomas but she hadn't heard it. Vonda picked up her phone and told her secretary to call Tony and ask him to come into the office.

While they were waiting, she explained Tony was the private detective she used to find the kind of evidence she needed. He was ex-LAPD and could dig out information others would miss. Ten minutes later Vonda's secretary called to tell her Tony had arrived and the door was opened by a short bull-necked man with slicked back black hair who instantly reminded Janine of her first husband Gerry. She did a double take as he walked in and sat down next to her but decided not to say anything.

Vonda asked her to give Tony as much information as she could about Ray's indiscretions so he could start making enquiries; in particular his affair with Josie Thomas, and a list of all his gigs.

He wrote down all the information Janine gave him and said he'd get back to Vonda as soon as he had anything to report. That was enough for this first consultation.

Pete and the band had arrived safely back in LA and Don had called Janine to check she was OK. She'd told him about her meeting with Vonda Statzler, and how she wanted as much evidence of Ray's philandering as possible. Don had always been reluctant to talk about the tape recording of Ray with Josie Thomas which had been made when they were in Van Nuys, but now Vonda's detective Tony was on the case he knew it would all come out in the open. He vaguely remembered him from when he was on the force but only by name.

They arranged to meet up later to go to Vince Boyd's TV recording and Janine briefly explained the events of her dinner with Charles Morse, and how Vince had saved her, which was why she wanted to go to the show to thank him again. She detected a note of jealousy in Don's voice as he said goodbye, although when she thought about it, Vince Boyd was a huge star who was paying her lots of attention, so she couldn't blame him. As if she needed another problem in her life!

The members of Peterson had a few days off before the West Coast section of the tour started and to save Dave having to go back home or across to his friends in Greenwich Village, Pete suggested he stay at the Red House with him.

Dave had picked up a copy of the LA Times at the airport and was flicking through it in the taxi when he suddenly froze. There at the bottom of the page was an article describing how a Mexican Cantina called Taco Taco in Studio City had been destroyed by fire. Firefighters had discovered two bodies at the scene who so far had not yet been identified, but Dave closed the paper sure they were Jorge and Rudy; his fellow members of the group responsible for the Maltrocorp disturbance. Whoever was behind the company, they were tidying up loose ends. First Jacob, now Jorge and Rudy. He felt sick. He needed to contact Claus immediately to warn him to be careful. They were the only two left and how long would it be before it was their turn?

Pete had consumed far too much bourbon before he called Judy and started getting all emotional. It was the middle of the night in Birmingham and she soon figured out what had happened, and tried to convince him it would be a better idea if he went to bed and called her later when he was sober. But he ignored her and sat in his chair trying to hold a conversation. At the same time he was slowly drinking himself into a maudlin state, and finally fell asleep still nursing an empty bottle. The trouble was Dave had gone to bed to sleep off his jetlag, and because Pete hadn't replaced the receiver Judy couldn't finish the call. Not only couldn't she make another outgoing call but Pete's bill would be astronomical. Thankfully Dave woke up and came downstairs looking for a glass of water and noticed what had happened. He replaced the receiver and carefully removed the empty bottle without waking Pete. He smiled at the snoring superstar and imagined the kind of headache he would have when he awoke later, especially when he received his phone bill.

Janine and Don were warmly welcomed at the TV studio and taken through to the Green Room where the presenter Alan Brookstein and Vince Boyd were sitting talking. Vince was there to promote his new album and would be singing one of the songs from it. While she was sitting watching the rehearsal the idea of a duet between Pete and Vince came to her. They'd got on great together and a country rock song might work. At the same time giving Pete a change of direction.

The show was fantastic with Vince's performance impeccable, and the more she watched him, the more her idea excited her. She would ring Pete and organise a meeting with him and Vince.

Ray was in Liverpool at the famous old Empire Theatre with the two Motown stars, and it seemed like everyone from his youth was there in the audience. The roar that went up as he walked on stage was deafening and he felt a shiver down his spine. Every song he sang was greeted with cheers and at one point he noticed both Edwin Starr and Jimmy Ruffin were standing in the wings watching. After the show the queue of people waiting to see Ray stretched around the block, and he was determined to meet them all. The biggest thrill was when the four guys who he was in a band with all those years ago came into his dressing room, and after handshakes and hugs they started to sing. He'd dreamed of this moment and here they were, the five of them together again. He turned around and there in the doorway was Edwin and Jimmy both clapping their hands. It was a very special moment and for a few moments he forgot his troubles.

Vonda called Janine early the next morning to say Tony had been busy and had some news she should hear. She arrived at her office an hour later wondering what it was he'd found. He was already sitting in the office and stood up when Janine walked in.

Vonda motioned for her to sit. "Well your husband has certainly been a naughty boy," she said lighting a cigarette.

Janine refused the offer of one.

"Tony, tell Mrs. Law what you found out."

"I was talking to an old LAPD buddy of mine, who told me he was called to a bar late one night about a month ago with a report of two people having sex in one of the booths. Turns out it was your man Ray being given a BJ by his girlfriend. My pal knew it was him because he signed an autograph for his wife so he let him off with a caution."

Janine sat listening as Tony described the details. When he had finished she opened her handbag and put a cassette tape on the desk in front of Vonda. "You should have this too," she said.

"What is it?" Vonda asked picking it up.

"Play it, I think you'll find it interesting."

Vonda slipped the tape into a player behind her and pressed play. A male and female could clearly be heard.

"Oh Ray you are so fucking big," the woman said. They were both breathing heavily. She started to groan, "Ray, you're gonna make me come." She cried out and then it went quiet. Then the man's voice said "Mmm that's nice." The woman laughed. "My turn baby. I need to taste you." His voice. "God Josie you are so good at that." Then the man shouted out, "Yes, yes, Josie yes."

Vonda switched the tape off and looked at Janine who sat impassively.

"I'd like that cigarette now if that's alright."

Vonda passed her the packet and she took one out. Her hand was shaking slightly as Tony lit it for her and she took a long deep draw, then leaned her head back and blew the smoke out in a slow stream. She'd asked Don if he could find a copy of the tape on their way back from the TV studio and he'd dropped it off before she left that morning.

Vonda had been writing on her notepad. "Well that doesn't need much explaining I must admit."

Tony stood up to leave. "Gotta go. I'm on the trail of some of the women he danced with on his shows. Shouldn't be difficult to find them. But here's a strange thing. One of them turned up dead last week. According to my pal the investigation's being run by a Detective called…"

He paused to look at his notes but Janine spoke first. "Detective Anna Delaney. She came to see me."

"Well this is getting interesting," Vonda said writing another note. "What did she want?"

"She wanted to know where Ray was two weekends ago and the name of the female singer in his band."

Tony carried on. "Yeah turns out he was dancing kinda close with this woman when the singer goes ballistic and whacks him with a microphone stand and grabs hold of her. Next thing you know the woman lays the singer out cold. Evidently she's some kind of martial arts expert. Anyway a week later she turns up in a burnt out wreck in the hills above Malibu. According to my pal, that Delaney's one tough cookie, never knows when to give up."

He left saying he'd be in touch.

"There's a Martini in Rico's with my name on it, join me?" Vonda looked at Janine.

"Jaysus yeah!" she replied.

Two Martinis later they were sitting on a pair of stools in Rico's Bar next door to the office. It was empty apart from the two of them and Rico who was busy polishing glasses. A juke box in the corner was playing sixties classics. Janine felt relaxed and they were telling each other their life stories. It turned out Vonda was a rock music fan, which should have been obvious by today's outfit of a Led Zeppelin t-shirt and jeans, and nearly died when Janine told her she was Pete Peterson's manager. She'd gone to the Whisky A Go-Go gig on Sunset Boulevard and already had a ticket for his Hollywood Bowl show.

Vonda had a rule not to bring business out of the office which was a relief to Janine, as although she had remained calm while Tony reported his findings and they listened to the tape, she was hurting inside. Vonda knew this, which was the reason why she'd suggested a visit to Rico's. Rico in turn knew Vonda well enough to leave her alone with the attractive lady and just serve the drinks when he was asked.

Vonda was fascinated by Janine's story of how she came to be in LA, and while she was telling it even Janine couldn't believe how things had turned out.

"You should write a book," Vonda suggested. "Or someone should make a film. Hey I know a film producer; I did his divorce; I'll give him a call." She laughed. "We're still friends even though I represented his wife and she took him for millions. He'd love it."

By the time Janine got back to Hermosa Beach it was dark and she was very drunk. She'd lost count of how many Martinis they'd had. She knew she should eat but she gave up on the idea and went straight to bed. She didn't hear the phone or the knock on the door when Don came round. He eventually gave up and went back home. Deciding the bottle of champagne would keep for another day, he put it in the refrigerator.

CHAPTER NINETEEN

Peterson's final leg of their tour was due to start in a few days when they would be playing large venues and stadiums along the West Coast, finishing at the Hollywood Bowl.

Dave went to visit the doctor in the private clinic he'd called from Scotland. He'd given an assumed name to avoid being recognised and sat in the brightly lit, air-conditioned waiting room waiting to be called. He'd worn sunglasses which shaded his eyes from the glare off the gleaming white walls, although in hindsight it was probably a bad idea as they drew more attention to him, and he was sure the receptionist had recognised him judging from the way she kept glancing over and smiling.

Eventually the doctor came out and asked him to come into his surgery. He carried out all the usual checks of blood pressure, pulse and general wellbeing which seemed to be normal. Slightly confused, he asked Dave the reason why he'd made an appointment.

Dave had pondered on how he would explain his problem and finally told the doctor he'd been bitten by a monkey while he was recently in the Far East. Although it hadn't broken the skin the scratch was concerning him, and he'd not been feeling well since returning. This prompted the doctor to take a sample of Dave's blood, telling him he would send it to a private laboratory where it would be tested for infectious diseases or any other abnormalities. He told him to call back in two days for the results.

Claudia Inestes was agitated and pacing back and forth across her meeting room. Her security guards sat around the table looking uneasy. Seeing their boss in a mood like this usually meant trouble.

"When I said deal with the Mexicans quietly I didn't mean burn their fucking restaurant down. Are none of you capable of doing what I ask?"

One of the men went to speak but she waved him down. "I don't like loose ends. Do we have any idea who the other one was from Maltrocorp?"

The men all shook their heads. She slammed her fist on the table. "I want every possible lead followed up. Do you hear me?"

The men all nodded and she dismissed them telling her driver to stay behind.

"Are you sure they're reliable? I can't have any more mistakes. The mayoral campaign is starting to get serious and the last thing I need is any links back to Maltrocorp and that shooting. Just keep your eyes on them at all times."

She held his chin in her hand and lifted it up as she bent down and kissed his lips. "I want you later, be ready."

He nodded and left the room wiping off her lipstick with his handkerchief.

Don had finally managed to speak to Janine after her session with Vonda the previous day. Her head was thumping as she answered the phone trying her best to sound normal. She convinced him it would be better if they met up later at the studio instead of having to entertain him at home. At least that way she had chance to take a long bath and get herself together.

Vonda had also called and thankfully she sounded as bad as Janine felt, so there was some justice in the world. She told Janine that Tony had located a few of the women Ray got up on stage, and although they were initially reluctant to come forward - two were married - they had confirmed his sole motive was to have sex with them after the show.

As she put the phone down she decided to call the locksmith and have the locks changed before he returned. It was only a matter of days until the tour finished and there was no way she was going to allow him back in the house. She had made a start packing his clothes in bags which she was going to send to SoulTown's offices. Looking around she remembered a package of laundry had been delivered which she'd thrown in the bedroom and hadn't unpacked yet. Opening it up she noticed his Piotr Pauli shirt which had been mended and automatically took the receipt off before pushing it into one of the bags ready to be sent.

Don was waiting at the studio with Randy the bass player, and welcomed her with a kiss on the cheek. He spotted straight away she was still a little worse for wear but decided not to comment. Evidently Pete was still suffering after his disastrous phone call to Judy and the fight with a bottle of bourbon which he'd lost. Fortunately there were still a few days before the first date of the tour up in Portland, Oregon.

Janine sat down and over a coffee explained everything that had been discussed with Vonda Statzler, including the hotel room in Birmingham, Ray having sex in a bar, the tape recording and the women at his gigs. All in all solid grounds for a divorce which would surely be in her favour.

Don listened and when she finished said. "Look, I'm not the expert but I would say if this Vonda woman is half as good as she's cracked up to be, you don't have anything to worry about, and Ray will be lucky if he gets out with the shirt on his back. Now, what would you say to a glass of champagne?"

The look on Janine's face gave him his answer and they decided to take a raincheck.

Dave had called the clinic to check if his results had arrived and the doctor came on the phone asking if he could get in that day. An hour later he ushered Dave into his surgery. He sat down and began reading a long list of numbers written on a letter. He looked up at Dave. "OK, I need you to be honest with me now. What kind of monkey was it that bit you and where?"

Dave knew that it was a lot worse just by looking at the expression on the doctor's face. "If I tell you this, you have to promise me you won't tell anyone else. People have already died because of it."

The doctor looked serious. "The Hippocratic Oath protects me, so you have no worries on that score."

Dave took a deep breath. "There was a break in at a laboratory in

Anaheim called Maltrocorp and some monkeys in cages that were being used for experiments were set free. I was one of the people responsible. My accomplice was shot dead, and one of the monkeys bit my hand, although I had a glove on so it only scratched the skin. I managed to get away with another man who has since been murdered, and last week I read two more who were involved were found dead when their restaurant was burnt down. So you see no-one else can know about this."

The doctor spoke again. "Well that explains the findings of the clinic who analysed your blood. You appear to have been infected by a rare strain of virus developed in the Cold War by scientists in East Germany, which works on the nervous system and over time results in total paralysis."

"Is there a cure?"

"I'm afraid not at the moment. But trials are continuing, as with the monkey at Maltrocorp, as yet without success. I'm sorry but that's all I can tell you."

"Do you know how long it will take?"

"No, that's where it becomes difficult to say. There has only ever been one previous case and he lived for ten years after being infected, but that was caused by a large dose received after an accident in the laboratory."

"So what's your advice?"

"I would suggest you come in for regular blood tests and we'll monitor your condition. And in the meantime pray that someone has a breakthrough with a cure. I'm sorry I can't be more helpful."

Dave sat very still before standing up and shaking the doctor's hand. "Thank you, I'll be in touch." He walked out of the clinic and looked up at the sky wondering how long he had to live, and what he could do to get revenge on Maltrocorp.

Ray's flight arrived back at two o'clock in the morning, and tired after the long journey he called Janine, waking her up.

She asked him what he wanted and did he realise what time it was.

"I was thinking I might come home and go to bed."

"Ray, I don't know whether you remember what I said in Birmingham, but this is not your home anymore. Your clothes are at SoulTown's office and as far as I'm concerned I never want to see you again."

"But I've got nowhere to go," he pleaded.

"You should have thought about that before fucking your friend the solicitor. Good night Ray!" Janine slammed down the phone.

Ray sat working out his next move. Then he dialled another number. "Hey babe it's me," he said as cheerfully as he could.

"Ray? What the hell do you want?"

"Listen, I need a favour. Can I sleep at your place tonight? Just for the one night until I get myself sorted."

"Screw you, Ray!" Josie Thomas slammed down her phone.

The guy lying next to her rolled over and mumbled. "Who was that?"

She lay back and started to stroke him gently. "No one, man, no one. Now where were we?"

Ray had one last hope and it was a long shot but in his situation worth a try. He flicked through the little book he kept hidden in his travel bag and found the number he needed.

A female voice answered just as he was about to hang up. "Hello?"

"Hey, I'm sorry if I woke you but it's Ray Law, you remember me from the party with Pete Peterson?"

Kathy Blake thought for a moment. "Hey Ray, yes of course I do. How are you?" She looked at the time. "It's kind of late."

"Yeah look I'm really sorry but I'm stranded at the airport and can't go back home at the moment. I was wondering if I could sleep at your place until I get myself sorted."

Kathy thought for a moment. "Yeah sure come on down, you know where I am. It'll be good to see you again."

He put the phone down and smiled to himself as he walked out to find a taxi.

It took him just less than an hour to reach her house and she opened the door wearing a very short nightie, high heels and luminous pink lipstick. There was a fug of marijuana smoke in the house as she grabbed his hand and pulled him in. Closing the door with her heel she took his bag and threw it down on the marble floor leading him towards the stairs. He glanced into the lounge and noticed there were about half a dozen couples lying across the furniture in various states.

"I remember thinking I'd love to get some of that cock of yours; is it still as big?" she said as she opened the door to her bedroom. She pulled her nightie over her head and lay down on the bed.

Kathy watched as he stripped off and squealed. "Oh my god it is!"

CHAPTER TWENTY

As the morning light was starting to shine through the wooden shutters on her bedroom window Kathy rolled off Ray, lay on her back and started to snore. He looked at her now in the cold light of day and thought she had become noticeably more haggard-looking since the day of the party. He'd never been fucked so much in his life and wondered how Pete had survived night after night of Kathy's insatiable appetite for sex. He had done his best to be in control but she was a sexual dynamo driven by a constant supply of top grade cocaine and for once he was going to have to concede defeat and make an escape before she woke up again and demanded more. He looked down at his battle weary member as he pulled on his shorts and promised it a rest. Even he wasn't capable of repeating last night in a hurry.

He crept downstairs and called a taxi to take him to SoulTown's office where hopefully his clothes were waiting for him. Once there he'd make a plan. While he was waiting he looked around at the state of her house. It no longer resembled the fabulous place where she'd thrown the party, and was in desperate need of cleaning with full ashtrays everywhere and dirty dishes lying all over the floor. Some of the couples from last night were still there, stretched out asleep on the various beanbags scattered around. He was about to quietly slip out of the house when he noticed an official looking letter on a table in the hall. Unable to resist, he picked it up and saw it was an eviction order. It would appear Kathy Blake was no longer the big star anymore, and putting it back where he found it he climbed into the taxi, closing his eyes as they pulled away.

The next thing he was aware of was the taxi driver poking his arm telling him they'd arrived and groggily realised where he was.

Eddy and Charles were waiting for him as he slumped down in a chair in their office.

Eddy laughed as he took in the dishevelled sight of their artist. "It's a tough life being a Sex God," he said with a chuckle.

Ray didn't have the energy to reply. Charles opened the other office door and pointed to a pile of black plastic bags. "Here's your stuff, man.

Your wife dropped it off the other day. She didn't seem too pleased."

Ray went on to explain what had happened in Birmingham and how Janine had completely overreacted, but Eddy commented that if his wife had discovered him with another woman blood would definitely flow.

Charles told him they'd found a cheap apartment in an area called Crenshaw where he could stay until he'd sorted out the situation with his wife. "It's not Hermosa Beach but, hey man, beggars can't be choosers."

Ray started to gather up his paltry belongings. He needed sleep. Long uninterrupted sleep.

Detective Anna Delaney and her partner Sergeant Joe Budd called that same morning at Janine's house to speak to Ray. When Janine opened the door in her dressing-gown she saved them the trouble of asking. "He's not here."

Anna looked annoyed. "Where is he then? We know he arrived back late last night on a flight from London."

Janine invited them in and poured herself a cup of coffee. She explained how he'd called her from the airport and that she'd told him in no uncertain terms he was not welcome there.

"And you've no idea where he went?" Anna asked.

"No, and I don't give a shite." Janine replied, then as an afterthought. "You might try his management, SoulTown off Sunset & Vine. I dropped his clothes there."

Joe Budd said they already had the address but as they turned to leave, Anna stopped, taking out a small plastic evidence bag from her pocket and showed it to Janine. "I don't suppose you recognise this, do you?" She watched Janine's face closely as she inspected the small button inside.

"No. Why, should I?"

"It was found in Laura Weiss' apartment and comes from a designer shirt made by Piotr Pauli. According to our research your husband bought a shirt from Piotr Pauli recently."

Janine felt her stomach flip as she remembered the missing button from Ray's shirt in the laundry. "Well I'm sorry but I can't help you. As I said all his belongings are at his management's office. Maybe if you call there they could let you search his clothing."

Anna smiled and nodded as she turned to leave. "Thanks Mrs. Law, we appreciate your help." On their way to SoulTown Productions she sat deep in thought while Joe drove. She turned to her partner. "Why don't I believe her?"

With perfect timing they arrived at SoulTown's office just as Ray was getting ready to leave, and showing their LAPD badges Anna introduced herself and Joe. She assured him they wouldn't keep him long, noticing how tired he looked, but they wanted to ask him a few questions in connection with a homicide they were investigating.

Anna explained that their victim was called Laura Weiss and she had danced with him during his performance at 'Kaleidoscope' in Santa Monica. There had also been an incident with his girl singer involving her. Ray said he remembered the night and that the singer had been sacked. Anna wanted to know if Ray had been back to the club since that night, and he said only once but didn't stay long.

"Did you meet Laura Weiss that night?" Anna asked.

Ray thought for a moment, suddenly on his guard. He'd been in Anna's position so many times he could almost predict her questions. "She was at the bar when I arrived, and I said hello, but the place was packed so I just had the one drink and decided to leave."

"Were you on your own when you left?"

"Yeah."

"And did anyone see you leave?"

"I don't think so. I just jumped in a cab and went back home."

"A long way for such a short stay don't you think?"

"Well to be honest I was still tired from the gig the night before. I was going away on tour the following week so I decided to call it quits and got an early night."

"And you don't have any witnesses to back up your story?"

"No. My wife was away in New York for the weekend."

"Mr. Law, do you own a Piotr Pauli shirt?"

"Yes, as a matter of fact I do."

"Would you mind showing it to us?"

Ray looked at the pile of black bags in the office next door.

"Well if you'd like to work your way through all that you're welcome, officers."

Anna looked at Joe and was about to say something else then changed her mind. They took a note of his new address, thanked him for his time and left him sitting in the office. She looked at her partner as they sat in their car.

"So why don't I believe him either? It was as if he was reading my mind. We need to go back to that club tonight and speak to the barman; see if he remembers anything."

Ray arrived at his apartment which was on the first floor of a condo situated just off Main Street in Crenshaw. It was exactly as Charles had described it, *beggars can't be choosers* he'd said. Bare walls and floorboards, furnished with a sofa and armchair in the small lounge and a double bed and an old wooden wardrobe in the bedroom. But it was clean, and he piled the bin bags in a corner and ran himself a bath. While it was filling he started to search through his clothes hanging up his shirts, trousers and jackets. In one of the bags he found the Piotr Pauli designer shirt he'd worn when he met Laura Weiss and wondered why Detective Delaney had asked about it. He vaguely remembered throwing it in the laundry when he'd got home that night and checked it over, but didn't notice anything different about it.

The bath was full and he lowered himself into the soothing warm water, closing his eyes. His mind went back to the interview with Detective Anna Delaney and Sergeant Joe Budd. She was definitely one to watch out for. He saw some of his old self in her, and if she was anything like him she wouldn't rest until she caught Laura's killer.

He went back over the events again, and the more he thought about it the more he was sure there wasn't anything to concern him. He climbed out of the bath and towelled himself dry, checking the scratches on his back in the mirror which were still sore from the night with Kathy Blake. He lay down, closed his eyes and was asleep in seconds.

Janine called Pete and told him about her meeting with Vince Boyd and the idea she'd had of them singing a duet. He'd initially been sceptical, but when she explained about his appearance on the TV show and how it would be an opportunity to open up another market, he began to warm to the idea. The royalties he was earning from producing Ray's hit were starting to come through, and if he could do it again with Vince then who was he to turn down the idea. Janine said she'd fix up a meeting at Whitland Studios while Vince was still in town, and he put down the phone already forming an idea in his mind. It would be useful to have Dave Sanchez involved, and although he'd originally talked about moving over to New York, as the tour of the West Coast was about to start he was still staying at Pete's.

Vince Boyd had jumped at the idea of working with Pete when Janine called him. She thought back to the first time they'd met on the flight over and how she'd been in awe of meeting him. 'How quickly things change in the music business' she thought.

Dave returned to the Red House after his doctor's appointment and had been intrigued about the idea of a collaboration with Vince Boyd. Like Janine, he'd been a big fan, and the prospect of working with one of his idols was exciting and took his mind off his ongoing problem. Pete had had a piano installed in his music room, and he and Dave worked late into the night on a song idea ready for their meeting with Vince.

Don took Janine to the studio the next morning and they met Pete and Dave who were looking tired after their late night. Janine was visibly excited that her idol was coming in to work with Pete. She told the guys how Vince had rescued her from an embarrassing situation with an inebriated Charles Morse, and then taken her to a bar where they drank Cosmopolitans. She explained how he had graciously put her in a taxi home even though he could have taken advantage of her.

Dave who had not really been listening suddenly looked up. "Well it would have been a surprise if he had; he's gay." Janine's mouth dropped open with surprise, along with Pete and Don. "You mean you didn't know?"

She was just about to speak when the door opened and Vince Boyd walked in. Four heads swivelled together towards him as, unaware of the previous conversation, he came over to them smiling.

"Hey everyone, how's things?"

CHAPTER TWENTY-ONE

Detective Anna Delaney and her partner Sergeant Joe Budd had gone back to 'Kaleidoscope' in Santa Monica that evening, and asked to talk to the barman who had been working on the night of Laura Weiss' murder. A tall well-built man with black slicked-back hair walked into the manager's office a few moments later, and introduced himself as Raul. Anna showed him a photo of Laura and asked if he remembered serving her on the night in question. He said he had because she was a good-looking woman, and also because she had been involved in the fight on stage with the girl singer. He thought at the time what a great right hook she had. Anna patiently let him finish and then showed him a photo of Ray, and asked if he remembered serving him on the same night. Raul thought for a moment then said yes he did. He remembered because he ordered two large brandies and poured them in the same glass.

Anna looked at Joe who was making notes of what Raul was saying.

"Think carefully. Did you see Ray Law and Laura talking together?"

"Yes. He kissed her cheek when he arrived like he knew her."

"Did you see them leave.?"

"No, I'm sorry. The bar was really busy and I was down the other end serving. The next time I came back up to where they were sitting they'd gone."

"And you didn't see them leave together?"

"Sorry, no."

Once again Anna and Joe were sitting in their car going through what they'd just been told. She thumped her fist on the dashboard. "Damn! There's something about Ray Law that's bugging me and I can't figure out what it is. Let's go back to the office."

They arrived back as Captain Lewis their boss was about to leave, but he called her into his office for an update on how the case was progressing. Anna went through what they had so far and was about to say how she felt about Ray Law when the Captain interrupted her. "Ray Law? English guy married to Janine?"

Anna nodded intrigued how Captain Lewis knew him.

The Captain went on. "Good guy. He was responsible for taking down the attempted bank note heist on Oscar's Night. Ex-detective from the Midlands in the UK. What's he got to do with it?"

She was now completely confused. Should she reveal her thoughts about Ray Law or keep them to herself? In the end she just said he had been interviewed because the victim had been involved in an incident during a show he was performing. This seemed to placate the Captain who left telling her to keep him up to date.

She was sitting staring at their notes when her partner suddenly sat upright. She looked at him.

"What is it?"

"Coming out of SoulTown's office after interviewing Ray Law you said it's as if he's reading your mind. Well if he's an ex-detective he knows what you're going to ask him because he's probably done it all himself before."

Anna gave him a hug. "Which now means we have a whole new ball-game on our hands!"

Claudia Inestes was feeling relaxed and positive. Her mayoral campaign was ahead in the polls, and she had just sold her house in Laurel Canyon for a tidy profit and bought herself a ranch in Santa Clarita. As far as she was concerned there was nothing to be worried about with the situation at Maltrocorp, which seemed to have calmed down. Security at the site had been improved, and things had got back to normal. She still hadn't had any news regarding the one missing person from the raid, but, since nothing further had been reported, she was inclined to let it go for the time being. If at a later date he raised his head then she would deal with it.

It occurred to her that she hadn't spoken to Janine, who she'd met at Renée's. She found her intriguing, but realised she had no way of contacting her. She did however know where she lived, since one of her men had tailed her home after the last time they'd met. Maybe she could use the excuse she was out campaigning and surprise her by knocking on her door. She called her personal assistant to pick her up and they set off for Hermosa Beach

Janine had got back home after watching Pete, Dave and Vince Boyd perform absolute magic in the studio. Irrespective of all her illusions about him being dashed, she had hugged Vince at the end of the session and left Pete and Dave finishing off the recording to drive back with Don to Hermosa Beach. She was opening a bottle of Bollinger to celebrate when the phone rang. It was Vonda Statzler wanting her to come by the office in the morning.

"Say what are you doing right now? Why don't you drop by the house, I'm just opening a bottle of champagne."

Vonda was thirty minutes away with Tony so they jumped in Tony's car and headed over to Janine's. Meanwhile she called the studio and invited the guys back when they'd finished, and then put a call in to Vince at the Beverly Hills Hotel. He was pleased she'd called and set off with his personal assistant.

An hour later the party was getting into full swing when there was a knock on the door. Don was the closest and opened it to find Ray, obviously drunk, standing swaying, holding a half empty bottle of brandy.

Janine had noticed what was happening and rushed over to confront him making sure he couldn't get in.

"So this is what happens when I'm not here, is it?"

He tried to push Janine out of the way but Don moved in front of her. "I think it would be better if you went home and sobered up, Ray." Don was trying to be diplomatic while at the same time protecting Janine.

"Fuck you, Don. Don't try and stop me coming in my own house." Ray made an attempt at a punch but Don easily dodged and caught him as he fell forward.

"Come on man, you're making a fool of yourself. Let's get you a cab before you do anything stupid."

But Ray wasn't finished and tried another swipe at Don catching him on the shoulder. This time Don decided he'd had enough and bundled him outside, closing the door behind him. "I'll not tell you again, Ray. Stop now or you will get hurt. Janine said she doesn't want you in the house, so let's calm down and I'll get you a cab home."

Ray was looking at him glassy eyed. "How come you're here then?" He staggered backwards almost falling over then regained his balance. "Oh I get it. You're fucking my wife. That's it, you bastard. I thought you were my friend and all the while you've been screwing her behind my back."

Don stood his ground trying to stay calm.

As they were standing outside, a taxi pulled up and Don took hold of Ray's arm leading him to it. He opened the back door and pushed him inside. Ray made an attempt to get back out but Don slammed the door knocking him over backwards. He leaned in to the driver and gave him a handful of dollars. "Get him out of here pal. He'll tell you where he lives."

Don turned round and walked back into the house and closed the door without looking back.

The atmosphere inside was a little subdued, but as he walked in, he rubbed his hands together and with a broad smile announced loudly. "Right! Who needs a drink?"

There was a collective sigh of relief and things quickly returned back to normal. Vonda was dressed in an 'In Flames' T-shirt, which Pete had thought hilarious and signed it across her breasts to much laughter, and was deep in conversation with Dave about the merits of synthesisers in rock music. Tony who didn't drink was sitting out on the balcony watching the waves, and Vince Boyd and his personal assistant were chatting with Don and Janine about how well she had done since he first met her; when they all flew out together from London. She secretly got the impression Vince was looking for her to manage him. 'Wouldn't that be a turn up for the books?' she thought taking a mouthful of champagne and secretly squeezing Don's leg. At least she thought it was secret, except Vonda had spotted the little token of affection and thought she would speak to her about it tomorrow. In her business it always paid to know everything about your client, just so there were no surprises to catch you out later.

They were all relaxing again when there was another knock on the door. Janine moved to answer it deciding if it was Ray back again she would call the police, and opened the door ready for an argument.

Instead of her drunken husband, standing in front of her was Senator Claudia Inestes. Janine was momentarily lost for words as she was the last person on earth she expected to see on her doorstep. She finally regained her composure and invited her in.

The guests had all stopped talking and were looking to see who the visitor was, when Janine introduced her friend the Senator and future Mayor, Claudia Inestes.

Claudia immediately apologised for intruding and said she should leave, but Pete intervened and with his best charming manner began introducing her to the other guests. Janine stood watching as she smoothly ingratiated herself with everyone and wondered how she had found out where she lived, positive that she hadn't even given Claudia her phone number. But Claudia the politician was in full flow explaining how she had been in the area canvassing and what a surprise to find her friend Janine lived here in such a wonderful house. Pete was relishing the moment holding her arm as he took her out to the balcony showing her the view, while at the same time watching Janine's face which had a look of bewilderment. After the episode with Ray she was wondering what could possibly happen next.

Suddenly Claudia was at her side holding a glass of champagne which Pete had poured for her. "Well you're the dark horse," she said. "I never knew you were the person behind such a successful star."

Janine was cautious how she replied, not wanting to let her know too much. "Yes it's a privilege to work with such a talented man." She looked over her shoulder at Dave Sanchez who was hovering, obviously wanting to speak to Claudia. "Claudia, may I introduce you to a wonderful musician, Dave Sanchez. He is an incredible keyboard player who works with Pete."

Claudia shook Dave's hand and smiled graciously. "It's lovely to meet you Dave. Maybe if I become Mayor you could play at my inauguration party?"

Dave was looking at her in a strange way still holding her hand when Janine spotted he was starting to embarrass her. "When you become Mayor Senator, when!"

Claudia made the excuse of having another engagement and thanked Janine for her hospitality, shaking hands with everyone. As she was leaving she leaned in close to her and whispered. "Give me a call, soon," and climbed in her limousine which was waiting outside.

As she drove off Vince Boyd suddenly spoke. "Well who'd have thought it. Janine you never cease to amaze me. A senator just drops in for a drink. How cool is that? Don't tell me you have any more surprises in store tonight."

Dave stood watching as Claudia drove away. He had a strange feeling that their paths would cross again.

CHAPTER TWENTY-TWO

At LAPD headquarters Detective Mike Downes, one of Captain Lewis' team of special investigators had been working late looking into the Maltrocorp incident. He was the legal expert and he'd been digging deep into the structure of the company. He'd found a couple of interesting pieces of information and spoke to Captain Lewis first thing the next morning.

"So what is it that's got you so fired up, Downes?"

"Well Captain, I've been chasing my tail for days trying to find out who's behind Maltrocorp. All I kept coming across are off-shore companies which are subsidiaries of other off-shore companies with no official directors' names shown."

The Captain looked at him questioningly and he quickly went on. "That is until last night. You see I happened to notice the purchase of a property over in Santa Clarita. It's somewhere my wife and I had been thinking about moving to, which is why it caught my eye."

The Captain shuffled in his chair. "Go on."

"Yes, well anyway, according to the property register the purchaser is a small set-up called Clarianest, which also happens to be part of one of the off-shore companies involved with Maltrocorp. And this is where it starts to get interesting. The sole director and shareholder of Clarianest is none other than Senator Claudia Inestes."

Captain Lewis sat up as if he'd had an electric shock.

"What! Are you sure? I mean really sure?"

Mike Downes passed a typewritten sheet across to him.

"It's all there in black and white. If you dig deep enough and long enough they always make a mistake. And she just made it!"

"Good work Mike. The question is, where do we go from here? Do me a favour, keep this under your hat for now. I need to seriously think about this."

Captain Lewis put the piece of paper into a file and dropped it onto the pile on his desk as the detective left his office. After a moment's thought he picked up his phone and called his ex-colleague Don Rosario, arranging to meet him later.

Sitting at a desk just by the door to Captain Lewis' office, Carlos Hernandez, another member of the special investigators team had been listening to the conversation and discreetly slipped out of the building. There was a public phone box just around the corner from the main entrance and he dropped a few coins in and dialled a number. He had a five-minute conversation before returning to his desk.

Don Rosario was busy getting ready to start the West Coast tour with Peterson. He was in the middle of packing his case when the phone rang. Expecting it to be Pete or even Manny he answered it with a short "Yes!"

He was surprised when it was his old boss Captain Lewis asking Don if he could spare him some time as he had something he wanted to discuss. He didn't want to go into any more detail over the phone, so they agreed to meet in his office. Don put the phone down wondering what could be so important and pulled on his coat hoping it wouldn't take too long.

Half an hour later he was sitting in Captain Lewis' office listening as his ex-boss told him what Detective Downes had discovered. When he'd finished they both agreed it had to be kept quiet until the right time. Don told the Captain how he'd been at Janine's last night when totally unexpectedly Claudia had arrived in her Senator's guise, and how Dave Sanchez had reacted. Don had a feeling there was something more that Dave hadn't told them. He wasn't sure what, but he intended to keep an eye on him during the tour.

Janine turned up at Vonda Statzler's office slightly hung over from the previous night's party. She couldn't believe what had started as a quiet drink had ended up a full-blown drama with first Ray turning up drunk, and then Claudia Inestes appearing as if by accident. Even Janine knew that was a lie, although she still wondered how she had found out where she lived. And then that whispered message in her ear as she left.

Vonda was looking great, wearing a 'Who's Next' T-shirt and her usual tight jeans and boots. She was smoking with her feet up on her desk as Janine entered. She flipped them off and stood up to greet her with a kiss on the cheek. She got straight down to business.

"So, having seen him in action last night I can get where you're coming from with Mr. Law. A real piece of work that one!"

"What's our next move?" Janine asked.

"We serve him papers. Simple as that. We've got so much on him there's a fair chance he'll just agree and go away quietly before we even reach court." Vonda carried on before Janine had chance to answer. "There is one thing I have to ask you though. Don Rosario? You and he seem to be a little more than professional acquaintances."

Janine felt herself going slightly red.

"Honey, there's not a lot gets past the Vondascope. It's just I don't like surprises further down the road and if your husband's got himself a sharp counsel they'll dig it out. You want to tell me?"

Janine sat and told her about the kiss in the hospital down in Miami and then the weekend in New York culminating in their night together at the hotel, and how he had become her knight in shining armour.

"Hey, he's a good-looking guy and who wouldn't want to know he was on your side. OK so now I know, anything else you need get off your chest?"

Janine started to cry and refused a tissue pulling herself together. She took one of Vonda's cigarettes and after she'd lit it described her affair with Mandy and how she had decided she wasn't going to be lonely when Ray went back to the UK. She told Vonda how she'd explained to Mandy that what they had was wonderful but it could never replace her husband, and then when he came back how she became cold towards her, culminating with her taking her own life in Boston screaming how she'd loved her.

Vonda sat taking notes without making any comments until she finished. "Wow, like I said before, you should write a goddam book! OK. I don't think we have any problems and I suggest we serve a divorce petition on him straight away."

She called her secretary in and instructed her to draw up the relevant papers. "We'll get those done and hopefully put this to bed as soon as possible." She stood and gave Janine a hug.

CHAPTER TWENTY-THREE

Don was sitting in the driving seat of the silver tour bus ready to set off on the first gig of the West Coast tour. He'd managed to get Manny to upgrade their transport to include individual aircraft seats for extra comfort and everything was loaded and everyone on board except Dave Sanchez.

Don sat drumming his fingers on the steering wheel trying his best to be patient, but if there was one thing that got his back up it was being late. It was a long trip to Portland, Oregon, and he wanted to get there as soon as possible to give the guys a good rest before tomorrow night's show at the Civic Stadium.

Finally, just as he was starting to get annoyed Dave came rushing up full of apologies saying he'd had a doctor's appointment which had run late. After apologising to everyone, Dave had settled down for the journey. The results from his previous blood test had shown no change so at least his condition hadn't worsened and he'd had another test before leaving. The doctor told him to make sure to keep in touch and reassured him everything was being done to find a cure and to stay positive. In fact he was actually feeling great after hearing the finished mix of the track he and Pete had recorded with Vince Boyd. It was an interesting change of direction for Pete and they'd come up with a really catchy Country-Rock song. Vince was over the moon and if it hadn't been for his personal assistant being so close all the time Dave might have tried a little harder to be more friendly. Vince knew though, he was sure of that.

Pete was reflecting back on events at Janine's. He couldn't believe what had happened to Ray. He'd become a completely different person since that night in Birmingham when he sang at his and Janine's wedding party. Pete almost felt responsible for encouraging him to sing more. But then there was the Senator and Janine. Very interesting, especially after seeing them together at Renée's; never mind her and Don. Like Don, he also knew something was going on with Dave but didn't know what, although it was funny watching how he'd spent the evening sending out signals to Vince Boyd without much success. He leaned back in his seat and closed his eyes. 'You couldn't write this'.

Ray Law had called Julia Davies at her office in Birmingham. He was sitting looking at the letter he'd received from Vonda Statzler informing him that her client, Janine Law, was filing for divorce on the grounds of adultery. She was not prepared to discuss any kind of financial settlement and was looking for nothing other than to walk away a free woman.

"She can't do that can she?" he asked, slurring slightly as he took another swig from the bottle of brandy in his hand.

Julia knew it would be difficult talking to him in his current state. "Listen Ray, I'm going to put you in touch with a friend of mine who's an attorney over there. She'll help you sort things out. Don't worry."

She cut the line before he had chance to say any more and dialled the number of her old university friend. They had been nicknamed 'The Devil's Duo' when they'd shared a room, and men on a regular basis.

Melissa Thomson-Howes had been pleasantly surprised to hear the Julia's voice after such a long time. They spent a couple of minutes reminiscing before Julia outlined why she'd phoned in the first place. Making notes as she listened, Melissa agreed to see Ray as soon as possible and to file a counter claim for half of Janine's estate. She agreed with Julia there wasn't much chance of getting it, but at least it would slow things down and make Vonda Statzler work for her money. She told Julia she knew Vonda personally and that they'd crossed swords on numerous occasions, so she would relish the challenge of coming up against her old adversary again. They said goodbye and promised to meet up again one day soon.

Melissa wasted no time in calling Ray to arrange a meeting. She could tell immediately he'd been drinking so told him to come to her office early the next morning, hoping that would give him time to sleep it off. She put the phone down and started to find out as much about Janine Law as possible. It was easy to discover her career since she arrived in

LA. Her rise from managing a new English singer to helping him become one of the biggest stars in the world was well documented, but it was the story behind the public persona that Melissa was interested in. She had to find some skeletons in her closet to throw back at Vonda who on paper had an open and shut case.

She knew Vonda had Tony who was regarded as one of the best investigators, but she had Dawson. Dawson played dirty, but Dawson got results. She called him and told him to be at her office first thing.

Ray was sober when he arrived at Melissa's office; just. He'd had a large brandy to steady his nerves before he set off. Dawson was already sitting in her plush second floor suite in Downtown drinking coffee when Ray was shown in by Melissa's secretary.

Melissa stood up and came round her desk to shake his hand. She was eloquently dressed in a grey, tailored jacket and pencil skirt with black high-heeled shoes. He could immediately see why she and Julia were good friends. They were almost like twins and it occurred to him as he held her hand, he would have to behave himself or he could end up in even more trouble.

She introduced him to Dawson who gave him a nod of acknowledgement.

Ray looked at him. "You got another name?"

"Just Dawson."

Melissa sat back down. "OK let's get down to business. I've spoken to Julia and to be honest what she's already told me doesn't look good Ray. I'd say as things stand you'll be lucky to come out with the shirt on your back, and that's if the judge is feeling generous." Ray stood up as if to leave, but Melissa carried on. "Sit down Ray. I said, that's as things stand. But before we start throwing in the towel let's look at the situation from your point of view. I don't for a minute think Janine's an angel. There's got to be something she's done that we could use against her."

Ray looked forlorn.

"Listen, this is a shitty business, and the only way you stand a chance of getting anything is to fight fire with fire."

Ray looked up. "She had an affair with a woman called Mandy Velasquez. It was when I went back to the UK. I called her at a hotel in San Francisco and then at home and both times a woman answered. The first time in the middle of the night."

Melissa encouraged him to carry on and he recalled how in the room where Pete was held hostage, just before she pulled the trigger Mandy had screamed how she loved her and they could have been good together.

Melissa wrote down everything he was saying. "That's great, is there anything else? Anything at all. Suspicions?"

He remembered the party at Janine's the other night. "Don Rosario, she's having a scene with him, I'm sure." He explained who Don was and how she had spent the weekend with him in New York.

Melissa asked Dawson to check it out. She decided to call it a day for now. "That's great Ray, at least we've got something to go on. I'll be in touch, but in the meantime keep away from Janine and Hermosa Beach."

Detective Carlos Hernandez had finished his shift and slipped into Claudia Inestes' office through the back door. He was sitting in her meeting room with the blinds closed bringing her and her personal assistant up to date with the news from police headquarters.

She slammed her fist down on the table. "Fuck! That useless accountant, Beckermann. I told him under no circumstances to involve me in any deals. We're going to have to deal with them. Carlos take care of this Detective Downes, and see to it that any relevant information disappears?"

"I'll deal with the accountant."

She lit a cigarillo and blew out a thin stream of smoke. "You can go now," she said and both men stood up. "Not you," she said to her assistant and smiled.

Detective Carlos Hernandez left the office trying to work out his plan of action. His first task was to get into Mike Downes' computer and erase the data he'd found on Clarianest. That was easy. Then he had to break into Captain Lewis' office and destroy the file he'd seen Mike give him. The hardest part was getting rid of Mike himself. He lived on his own since being divorced and had no children, which made Carlos feel a little better.

The challenge was to make it look like an accident.

During his time as a detective Carlos had built up a network of informants, a lot of them ex-cons who for a few dollars would arrange for someone to be taken care of. He knew a serving cop would cost more and require a certain kind of person but he was sure it was possible. He made a call and arranged a meeting later that night.

Claudia climbed off her assistant's body as he lay on the meeting room table. She decided to go to the council committee meeting without her panties and as she was sitting in the back seat on her way to the council house she could feel the draft from the air conditioning between her legs. She watched the streets flash by as she lit one of her cigarillos and thought to herself, 'Soon this will all be under my control'.

She reached between her legs and began to stroke herself. Her assistant had been watching her in the rear-view mirror and smiled to himself as she closed her eyes and slid down the seat. At least he probably wouldn't be called on again tonight to service her constant demands.

Carlos was sitting in a deserted parking lot in the Fashion District waiting for his contact. It was dark and dimly lit with only a few of the streetlights working, so when his passenger door opened and a man slid into the seat it took him by surprise.

"What the fuck, you scared the shit out of me!"

The man smiled showing a row of decayed teeth. His clothes smelled of damp and stale urine.

"And you stink. Don't you ever wash?"

"It'll cost you a grand, up front," he said.

"Up front! Don't make me laugh. You think I was born yesterday? Half now, the rest on completion."

"And I need two fifty for a piece."

Carlos breathed out and took an envelope from his pocket. "There's a photo in there. Make sure it looks like a failed mugging. His address is on the back."

The man took the package and was gone as fast as he arrived. Carlos drove off, opening the windows to get rid of the smell.

CHAPTER TWENTY-FOUR

Vonda had asked Janine to call in at her office and opened the door herself explaining her secretary had phoned in ill. Janine noticed it was a 'Jimi Hendrix - Are You Experienced' T-shirt today and a clean pair of tight jeans with her usual boots. She followed her into the office and sat down.

Vonda picked up a letter from her desk. "OK so we've had a response from your husband's attorney; an old adversary of mine, Melissa Thomson-Howes who by all accounts went to university with Julia Davies, the woman you discovered in bed with him in Birmingham. Anyway the reason I've asked you to come over is they're saying they have evidence of your infidelity with Don Rosario in the hotel in New York and will be presenting it in their defence. Like I told you before, it's always best to come clean so there's no surprises later down the line."

"Shit! How did she find out about it. We were so careful."

"Obviously not careful enough," Vonda replied. "A few dollars to the bell hop, doorman, chamber maid and someone's memory can always be jogged."

"So what do we do now?"

Vonda lit a cigarette and offered one to Janine who took it, and as they blew out their smoke she explained they had two options. "We go to court which would entail lots of sworn statements and costs, and ultimately let a judge decide; which might not end with the desired outcome. Or, agree to a deal."

"What kind of deal?" Janine asked.

"Well let's look at your original proposed terms of divorce which were Zilch! Fine so long as he's prepared to walk away with his, ahem, well-used tail between his legs. But as we've discovered today he's not going to do that. Or should I say Ms. Davies back in the UK is not letting him do that."

Janine was silent.

"You're looking confused, can I make a suggestion?"

Janine nodded.

"Admit joint infidelity and offer an immediate cash settlement."

"But he doesn't deserve it. He doesn't deserve anything."

"Well that's your opinion, but it might not be the opinion of a learned judge, depending on who you get or what mood they're in."

Janine lit another cigarette and stood up pacing around the office looking markedly disturbed. "Is what I say in here confidential?"

"Yes of course it is."

"There are two things I have to tell you." She paused as if considering her next action. "I had a meeting this morning at Westoria Records, and Manny Oberstein and his son told me that due to Ray's high profile and his unacceptable behaviour they are cancelling his contract with immediate effect. I asked them to reconsider but they have made the decision. I'm sure it will be blamed on me, but I swear I had nothing to do with it."

Vonda looked shocked. "Does his management know?"

"They were in the meeting. They intend to sever links with him too."

"Oh shit that's bad. What do you think he'll do?"

"Well on the face of it his career's over in the States. He'll struggle to find anyone else to touch him especially after being dropped by Manny. He could go back to the UK and try and carry on there. He seemed pretty popular and they're more forgiving."

"In that case as a positive gesture you could offer to pay his fare back to the UK in your settlement offer. But you said there were two things you wanted to say."

"Yes and this is where I have a major problem."

"Well I am your attorney so if there's anyone you can confide in, it's me."

"Do you have anything to drink?"

Vonda was taken by surprise. "Yeah I've got some Vodka somewhere will that do?"

She poured Janine a large glass and she swallowed it in one gulp.

"I think Ray murdered that woman, Laura Weiss."

"What!" Vonda poured a glass out for herself and knocked it back. "What makes you think that?"

Janine accepted another glass of the Stolichnaya and related how she had arrived home from New York and found Ray's shirt in the laundry and how it had a button missing. Then when the two LAPD Detectives had turned up and showed her the button, she'd known but said nothing.

"You're gonna have to say something," Vonda said.

"I know! I know what a bastard he is, but I can't shop him. I'm sorry, I had to tell someone and I'm sorry it was you." Janine broke down and sobbed.

Vonda had another shot from the bottle and sat thinking until Janine had stopped crying.

"Alright! Look, attorney client privilege says I don't have to disclose what you've just told me and I won't. But fuck Janine, you never cease to amaze me."

Detective Mike Downes had driven home after having a quick beer with a couple of other guys from the, including Carlos Hernandez. He'd told them he was picking up a pizza on the way and left the bar across from headquarters about seven-thirty. It was a twenty-minute drive to his small apartment in Los Feliz and he was leaning in to the passenger side to pick up his pizza box from the seat when he was aware of someone standing behind him. He stood up slowly and was confronted with a man wearing a Ronald Reagan mask pointing a gun with a silencer at him.

He put his hands up. "Look I don't have much money, but you can have it all."

He went to pull out his wallet but before he had chance to reach it the man shot him through the heart, and he slumped back on top of his Marguerita already dead.

Carlos Hernandez had made an excuse to the others in the bar that he'd forgotten something and slipped back into headquarters. Unnoticed by the night staff, he crept into the Captain's office and flicked through the stack of files on his desk finding the one marked Clarianest. He removed the single printed sheet of data putting it inside his jacket and quietly pulled the door closed behind him. Five minutes later sitting at his desk, he'd accessed the list of information Mike Downes had printed out and deleted the source file. The password he'd used was the generic one that all the team had access to, so he thought there was no way it could be traced back to him. He closed his terminal down and left by the rear exit.

Senator Claudia Inestes had called George Beckermann, her accountant, as she left her council meeting, and asked him if he could meet her at the house she had just sold in Laurel Canyon. She'd made an excuse of wanting to go through a few accounts linked to the property before she left, and was already waiting when he arrived. She'd changed out of her business suit into a pair of jeans and a jumper and let him into the empty property. All of the furniture had gone and the bedroom was empty as she led him through and out onto the balcony. The view was magnificent and the fact they were standing over a sheer drop made it even more exhilarating. She poured them both a glass of her Cristal champagne and raised her glass. He did the same and in the total darkness failed to see the figure dressed all in black silently walk up behind him.

Suddenly he was physically lifted off his feet and thrown over the rail into the valley below in one swift movement. It happened so quickly he didn't even have time to call out before his body smashed onto the rocks at the bottom. She finished her glass and threw it over the rail turning to her assistant. "Waste of a good glass of champagne." She lifted his black balaclava and kissed him hard on the lips.

His services would be required tonight after all he thought, as she roughly undressed him.

The news of Detective Mike Downes' murder was all round the building by the time Captain Lewis arrived the following morning. Nobody could understand the senseless gunning down of the quiet unassuming guy. It appeared from the CSI report that it was a mugging gone wrong. There were no eyewitnesses and the lack of evidence at the scene made the investigation almost impossible.

Captain Lewis had called Detective Anna Delaney into his office to discuss the case. He'd told her to close the office door and asked her to sit down. She pleaded that she and her partner were already heavily involved in the Laura Weiss homicide, but admitted they were nowhere near an arrest. Captain Lewis explained he wanted her on this case, especially as she was one of his best detectives and it was one of their own. Then he said that what he was about to tell her could not be repeated outside of his office.

Then he told her he was of the opinion that it could be an inside job connected to something Mike Downes had found as part of looking into the Maltrocorp company. He told her that Mike had shown him how Senator Claudia Inestes could be linked to Maltrocorp via a property deal she'd recently done, and given him a printed sheet of data which proved it. Mysteriously at the same time as Mike was murdered the sheet had disappeared from the file, and all trace of his work had been erased from the computer. He said he hadn't revealed any of this which is why he wanted it to remain between them. One of the team outside in the office was responsible and they had to be found.

She listened intently as the Captain talked and when he finished thought for a moment before speaking. "Isn't she odds on to be the new mayor?"

The Captain nodded. "So it's even more important you handle this carefully. The last thing we need is animosity between her and the department."

She left his office frowning and asked Joe her partner to follow her.

They sat in their car as she explained what she'd just been told. Joe whistled. "Wow, that's really heavy. So what are you going to do?"

"We are going to find out what went on last night before Mike was killed. I know he went for a drink with a few of the guys after work, so we need to speak to them without getting them suspicious."

They went back up to the office and one by one found out who had been in the bar with Mike. One of his colleagues said that he'd told them he was picking up a pizza on his way home and that he'd left about seven-thirty. He and the others had stayed on for another beer before leaving about eight. Then he remembered that Carlos had said he'd forgotten something and went back to the office shortly after Mike had gone. Joe reported back to Anna that it might be interesting to speak to Carlos Hernandez on his own.

Carlos had been sitting at his desk taking in all the activity since he'd arrived and was starting to get worried. He watched as Anna Delaney was called into the Captain's office, and although he couldn't hear what was being said he could work it out for himself, especially when he saw the Captain pick up the empty file on his desk. He'd also noticed someone had accessed the Clarianest folder which was now empty. He knew it would be difficult to trace anything back to him, but he had made the stupid mistake of saying he'd forgotten something and returned to the office.

Anna Delaney had decided to speak to him but by the time she got back to the office Carlos had gone. Nobody had seen him leave, and unbeknownst to her he was now on his way to Claudia Inestes' office. The senator had agreed for him to come over when he explained what was happening at headquarters and was waiting for him in the meeting room with the blinds drawn.

He was shaking as he walked in but she told him to calm down. She said it was a mistake anyone could make and asked her assistant to join them. Her secretary had brought in a tray of coffee and Claudia waited until she left the room to offer Carlos a cup. As he leaned forward to take it from her, the assistant moved behind him, and in one slick movement dropped a garrotte over his head pulling it tight and wrenching him backwards, Carlos bucking up into the air dropping his coffee as he tried desperately to get his fingers under the rope, but the man was too strong for him and moments later his fight was over.

Claudia's pulse was racing with morbid excitement. She lit one of her cigarillos and watched while her assistant picked up the limp body and removed it through a side door into an alleyway where her limousine was parked. He heaved the lifeless corpse into the trunk and slammed the lid down before returning and pulling the door closed behind him. He then went round and locked the other door as Claudia, visibly excited by what had just happened pulled up her skirt and sat on the edge of the table as he opened his trousers. She hooked her legs around his waist as he ripped her knickers aside.

Outside in the office her secretary informed one of her fellow councilmen she was in a meeting and couldn't be disturbed as Claudia's moans of ecstasy came from the other side of the door.

CHAPTER TWENTY-FIVE

Ray Law was sitting staring at Eddy and Charles, his managers, in their office. They had asked him to come in for a meeting and he was speechless as they told him the news they had received from Westoria Records that morning. According to Joel Oberstein, the new Chief Executive and Manny Oberstein's son, they had decided to terminate their agreement with Ray Law with immediate effect. This was due to unacceptable behaviour on his part with female members of his audience. According to the letter there were numerous women prepared to come forward and testify that Mr. Law had enticed them up on stage with the specific purpose of having sex with them after the show. As a result Westoria Records, had taken this action in order to protect their integrity.

Ray laughed. "This is bullshit! It's my wife trying to get her own back. So what are we gonna do guys?" He looked between Eddy and Charles waiting for them to reply. Eventually Eddy passed him a letter.

"That's our letter terminating your contract. We're sorry man, but we can't deal with this and the best way is to call it quits, hopefully with no bad feelings."

"No bad feelings!" Ray jumped up. "No bad fucking feelings! Are you kidding me! Why can't you stand up for me and fight them?"

"We just don't have the resources," Charles said. "Do you have any idea what it would cost to try and fight Westoria in the courts?"

Ray was shaking with rage. "Fuck you guys, fuck you!"

He slammed his way out of the office and found himself on the street desperate for a drink. There was a bar on the next block and he walked straight up to the barman and ordered two large brandies. When he put them down on the bar Ray picked one up and poured it into the other glass and immediately drank half of it down before looking around him and spotting a public phone at the end of the bar. He dialled Janine's number.

"You and I need to talk," he said when she answered.

She told him that she was not supposed to have any contact due to their impending case but he ignored her.

"I don't give a fuck, I'm coming round now and you'd better let me in," and slammed down the phone. He drained his glass in one and threw the money on the bar as he walked out.

He was swaying noticeably when she answered the knock on the door but let him in. He slumped down on the sofa smelling of alcohol. Janine stood looking down at her soon to be ex-husband wondering what on earth had happened to him, and them.

"You're here now, so talk before I call my attorney and get you thrown out."

"You've fucked my record deal!"

"No Ray, you've fucked your record deal. I didn't have to do anything. Are you so blind you can't see what's happening? Look at the state of you; you can hardly stand up. I just want you out of my life and we can do it the easy way or the hard way."

He stood up looking round the lounge. "Have you got a drink?"

"No I haven't got a drink, and you need to go home and sober up. Then maybe we can have a sensible conversation. I want you to leave Ray. Now!"

He made his way unsteadily to the door and left without saying another word.

Janine sat down and cried. She couldn't believe how the wonderful caring man she'd married had turned into the alcoholic sex-crazed person she'd just thrown out of her house. Then she thought about what she'd told Vonda of her suspicions. She didn't want to believe them, but the more she considered the button Detective Delaney had shown her and how she'd sent Ray's shirt to be mended, the more she was convinced he had done it.

Detective Anna Delaney was in Captain Lewis's office. He'd summoned her first thing and he wasn't happy.

"Two of my officers found dead in the space of twenty-four hours. First Mike Downes is shot and then Carlos Hernandez strangled. What the hell is going on Anna?"

Carlos Hernandez's body had been found in a dumpster down a back alley in the Fashion District. Anna and her partner Sergeant Joe Budd had been called out to the scene but so far there was no hard evidence for them to go on; apart from the nagging suspicion in her mind that Carlos was somehow linked to the disappearance of the Clarianest data. And then another question going round in her mind was what connection did Senator Claudia Inestes have to the case? Her image remained squeaky clean and her mayoral campaign stronger than ever, but Anna had a feeling that somewhere along the line she was involved. The fact her name, if only fleetingly, had shown up in Mike Downes' investigation was enough for Anna to want to know more. Also how strange that the moment her focus turned to Carlos and the missing files, he turns up dead. She didn't believe in coincidences and suddenly they were happening on a regular basis. Time for her and Joe to get busy she thought, as she left the Captain's office.

It didn't take them long to find the evidence that Carlos was responsible for erasing the Clarianest data. Even though he'd tried to disguise how he'd done it, there was a trail identifying his computer responsible. It was assumed he had stolen the print-out from the office as well, but after that the trail went cold. No one had seen him after he left the bar until he turned up as a corpse the following morning.

Joe had managed to find the address of an accountant involved in the recent sale of the house belonging to Claudia Inestes in Laurel Canyon, but attempts to speak to him had so far failed.

He and Anna had visited his office but his secretary had not seen him for a couple of days, which she said wasn't unusual as he often disappeared for days on end. Anna flicked through his appointment book as they were talking and noticed an entry marked C for a couple of nights ago which had been ringed. The girl hadn't any idea what it meant, but Anna asked if she could take the book with her, and they were sitting in their car outside the office when she shut it with a bang.

"Clarianest!" she said. "It has to be. It's so obvious. Maybe we should pay the senator a call."

Claudia Inestes was waiting for them in her meeting room looking relaxed, smoking one of her cigarillos. She offered them coffee which they politely refused. Anna was well aware of the warning Captain Lewis had given her about how she dealt with the senator.

"Thank you for seeing us at such short notice. We appreciate how busy you must be."

"How can I help, detective?" Claudia replied crushing out her smoke.

"We believe you employ an accountant called George Beckerman."

"Well, I did but I fired him."

"Can I ask when that was?"

"Yes, two days ago. In fact I arranged to meet him at my old property in Laurel Canyon but he failed to turn up, which was one of the reasons I decided to dispense with his services. His unreliability."

"What was the address of the property in Laurel Canyon, Ms Inestes?"

"The Ledge, Lookout Mountain Road. It's empty at the moment, but I believe the new owners are due to move in any time."

Joe wrote down the address in his notebook.

"Thank you for your time Ms Inestes, and good luck with your campaign."

Anna and Joe left her sitting in her office and Joe laughed as they opened their car doors. "Good luck with your campaign! You told me you can't stand her."

"I can't," Anna replied. "But there's no harm in making your suspect think you like them. I don't trust the Senator as far as I could throw her. She seems to be one step ahead of us all the time and I intend to find out why."

When Janine told Vonda in her office that Ray had been to the house she went ballistic.

"I told you under no circumstances were you to talk to him, let alone allow him to come to your house. Are you crazy!"

"I know, but there was nothing I could do, and to be honest having seen him again I felt sorry for him. So I've made up my mind to make him an offer. And before you say anything." Janine held up her hand to stop Vonda speaking, "I'm going to pay his air fare and all his expenses back home as we agreed and I'll give him ten thousand dollars cash. I'll also talk with Manny Oberstein to see if I can buy the rights to his album for the UK, which if he carries on working over there should give him an income. But that's it, and if he doesn't see sense and agree I'm happy to go to court and fight the bastard!"

Vonda stood up and came round her desk to give Janine a hug. Her T-shirt for today was Sgt Pepper's Lonely Hearts Club Band by the Beatles. She certainly had an eclectic choice.

"I'll get that over to Melissa Hobson-Howes today. If she's got any sense, she'll tell him to take the money and run."

Vonda asked her if she was quite sure, considering she'd certainly mellowed out from her original proposal, but Janine said she was happy to do that so long as he agreed. She could imagine Ray's reaction when his attorney read him their latest offer, but she had a feeling once he'd calmed down he would accept it. He hadn't any alternative now his career was over, certainly here. But if he was clever he could use his name back home and probably earn a decent living around the clubs.

CHAPTER TWENTY-SIX

The scene outside in the arena was chaotic as ten thousand Peterson fans from Washington chanted, "WE WANT MORE, WE WANT MORE"

Pete Peterson and his band sat in their dressing room exhausted, soaked in sweat with towels draped around their shoulders.

Don Rosario burst through the door. "Come on guys, you need to get back out there otherwise there'll be a riot."

Pete looked up at him. "Man, I'm gonna need a quick production meeting."

Don shook his head. "That stuff's gonna kill you, you know that!"

"Right now there's ten thousand people don't give a shit," Pete replied. "Just do it will you!"

Don threw the small plastic bag to Marshall the drummer who quickly chopped out three lines of the white powder which he, Pete and Randy the bass player snorted through a rolled up hundred-dollar bill. Sniffing back the pure cocaine they rushed onto the stage followed by Dave Sanchez who looked at Don and shook his head. The roar from the crowd was deafening as they reappeared and ten minutes later they were once again slumped in the dressing room having played two frantic encores.

Pete was visibly drained and waited until Don returned.

"Man, that's it! After this tour I'm done. I can't keep it up anymore."

Don laughed. "I didn't hear that pretty blonde complaining last night."

"No! This time I mean it." Pete stood up and addressed the room. "Guys I'm making this official as from right now. After this tour that's it. Six platinum albums and five sold-out world tours. Not bad don't you think."

Don allowed him to finish. "You'll feel different in the morning. You always do."

Pete was shaking his head. "Not this time, my mind's made up. It was as I was screwing that blonde last night that it all came home to me. I didn't know her name and what's more I didn't care. She was just another in a long line of faceless fucks. They want me just so they can say to their friends, 'Yeah I screwed Pete Peterson' but do they really give a shit. I don't think so! I have a beautiful woman and a child back in the UK and I've decided it's about time I became a real father."

Don stood back and listened as Pete talked earnestly. He asked as Pete paused. "Have you spoken to Janine about this?"

"Janine will understand," he replied. "And let's face it everyone's done really well for the past few years, and nothing lasts forever." He waved his arm around the room. "These guys are great players and they won't have a problem picking up top gigs. Plus they'll earn well from the royalties off album sales for years to come. I just thought when I needed to have another line to go back on again. That's not right! I've been there before and last time it nearly killed me, so I've got to stop now before it's too late."

The three members of the band sat listening to Pete and knew in their hearts that he was talking sense. It had been amazing since they first met and they all recognised it was probably a good time to move on. In truth they each reflected it wouldn't be that much of a problem, as individually they had built up their own successful businesses that gave them a good income irrespective of the wages paid by Pete.

Randy Jones the bass player had taken the opportunity to buy Whitland Studios, the place where they had all first met. Along with the attractive receptionist who was now his wife, he had turned it into one of the best rehearsal and recording studios in Los Angeles. Record labels such as Westoria were regular customers and Peterson had recorded their last two platinum-selling albums there. Major artistes rehearsing for tours kept its diaries full and it was virtually impossible to book time unless it was done well in advance. He had also invested in a fledgling video company which had become a successful part of the setup, and was spending more and more of his spare time filming bands for a new TV channel solely playing music videos.

Marshall Thomas the drummer had his own management company, and was the go-to person when singers or producers needed musicians for touring or recording. He himself was constantly in demand and reflected on the offers he'd been forced to turn down in the past due to Peterson's touring commitments.

They were brought back fromreverie by Don announcing it was time to meet their adoring public, and the latest batch of young women eager to have a piece of Pete were corralled into the green room.

Dave had stood at the back watching the sexually charged procession make its way through, when his attention was caught by an attractive man standing on his own who appeared to want to speak to him. Dave had always kept his sexuality private and was surprised when the man, dressed in an expensive dark blue silk suit and ivory open-necked shirt approached him, making it his intentions quite obvious. All the others in the dressing room were busy and didn't notice as they slipped out, and spotting an open side door they found themselves in a small room at the back of the stage area used to store lighting. Dave had hardly closed the door when the man gripped his arms and forced him back against the wall, his mouth finding Dave's as he kissed him sensually. His hands strayed to Dave's belt and he swiftly unzipped his jeans. He then dropped to his knees and Dave found himself unable to resist his skillful attentions and crying out he exploded. Satiated the man finally stood back up and kissed Dave again.

"I suppose I should introduce myself," he said grinning slyly. "My name is Henry Walton. I'm from Palm Springs and I've been a fan of yours for a long time. I flew here hoping I would get a chance to meet you."

Dave stood, his legs still shaking slightly and was speechless. He smiled and reached out to touch Henry's face. "So now you have, what do you think?"

Henry took Dave's hand from his cheek and sucked his fingers.

"Well you taste nice, that's for sure." They both laughed. "Look I'm not usually this forward with guys I meet. In fact I don't meet many guys, but you're special. I've never heard a more talented musician in my life. I've followed you since you first joined the band. I love Pete Peterson's music and when I found out that you had written a lot of the songs with him, I was blown away."

Dave was suddenly aware that they had been gone quite a while and Don would be wondering where he was. "Look I'm going to have to go soon, but can we meet again? I think I owe you," he said smiling. "We only have a few more dates before the tour ends and then maybe we could get together?"

"I'd like that," Henry said. He reached in his jacket pocket and gave Dave an embossed business card.

"Fine Art Dealer; impressive!" Dave said reading the card. "Listen, I'll call you, I promise."

Henry leaned in and kissed him again slowly. "You better!" He turned and walked out of the room leaving Dave breathless.

Don was alone in the dressing room when Dave returned. Pete and the band had dealt with the horde of girls and had left to wait on the tour bus. He thought to himself that Dave seemed different and watched as he gathered his clothes together. He couldn't put his finger on what it was, but there was certainly something about him. "Hey Dave, are you OK man? Everything alright?" Don asked.

Dave was dying to tell someone what had just happened but he knew he had to keep it to himself. Being gay in a band was difficult and although the guys all knew, he rarely talked about it. What he did know was that he couldn't wait to see Henry again, and felt that maybe for once in his life he'd found someone special. Time would tell, and he kept his thoughts to himself as he climbed on the bus to join the others.

CHAPTER TWENTY-SEVEN

Detective Anna Delaney was once again in Captain Lewis' office. She was stomping backwards and forwards in frustration.

"I'm absolutely nowhere," she said. "I can't get anywhere with that bloody Senator. Wherever I go she seems to have been there before me. That smug look she has whenever she answers one of my questions is driving me mad. I'd dearly love to wipe it off her face. And now it's virtually confirmed she's going to be the next mayor she'll be untouchable. I know she's involved but I can't prove it. Mike Downes finds the clue then he's mysteriously shot, and Carlos Hernandez who was the mole is strangled but by who? No clues, no witnesses. Then the one possible witness, the accountant, disappears before we have chance to speak to him."

"Hang in there Anna, you know she'll make a mistake eventually, they always do." The Captain was doing his best to sound positive, but she carried on.

"Then there's the Laura Weiss case. I thought I'd got him, the singer Ray Law. I know you have history with him and the bank job, but he did it, I know he did, but again I can't prove it. The barman says he saw them together at the bar for a short time, but nobody saw him leave the club with her. Just like the Senator, he seems to always be one step ahead, knows what I'm going to ask him."

The end of the tour couldn't come too quickly for Dave Sanchez. He'd contacted Henry and arranged to fly up to Palm Springs as soon as possible and was in his doctor's surgery giving another blood test. His last results showed no change in his condition although with no sign of a cure it was hardly good news. Dave had learned about the possible link of Claudia Inestes to Maltrocorp, but Don had warned him not to do anything foolish because the police weren't a hundred percent sure yet, and with her recently becoming mayor in a landslide victory she was now a very important person. Walking out of the clinic with a time-bomb ticking inside him Dave knew he had to do something in retaliation, although what and how he had no idea.

Strangely the opportunity came about without him having to try. When he got back to The Red House, Pete told him that Westoria Records had received a call from the mayor's office asking if Dave Sanchez from Peterson would be available to play piano at her inauguration ceremony. The new mayor had remembered meeting him at Janine's house and requested his talents especially. He couldn't believe his luck. It was the ideal opportunity to strike back at her but he hadn't a clue in what way. Then he remembered Claus who was the master organiser and decided to give him a call.

They met the next day and Dave explained how he'd learned about the possible link between the mayor and Maltrocorp, and that he'd been invited to play at her party. They both agreed it was a chance they couldn't afford to miss to revenge the deaths of their friends. Claus had immediately began analysing the situation looking at possible ways of causing the most damage, when Dave shocked him by revealing his condition. He said he was prepared to sacrifice his own life as long as Claudia Inestes died too.

They sat in silence for a while whilst Claus took in the enormity of what Dave had just said. There was a week before the event and he told Dave he would go away and think about it.

Pete had followed up his announcement in Washington by telling Janine what he planned to do. She had been upset, but not really surprised. She had to agree it was probably the right thing for him having already witnessed first-hand his collapse in London. He'd told her he'd already been in touch with Judy and once everything was sorted out he would be flying back to Birmingham. She noticed how he seemed genuinely excited about his decision and secretly hoped his life would turn out better than her own.

Ray's attorney, Melissa Thomson-Howes had been back in touch with Vonda, telling her that he would settle for nothing less than half a million dollars. Without telling Vonda, Janine had called Ray and asked him to come to the house in Hermosa Beach, and as she sat waiting there was a knock on the door. He was smartly dressed in his Piotr Pauli shirt, beige trousers and brown leather jacket when she opened the door, and she noticed as he walked past her there was no smell of alcohol. She was nervous and didn't know why. Whatever they had between them was gone and there was no way she would ever have him back again, but the arrogant way he strolled around the house annoyed her.

"I want half a million and nothing less."

"No Ray, you'll get what I've offered and not a penny more, and be thankful you're getting that!"

"I don't think so! We've got stuff on you that Melissa will use in court."

Janine was thoughtful, weighing up carefully what she was about to say to him.

"Did you ever wonder why the police asked about that shirt you're wearing?"

Ray looked puzzled.

"When I returned from New York I found it in the laundry. It was missing a button and I sent it off to the cleaners and asked them to repair it. It was the weekend that Laura Weiss was murdered and when the detective showed me the missing button which was found down the side of her sofa I knew what you'd done. You murdered her didn't you! Probably because you were drunk and couldn't get your way."

He went pale and started to make an excuse but she carried on.

"There's no need to panic, I didn't say anything, and I don't think she suspected. But I knew." She watched as he sat down confused. "So that's why you're going to go back to your attorney and tell her to accept the offer and go back to the UK. I'm giving you this chance because there was a time when I loved you, and I think you loved me. But that's gone. Now get out of my house and don't ever try to contact me again. And remember, I will always know what you did."

Three days later Ray was sitting on a Pan Am flight as it took off from LA. He was in First Class due to his ex-wife's generosity and looked down as the majestic Jumbo jet crossed the sun-kissed coastline on its way to London. He'd agreed to all the conditions from Vonda Statzler even though Melissa Thomson-Howes had told him he was making a big mistake. Her protests fell on deaf ears though, as there was no way he could explain the reasons why he'd accepted Janine's offer.

Claus and Dave were sitting in a café on Wilshire Boulevard deep in conversation. There was a steady stream of customers who didn't notice the two of them in the corner with sheets of paper covered in drawings on the table in front of them.

Since Dave's revelation of his illness and his desire to exact revenge on the new mayor Claudia Inestes, Claus had been working nonstop on a plan. He told him how it would be confined to the room in which the ceremony would take place and have a devastating effect on all the guests there. He explained using the diagrams, that he could create a device small enough to be fitted into the piano Dave would play. It was an aerosol containing a minute amount of hydrogen cyanide (HCN) which when released would be enough to poison everyone in the room within a matter of seconds. It would be triggered by Dave playing a note on the keyboard while at the same time pressing the loud pedal. Claus would fit the device while masquerading as a piano tuner on the day and once installed it would be all down to Dave. He would use it in the 'Star Spangled Banner' which meant it would need to be linked to the high 'F' note when the guests would sing the word 'Free' in the line 'O'er the land of the free and the home of the brave' at the end. Claus was worried about using the HCN and its dire effects, but Dave was insistent saying it was payback time for not only him but all their other friends; Jacob, Alice, Jorge and Rudy.

In the end he reluctantly agreed and they set about making their plan happen.

Ray was back in Birmingham staying with Julia Davies. It wasn't an ideal situation, but until he found himself somewhere better it would do. Although he had the money Janine had paid him he knew it wouldn't last forever, and called a few agents he'd met on the Soul tour to try to arrange some gigs. But word had evidently travelled quickly and most of them subtly said they had nothing at the moment. Undaunted he kept trying until finally he found one who said he could put something together for him. There was still mileage in his hit 'The Love Game,' especially around the holiday camps, which according to the contact were big business. He said he could sell him as the 'Hit Motown Singer' even though Ray told him he wasn't actually signed to Motown. The agent had laughed. "Since when has that made any difference?"

So it was, that 'Hit Motown Singer Ray Law' set off on a month-long tour starting down on the south coast at a large holiday caravan park. Accompanied by the resident organist and drummer on his first night, he nervously waited for his introduction.

"Ladies and Gentlemen please put your hands together for Hit Motown Singer, Ray Law."

As the curtains opened he was faced by a club full of drunken holidaymakers whose children were running up and down sliding on their knees in front of the stage. He wanted to strangle every one of them but managed to remain professional and performed his first few songs to polite applause.

Things changed dramatically however when he asked an attractive young woman he'd spotted earlier if she would dance with him during his next number. She eagerly jumped up on stage and they began to move together to the slow sexy rhythm. She was obviously enjoying herself playing up to him, when a well-built man standing at the bar walked across the room and grabbed hold of him by his collar.

Taken by surprise Ray tried to defend himself but wasn't quick enough and received a punch on the cheek which sent him flying.

"Get your filthy hands off my wife, you dirty bastard! I've read all about you and what you get up to," the irate husband was shouting.

The musicians had stopped playing and there were screams from some of the women in the audience as Ray scrambled to pick himself up.

Hearing the commotion, the doorman rushed in and pulled the man away, while Ray managed to get off the stage. Once everything had eventually calmed down he made his way to the caravan he was staying in that night. It was cold and damp and he'd just finished pulling the tatty curtains and lighting the old Calor Gas fire when there was a knock on the door. He cautiously opened it, but standing there shivering was the woman he'd got up on stage earlier who pushed past him. "Hey now listen, I don't want any more trouble," he said taken by surprise.

"Ah, don't take any notice of him, he's a fuckin' arsehole."

Ray still wasn't sure. "Hang on a minute, what happens if he finds you in here?"

"He won't. He's pissed out of his brains snoring his head off back in the van," she replied looking round. "You got anything to drink?"

"I've got some brandy in my bag."

"That'll do. Where's the glasses?"

She opened a cupboard and found two tumblers which she half-filled and passed one to Ray.

"Now are you gonna shag me or what?"

There was a message for him to call the agent the following morning and fearing the worst Ray dialled his number.

"It doesn't take you long to cause problems does it," he said laughing. "But the good news is they loved you and just added another month of shows at their other sites."

Ray was stunned and rubbed the bruise on his cheek wondering if he could keep it up. Then smiled as he remembered how he hadn't had any problems with the young housewife last night.

CHAPTER TWENTY-EIGHT

Claus had called Dave and they had met to go through the plan. He'd shown Dave the device he'd created which would fit inside the grand piano he would be playing on the night. The tiny aerosol spray canister containing the HCN gas would be fitted inside one of the sound holes in the frame of the piano. There would be a minute trigger which would be attached to the middle or sostenuto pedal which only works on the notes that are being held. That would mean as soon as Dave pressed the pedal and hit the top F at the end of the anthem the poison would be released. All that remained was for Claus to get access to the piano on the day to fit it.

Dave said he would contact the venue to say his personal tuner would be attending during the afternoon of the ceremony.

Once again Claus questioned Dave as to whether he was quite sure he wanted to go ahead with the plan, but he was positive.

It was the day of the inauguration of the new Mayor of Los Angeles, Claudia Inestes. The room had been lavishly decorated, the tables and chairs arranged with sparkling glasses and cutlery and the food preparation was in full swing. Everyone was so busy it had been easy for Claus to walk in and pretend to tune the piano while carefully fitting the device.

Dave arrived early dressed in a dinner suit he'd hired complete with bow tie, and was sitting in his dressing room when Claudia came in to see him and give him his instructions. He was to come onstage while she was making her speech and immediately after she finished begin to play. She thanked him and wished him luck before leaving to welcome her guests. As he stood alone he began going back over his life; thinking of all the great times he'd had and how it had all come down to one tiny scratch on his hand. He automatically stroked it and took a deep breath to stop himself becoming emotional.

He told himself he knew what he was doing and nothing was going to stop him. He and Claus had arranged for a letter to be delivered immediately afterwards to the LA Times explaining why the action had been taken, exposing the new mayor as the fraud she really was.

He could hear sounds coming from the room and began to make his way to the stage where Claudia Inestes was making her speech to the invited guests. He walked up to the piano and sat down. The mayor finished her speech and the guests all stood up clapping and cheering. When the clamour had finally died down it was Dave's cue to start to play.

This was his moment.

His chance for retribution.

In a matter of minutes it would all be over. He looked around at all the faces gazing up at him as he began the opening phrase of the anthem and froze.

There sitting at a table in the middle were Janine, Don, Pete and Henry the man he'd met in Washington. His hands started to shake as Janine spotted him, waving and giving him the thumbs up. His friend Henry smiled and Don and Pete raised their glasses. He was playing on autopilot now, not thinking about the music. His heart was beating so fast he thought it was going to explode.

WHAT SHOULD HE DO?

It wasn't too late to abort it. Was it?

WHAT SHOULD HE DO?

He realised he was coming to the end, everyone was standing up, singing and this was the moment.

OH GOD! WHAT SHOULD HE DO?

He looked down at his friends standing now and singing. His foot hovered over the pedal.

'O'er the land of the

FREEEEEEEEEEEE..........................and the home of the brave.'

The whole room was cheering. The mayor walked across to the piano and hugged Dave kissing him on both cheeks. He stood up and bowed then suddenly the room started to spin and he collapsed. There were gasps as two security men ran over and carried him off the stage into his dressing room.

He came to moments later and looked up into the worried faces of Don and Henry who had followed the two guards. They were all fussing about him making sure he was OK when he realised he had to speak to Claus to stop him from delivering the letter. Pushing them all away he rushed out looking for a phone box hoping he could catch him in time.

In fact Claus was waiting for the news announcement before making a move and Dave managed to stop him.

"I couldn't do it! I couldn't do it! I'm so sorry."

Claus told him to calm down saying he understood.

He eventually walked back into the room to say thanks to Don and Henry and get a hug and kiss from Janine - who was extremely concerned - and a handshake from Pete.

Henry had already introduced himself to the others, explaining how they'd met, and managed to prise Dave away. They sat in a bar nearby talking for what seemed like hours. Henry was such an easy person to talk to, Dave found himself telling him everything including his mystery virus. Henry was the only other person apart from Claus he'd told and somehow it was a relief to be able to share his feelings.

They went back to The Red House where Pete and the others were having a drink and Henry revealed Dave's secret. He told them he was in love with him and was going to help him in any way he could. He had lots of money and was prepared to spend it looking for a cure. What he said came as such a shock they were all speechless and in tears as they embraced each other.

Dave was relieved everything was out in the open except for one thing. How close he had come to killing the mayor with one press of his foot. Only he and Claus knew and that was how it would stay.

For now!

CHAPTER TWENTY-NINE

Shortly afterwards Pete finally made the move back to Judy in Birmingham. He'd managed to sell The Red House for a tidy profit. He'd shipped his belongings back to the UK and was saying goodbye in Janine's house in Hermosa Beach to her and Don.

"I'm gonna miss you guys," he said desperately trying to hold back the tears.

Janine was leaning against Don who had his arm around her waist.

"I know we'll say let's keep in touch, but you know we probably won't. Judy has still got the club so there'll always be a link. Go and enjoy your life and look after your family. And remember, we don't say goodbye, only until the next time."

Pete embraced her and this time they did cry. Don gave him a bear hug and they both watched as he climbed into the taxi and waved as he left.

Ray was fed up of playing holiday parks and wanted to get back in the studio to record some new songs. He'd contacted a producer in London recommended by the agent he was working for, and he and Julia went down to meet him. The producer had put together a tape of some new songs he thought would suit Ray and they met in a small studio at the back of Marble Arch.

It was noticeable from the outset that Ray's voice wasn't up to the standard of his previous recordings. Julia was very supportive and argued that maybe it was the songs that were wrong. Being an experienced professional and recognising that they were the paying customers, the producer agreed to try some more songs. This made no difference whatsoever, and if he had been honest he should have told them to forget it, but he persisted and encouraged Ray to record some guide vocals. He knew if he got the girlfriend on his side it would be a lot easier and began a charm offensive on Julia. He even convinced her she could sing and got her to record a harmony to Ray in the chorus of one of the songs. By this time they'd spent most of the day in the studio which at forty pounds an hour was beginning to mount up but Julia, who'd always wanted to sing, was hooked, and they arranged to come back the following day to record some more.

They had booked into the Metropole for the night and high on adrenaline after the atmosphere in the studio they drank champagne and screwed for most of the night, ending up only getting a few hours sleep before they were due back in the studio again.

Eventually turning up two hours late and feeling hung over, Ray began trying to sing the vocals on the songs but Julia immediately commented that his voice didn't sound right and once again blamed the studio. At this point the producer who had done his best to remain quiet the previous day had had enough and stood up. He told the pair of them there was no way he was going to carry on trying to *polish a turd* and walked out the studio slamming the door behind him.

Julia called him all the names under the sun, threatening to sue him and the studio, and they eventually left having paid their bill of five hundred pounds, with a tape of the half-finished songs. They drove back to Birmingham in Julia's Porsche listening to the cassette on her stereo and reluctantly agreed that maybe the producer had a point. In fact, Ray was so disgusted with what he was listening to, he ejected the tape and threw it out the window watching in the wing mirror as it was crunched under the wheels of a truck they were overtaking.

Pete had arrived back home to Judy's house and was having a happy reunion with her and Rick. She'd cooked a traditional roast dinner to celebrate his return and they were all sitting watching the television. Pete had bought them presents from the airport and Rick played his guitar before going off to bed enabling Judy to sit down and cuddle up next to Pete on the sofa.

"I've got something to tell you," she said looking up into his eyes. "I know you've only just got here and everything, but I've been bursting to tell you."

"Go on, I'm all ears."

"You remember you said about looking for a house? Something that possibly had lots of space?"

"Yes, yes!"

"You're not going to believe what I've found, and it's well within what you want to pay."

"Tell me, before I burst."

"Gerry and Janine's old Georgian mansion house in Warwickshire."

"What! The place with the stables and everything? Are you sure?"

"Yes, I spoke to the estate agent, he's meeting us there tomorrow."

Pete couldn't stop smiling. "Oh my god that is incredible. Just wait until I tell Janine, she'll be over the moon." They hugged and kissed each other and then Judy noticed Pete was beginning to fade fast as the jetlag began to kick in and she led him up to bed. Within minutes he was snoring as she lay at his side still pinching herself; he was really there.

estate agent was already waiting as Pete and Judy drove down the gravel drive and pulled up at the front entrance. He led them through the oak-panelled hallway which still had the suit of armour standing at the bottom of the stairs and took them on a tour of the eight bedrooms, four bathrooms, through the huge lounge with its inglenook fireplace, into the ultra-modern kitchen which Janine had designed and finally the heated swimming pool. They were standing outside again when Pete pointed to the group of buildings a few hundred yards away. The agent told him that at one time Gerry had thought he might convert them into offices and a recording studio which Pete remembered him once mentioning, but had never bothered.

"We'll take it!"

The agent stopped dead in his tracks. "Are you sure you don't need any more information?"

"Janine trusted you, so I don't see any reason why I can't. Just get all the paperwork sorted and let me know when we can move in."

He turned round and kissed Judy and they drove off leaving the estate agent mentally counting his commission.

Two weeks later they moved in. They'd spent the time buying new furniture to replace the remnants that had been left by the previous owner; a property developer who had gone bust, which was the reason the price had been so low. In fact Pete had paid much the same price Janine had sold it for he was well pleased and Rick had a ball playing in all the space he'd never experienced before and had taken to the swimming pool straight away.

Pete was sitting in the lounge one night watching the television, drinking a glass of red wine, when the phone rang. They'd been in the house now for a month and he suddenly realised in that time he hadn't spoken to anyone other than Judy and Rick. He picked up the phone and Janine's voice greeted him.

"Hey Pete, how're ya?" He was pleased to hear her Irish-American brogue. "How's the old house? I hope you're looking after it."

They laughed and she quickly brought him up to date with all the news, how she and Don had become an item now her divorce was through and that they were looking at the possibility of setting up their own management and agency. "But there's something come up over here that we have to deal with. You remember the song you and Dave wrote for Vince Boyd? Well it's become a huge hit on the Country Music scene and they're crying out for the pair of you to perform it."

Pete was silent for a while and she asked if he was still there.

"Yeah I'm here. I know you can keep this news to yourself, but I had to go to the doctors for a check-up and he's told me I have a dodgy heart." He laughed. "Probably all that shit I've taken over the years hasn't helped. But anyway he's told me to pack it all in. No more gigs otherwise I risk having a heart attack. I mean it's not as if I need the money. So I don't think I can help you."

Janine thought for a moment.

"OK, so what if Vince came over to you and the pair of you recorded a video? It's the new way of promoting records now. It gets shown on all the TV channels, there's even one that just shows music videos and you don't have to perform, just sit back and count the pennies. I'll get back to you with the figures."

He had to admit she had become the perfect saleswoman and it did sound like a good idea. He told Judy that night when she got home and surprisingly she already knew all about it having spoken to Janine earlier that day. Judy was still managing The Hexxicon and at the same time running FAM the artist management company Gerry Fortuna had set up in which Janine still had an interest.

So two weeks later Vince Boyd arrived at Pete's mansion complete with a film crew, and they spent a fantastic three days filming the music video for 'It Can't Be Love' the Number One hit on the Country Music chart. Pete enjoyed the experience and was sorry to see Vince leave but realised something strange had happened to him since he'd been back. He no longer felt the urge to play again. Maybe it was because he was enjoying family life or perhaps he was taking notice of what his doctor had told him, but sitting down with Judy and Rick, eating wonderful home-cooked food with a glass of wine was all he wanted to do. Sure he loved playing his acoustic guitar with Rick and teaching him chords and new songs but that was it.

Coming up to the six-month anniversary of them moving into the house Judy made an announcement at dinner. She was pregnant. Pete was overjoyed and couldn't contain his happiness. He spent the rest of the night with a beaming grin on his face and the following morning as they sat down to breakfast he got down on one knee and asked Judy to marry him. Rick thought it was hilarious but Pete was deadly serious and Judy burst into tears as she said "Yes, of course I will."

They decided to do it more or less immediately without any fuss and a month later in a private ceremony in Warwick Registry Office they became Mr. and Mrs. Pete Peterson with Rick present. They stopped two people in the street and asked them to be their witnesses and it was all over in half an hour. Pete was happy that his children would have his name and everything was legal.

Seven months later their daughter Lucy was born.

CHAPTER THIRTY

Ray Law had finally given up on his singing career. He'd made a further two attempts at recording some new songs but eventually admitted his voice was no longer good enough and studio time was a waste of money. His fondness for brandy had taken its toll and he had accepted he was an alcoholic. Julia and he still had a relationship which went from full-on sex romps one night to tempestuous arguments the next. They had become well known in Letton, where they lived, for their public performances usually in their local pub, The King's Head. Ray would spend most of his day there and was always charming, especially with the women, but as the night wore on he would become maudlin, talking about his former career as a Motown star. He developed an acute ability to pick on a newcomer who would gladly buy him large brandies to hear him recount his endless showbiz stories, while the locals who'd heard them time and again began to avoid him like the plague. Julia would then appear after a day in the office and try to drag him home usually ending up causing a scene shouting at each other with the odd glass of wine being thrown.

One day Ray had shown up at his usual seat later than usual dressed in a suit looking every inch the businessman. When quizzed by the landlord he revealed he'd just been appointed chairman of a new film company which would be making a feature-length drama using local talent. He was currently in talks with major private investors and his legal team were in the process of setting up the studio. He went on to explain how this would be a massive boost to the area creating jobs, and how it was possible they could use The King's Head as a location. He had been more than grateful to receive a large brandy in return.

At the same time out of the corner of his eye he'd spotted a group of women who had just walked in for an afternoon drink. He was soon introducing himself as the former Motown singing star now head of a new film company coming to the area, who were looking for talent. Using all his old skills he soon identified the attractive divorcee who happily stayed behind for another drink when the others left, and then invited him back to her place just round the corner. With the knowledge that Julia was away for a couple of days on a case, he listened attentively as the woman told him all about herself and how she always dreamed of being an actress, whilst at the same time charming her into bed. As he left her house the following morning he thought this film company idea could turn out to be fun. His next challenge would be to how to make money from it.

In Palm Springs Dave had been responding well to treatment in the clinic Henry had discovered. They now lived together in Henry's luxurious apartment and Dave played Henry's Bechstein grand piano in the enormous lounge every day, and at the lavish parties he threw for his multi-millionaire clients. There were extortionately expensive paintings regularly displayed in private viewings and although he was the first to admit he didn't understand anything about art, Dave was beginning to love the lifestyle. The memories of touring and the rigours of life on the road as a rock star were beginning to fade and his previous life in Los Angeles had long been forgotten.

Until one night, when Henry and Dave were watching a news broadcast from Los Angeles City Hall given by Mayor Claudia Inestes. She was announcing the investment of a huge sum of taxpayers' money into the research of viruses to be carried out by a company called Maltrocorp.

Dave nearly jumped up off the sofa as they watched her talking about her new scheme. He was shaking with rage as Henry wrestled the remote control from him and switched off the screen.

"You should calm down. It doesn't affect you now, you're in Palm Springs remember."

But it did affect him and a few days later while Henry was visiting a client, Dave made a phone call to his old associate Claus. They agreed to meet and were soon sitting at the same corner table in the coffee shop on Wilshire Boulevard once again. This time it was Dave who outlined his plan to Claus who sat making notes. They shook hands and both went their separate ways.

A week later Mayor Claudia Inestes emerged from the front door of her ranch nestling in the hills of Santa Clarita. It was a clear sunny day with hardly a breath of wind and she had decided to wear a new white linen jacket and skirt over a dusky pink silk blouse. She was on her way to the weekly council committee meeting over which she now presided, and she carried her notes in a brown leather briefcase which she passed to her assistant as he opened the rear door of her black limousine. She turned to admire her home once more before settling into the soft leather of the back seat. The assistant closed the door and climbed into the driver's seat making sure all the windows were closed before activating the air-conditioning. Claudia crossed her legs, her silk stockings shining in the sunlight and lit her cigarillo, despite her doctor's warning about them being bad for her health. 'What harm will the occasional one do anyway?' she thought.

The assistant pulled away and drove down the long winding drive towards the highway. The surrounding hills were covered in verdant foliage and Claudia had just noticed a beautiful flowering shrub when the car came to a sudden stop jolting her forward. Her driver had jumped out of the car and was standing with his hands on his hips looking at a truck slewed sideways across the road blocking them. Claudia lowered the window leaning forward to see what the problem was as a quarter of a mile away her head filled the scope on the M21 sniper rifle.

Claus breathed in and held his breath as he slowly squeezed the trigger. He watched as she began to speak to her assistant but before she finished her sentence the top half of her head exploded and splattered against the cream interior of the car, the sound of the shot arriving a second later as it echoed around the hillside. The driver had thrown himself to the ground and scrabbled around behind the car, as Claus dressed in his camouflaged ghillie suit stood up and walked away down the other side of the hill, where he'd waited since dawn to take his shot.

The brother of Jacob who had been murdered by Claudia's security guards had been responsible for parking the stolen truck across the road. He watched through binoculars from behind a bush further down the track and made his way back to the highway where Dave was waiting to pick him up. Hours later a letter was delivered to the LA Times stating the reason behind the assassination of the mayor, outlining her connection with Maltrocorp and the murders of four civilians. It was the headline on that evening's News bulletin on all the TV channels and in the newspapers the following day.

CHAPTER THIRTY-ONE

Pete had seen the item on the news in the UK and knew immediately that Dave must be involved. The report said that so far the police had been unable to make any arrests and investigations were ongoing. He thought back to seeing the then senator and Janine leaving the bar in Santa Monica together and wondered how she felt, and if she knew it was Dave. But they were all over five thousand miles away and it was none of his business anymore. Even so he couldn't help thinking about them. His life was so different now, and if he were to admit it he was getting bored of doing nothing.

A chance meeting at a party changed things completely. He and Judy had gone to a neighbour's birthday celebration in a nearby village hall and after a few beers Pete had ended up strumming an acoustic guitar and singing a couple of songs. Having kept his identity a secret up until then he was now a celebrity again. He'd mentioned to one of his other neighbours who he knew had horses, that with all the empty stables on his land he was thinking of buying a pony for his daughter Lucy, and the neighbour suggested Pete talk to Tommy Douglas a well-known ex-trainer who lived in the village.

After a phone call from Pete, Tommy had turned up at the house and they surveyed the empty stables together. Tommy admired them saying it was a shame such wonderful facilities were going to waste, and when Pete mentioned he was interested in buying a pony for his daughter Lucy he arranged to take him to the auctions. They brought back a friendly little chap called Sparkle who Lucy took to riding like a duck to water and with Tommy's encouragement Pete began to get interested in all things equine.

Within a month they had been back to the auctions and with Tommy's advice bought two young mares. He offered his services to train them for a small fee and suddenly Pete found himself involved in 'The Sport of Kings.'

The first lesson he learned was it wasn't cheap. Tommy had enrolled a vet he knew whose monthly fees were eye-wateringly expensive, but vital according to the trainer. The top of the range horse box had cost more than a luxury car, but was equally necessary and by the time they came to entering their first race Pete had spent the best part of a quarter of a million pounds. Granted they'd bought two more horses, both highly rated by Tommy and for what he termed bargain prices.

The day of the first race arrived. It was a two-year old race at Chester racecourse over five furlongs and Pete, Judy, Rick and Lucy were excitedly cheering from the stand as their horse, Firefly romped home to win by a length. Tommy led the victorious jockey into the winner's enclosure and the Peterson family were photographed with the trainer and jockey proudly holding the trophy in front of the triumphant horse.

Not knowing anything about the sport, suddenly the euphoric rush of victory made Pete feel like he was back on stage again and he loved it. The fact the winner's purse was only a couple of hundred pounds didn't seem to matter as they celebrated with a slap-up meal on the way home. Had he known then what was in store perhaps he would have thought differently.

Ray had convinced Julia his film company and studio was a great idea and between them they were spending their time schmoozing all the high rollers of the city. Through Julia's company they had befriended a couple of media lawyers, and using their contacts had managed to get invitations to every event involving the creative sector, as well as setting up meetings with potential investors who were attracted to the glamour of the film industry. Ray quickly became known as *Mr. Showbiz*, the Motown legend, and was happy to pose for photos. Somehow though he always managed to avoid the questions relating to his relationships with the likes of Marvin Gaye, Diana Ross and Berry Gordy, changing the conversation to his touring with Edwin Starr and Jimmy Ruffin instead.

Unfortunately the one area where he wasn't having any success was raising money for his project. All the people he spoke to were happy to endorse him and his rapidly growing team, but not one of them had yet to put their hand in their pocket. Julia, the ever-faithful supporter was becoming frustrated by the lack of cash and was watching her financial input increase as Ray ran up bills everywhere he went. His money from

Janine had long gone and his dependence on Julia was now total. Her other concern was having set up the company for him in the first place, she had no actual shares despite his continual promise to change the agreement. This gave Ray complete control, and meant if she or any of the other directors had a suggestion, Ray could overrule them, which he did on every occasion. He had also amassed an army of women who were under the misguided impression they had a part in the soon to start production, and his casting couch was becoming legendary in the bars and restaurants in the city.

He constantly boasted of his connections with the rich and famous, from racing drivers to rock stars, although none so far had materialised. Then one day sitting in The King's Head reading the sports section of the newspaper he spotted the photograph of Pete Peterson and his family with their winning horse 'Firefly'. Could this be the answer to all his prayers? He didn't even know Pete was living back in the UK and according to the report not far away either. Ray knew Pete had a fortune and once he told him about his company and the plans he had, he was sure he would invest. After all what was a million pounds to someone like Pete Peterson?

He immediately began concocting a plan. He would need to find an excuse to meet Pete and become friends again, maybe through a musical connection. Then he would subtly introduce into the conversation the news about his new company, and once he was interested, let Pete think he was being offered the golden opportunity to get in first before anyone else. He sat there pleased with himself and couldn't wait for Julia to get back so he could tell her the great news.

In fact she walked through the door moments later carrying his suitcase which she threw across the room at him with a face like thunder. He looked at her confused.

"So there I was in a bar at lunchtime with a client having a drink, and I happened to overhear a conversation between two waitresses. One was telling her friend how she'd met this cool film director and how he said she could be in this film he was making. Oh yeah, and how she gave him a blowjob in her car. Sound familiar, Ray?"

He started to make an excuse but she picked up his glass off the bar and threw the contents over him. "Don't bother coming back."

She walked out of the pub and moments later her Porsche roared out of the car park.

CHAPTER THIRTY-TWO

Don had moved into Janine's seafront house in Hermosa Beach and their thoughts had turned to the possibility of starting a family. It was something Janine had longed for, but after the accident in Miami and her subsequent miscarriage they had sought specialist medical advice. Sadly all the tests came back negative and finally they were forced to admit that Janine would be unable to have a baby. It was heart-breaking news for her to have to come to terms with, but Don was supportive and knowing how much she wanted a child asked why couldn't they adopt. After all neither of them were getting any younger and maybe there was the possibility of an older child needing a caring home.

They decided to make enquiries and contacted a couple of agencies they were recommended, but without success. They were deemed too old and didn't match the criteria. Janine was beginning to become despondent and had accepted that she would never have a family of her own when Don received a message from an old friend in the force who'd heard that they were trying to adopt. He'd said it was a long shot, but he had recently attended a serious road traffic accident involving a family of three, mother, father and twelve-year-old daughter. The father had been a cop and along with the mother had been killed but the daughter survived. The social services had tried to contact any relatives, but it turned out there were none and this young girl had become an orphan. His friend said they shouldn't get their hopes up too high, but it was worth a phone call to explain their situation.

Two days later Janine and Don visited the young girl who was still in hospital, accompanied by the head of the social services department responsible for her. Her name was Fleur and she was absolutely beautiful with long blond curly hair and bright blue inquisitive eyes. She was old enough to understand what had happened, and with the only other option being for her to be put into care they were all desperately hoping they could resolve the situation without upsetting Fleur any more than necessary. Janine and Don visited her regularly over the next few weeks, and by the time she was ready to be released from hospital they were all good friends so she was happy to come and stay with them in Hermosa Beach.

They had found out during the course of their visits she was interested in sport and liked music, and when she found out Janine managed Pete Peterson she tearfully remembered her mother was a big fan and had all his records.

One night when they were all sitting on the balcony watching the waves crashing on the beach she questioned Don about his time with the LAPD. She said how she'd told her dad she wanted to join the force when she was old enough, but he refused to discuss it. Don sat back and looked at Janine and thought this parenting lark might not be quite as straight forward as they first thought.

After being kicked out by Julia, Ray had managed to charm his way into staying with Sylvia, the divorcee he'd met who conveniently lived near The King's Head. Eventually he had managed to contact Pete, who although at first reluctant, had finally agreed to meet up for a drink.

Pete had suggested the bar in the Crowne Plaza in the centre of Birmingham. Ray, with Sylvia, now his official secretary, had arrived early and dressed in his business suit. He had quickly downed a couple of large brandies as 'looseners' to give him a boost.

Pete walked in wearing jeans and a black leather jacket, still looking like the rock star he used to be. Every female head in the bar turned as he strode up to Ray, and putting all things behind them shook his hand and sat down, lighting a cigarette. Ray introduced him to Sylvia and told her to order him another brandy and Pete said he'd have the same.

"So, Ray, how are you? I can't say I was looking forward to seeing you after the last time we were in the same company, but then I thought we should let bygones be bygones, draw a line and move on. So what can I do for you? You mentioned something about a film company when you called."

Ray explained about the new project he was looking to put into action once he had the funding in place.

Pete listened to his pitch, then without commenting asked what had happened since he last saw him.

"Well, after Westoria dropped me along with SoulTown I didn't have many options so I decided to come back here. It was OK for a while and I played gigs on the circuit but I wanted to record some new material, and although we went down to London I couldn't find the right producer and songs. I mean everything was an anti-climax after 'The Love Game.'"

Pete smiled. "Yeah that was a good song. So tell me more about this film company. Who else is involved apart from you?"

"My solicitor Julia Davies helped me set up the company and I have a production team and a legal team who are directors. Sylvia here is my official secretary."

"And how are the shares allocated?"

"It's my company - my idea. I own all the shares."

"But if you've got a production team and legal team as you say, how do you expect them to work with no incentive? They might be directors but without shares it means nothing. And what's the project? Do you have a script? I'm presuming you've invited me here to talk about investing? So what can you show me?"

Ray explained that the script was currently being rewritten and he would have a final edit soon. But it was looking great and his team were working hard.

Pete finished his drink but refused another.

"So let's get down to the bottom line. How much do you need and what's the deal?"

Ray swallowed the rest of his brandy and ordered another.

"One million quid for five percent."

Pete looked at him and laughed. "So you're valuing your so called film company of which you own one hundred percent at twenty million pounds? You're having a laugh! You haven't got a finished script yet, never mind a studio. And where's your business plan?"

Ray couldn't answer him and took a mouthful of his brandy.

Pete looked at him and pointed at Ray's glass.

"There's the reason why you couldn't record a new song. Not the producer or the choice of material. I know the guy and he was trying his best to help you, but you couldn't come up with the goods. I warned you ages ago about how much you were drinking, but you wouldn't listen and you fucked up your marriage and now you've fucked up your career. So I'm sorry Ray, I wouldn't trust you as far as I could throw you. Good luck if you can find another victim, but it's not going to be me. Oh and by the way, drop the 'Hit Motown Singer' shit; it's a lie and you know it."

Pete stood up, and without shaking his hand, left Ray and Sylvia at the bar.

Pete drove straight home from the meeting with Ray to speak to Tommy Douglas his trainer about what was happening with his horses. With Tommy's advice he had now bought five race horses which had cost him a million pounds, but since installing them in his stables nothing had happened. After Firefly, his first winner, none of his string had had any success due to a constant string of excuses from Tommy, and Pete was becoming frustrated. He'd talked to one of the jockeys who despite his best efforts came next to last. He was reluctant to comment as he was an old friend of Tommy but finally admitted that the horse was obviously under trained. He said if it had been fit it would have won by a mile.

Alarm bells started to ring in Pete's mind.

He'd recently become good friends with a retired owner called Monty, a real character who had great stories to tell and he'd been to his house for dinner. Over coffee and brandy he had complimented Pete on his stables and his collection of horses but in confidence told him to watch Tommy Douglas. He explained there were rumours that Tommy had a connection with the auctioneers. He would fix the prices artificially high by getting his contacts to keep the bidding going longer, then at a given signal pull out leaving the buyer with a grossly inflated price. Tommy would then take his cut from the profit.

This made Pete feel sick when he thought that he'd always given him a bonus when they made a good buy, and now to find out he was skimming off the top as well. He'd not said anything at the time, but decided it was time to have a word with his trainer.

Fleur had settled in with Janine and Don and quickly became one of the family. Academically she was bright and enjoyed reading, but when it came to sport she excelled. She could easily outrun anyone in her year and was tipped as an athletics major. She had a way of taking everything in her stride and accepting her abilities, but her main ambition was to join the LAPD and become a detective. She bombarded Don with questions at every opportunity and he was happy to answer, although the one sticking point was when she asked him to teach her to shoot a gun. Janine who so far had listened and encouraged her, was adamant that she would have to wait until she was old enough and would not be convinced otherwise. She explained how she'd experienced too much death due to guns and Don had to agree.

Since they were now all living together Janine had decided she finally wanted to move into a bigger house and had found the ideal property further down The Strand. It had three bedrooms, a study for Don, a huge rooftop patio and a garden. It was perfect for their needs and she wasted no time doing a deal. As with all the other properties on the twenty-mile seafront pathway every one was different. Her last house was modern with steel and lots of glass whereas this one was a more traditional colonial design with a garden. She loved the thought of being able to grow things and set about planting vegetables.

If life for Janine was becoming wonderful, her ex-husband was not faring so well. He was still living with Sylvia although she was becoming a nuisance. She, like Pete, wanted to know why Ray refused to give away any of his shares in his company. Three of the directors had already resigned and he was in danger of his legal team downing tools unless they were paid, but he still stubbornly refused to give anything away.

The obvious problem was Ray's dependance on his glass of wine first thing in the morning to kick-start his day, followed by a large brandy, beers at lunchtime and depending on who he could bore with stories of his time at Motown, more brandies until he stumbled into bed with

Sylvia assuring her everything was going fine and investors were coming on board. He would then attempt to have sex which would usually end up with him falling asleep before either of them were satisfied.

One night after a particularly disappointing day of more rejections and resignations, Ray was sitting in the bar of The King's Head when Julia Davies walked in accompanied by a well dressed, handsome middle-aged man. Their body language seemed to indicate they were more than colleagues as they sat sharing a bottle of champagne. Julia had ignored Ray and was holding her partner's hand as they laughed and joked when, having had far too much to drink, Ray stumbled off his stool and made his way unsteadily across to their booth.

"It didn't take long for you to find someone else to screw then?" he slurred.

The man went to stand but Julia motioned for him to stay where he was. They turned away and continued to talk.

"You didn't ignore me when you needed it before though. Eh?"

Ray swayed and caught hold of their table knocking a full glass of champagne over.

This time the man brushed Julia's arm away and stood up grabbing hold of Ray and without saying a word pushed him backwards towards the Fire Exit. Using him to open the crash bar he shoved Ray through the doorway and went to pull the door closed, but Ray somehow held onto his arm stopping him.

They stood facing each other momentarily before the man clenched his fist and taking one quick step to the side went to punch Ray on the chin. Before heconnected Ray fell backwards landing on his backside. The man turned away and came back into the pub slamming the door behind him. He sat down next to Julia to a round of applause from the locals and filled the empty glass again.

Sylvia had watched the whole thing from the doorway and turned around to walk back home. She had only gone a few yards when she heard Ray's voice calling her. Her first thought was to ignore him, but then she actually felt sorry for him and went over to where he was still sitting. She helped him to his feet and they started to walk unsteadily back to her house.

The King's Head was situated on a busy main road with cars parked on either side. For once, instead of walking the extra few yards to the pedestrian crossing, Ray pushed her away and without looking staggered out into the road from between two parked cars.

Before Sylvia had chance to stop him there was a squeal of brakes and a loud bang as a white estate car hit Ray. It knocked him up into the air and he landed with a sickening crunch head-first on the tarmac. The car's engine was still revving loudly and instead of stopping it drove off at high speed.

Sylvia screamed for someone to help and ran over to where Ray's body lay motionless in a rapidly expanding pool of blood. She was so shocked she hadn't thought about getting the registration number of the white car and the road was now completely empty. Panicking she ran to a nearby house and asked them to call an Ambulance and the Police. By the time she got back to Ray there was a crowd developing, mainly drinkers from The King's Head who'd heard the noise and came out to see what had happened. Ironically the man now kneeling at the side of Ray's body was the same man who had thrown him out moments earlier. He told her he was a doctor and from the grave look on his face Sylvia feared the worst.

Moments later an ambulance arrived followed closely by a police car and they quickly assessed the situation confirming Ray was dead.

Julia had followed everyone out and stood apart from the group of onlookers. She felt sick and started to cry. Her boyfriend spotted her and came over putting an arm around her shoulder and steered her back into the pub where he bought her a large brandy and told her to drink it down. He wasn't insensitive enough not to realise she once had feelings for the man lying dead in the road even though their last meeting had hardly been friendly. He suggested they go back to her house and guided her to his car. Later, as he lay at her side in bed he gently caressed her and held her tightly as she quietly sobbed.

CHAPTER THIRTY-THREE

Pete had been sitting with Judy watching the TV when they saw the news report about the death of 'Hit Motown Singer' Ray Law in a hit-and-run accident. The vehicle believed to have been involved had been found burnt out on a trading estate nearby. There were no witnesses to the accident although police were continuing with their investigations. They were both stunned at the news; Pete in particular since he'd only met with Ray a few days ago, and Judy who had been with him when the Soul tour played at The Lexxicon.

Their first thought was did Janine know? It was not a phone call either of them wanted to make, but they knew she would appreciate them telling her even if she and Ray had not parted on the best of terms.

It was one o'clock in the afternoon when the phone rang in Janine's new house. She picked it up and was surprised to hear Pete's voice. But from the tone she knew straight away something was wrong.

"Hey Pete, is everything OK? How's Judy and the kids?"

"They're fine, we're all fine. I guess you haven't heard yet?"

"Heard what?"

"There's no other way to tell you this. Ray died last night. He was killed by a hit-and-run driver. I'm so sorry Janine, but we thought you should know."

Janine was silent. She couldn't describe the feeling, it was almost as if it was a relief. She wanted to cry but tears wouldn't come. She'd loved him and she'd hated him probably in equal amounts and now he had gone. She took a deep breath. "Thanks for telling me."

There was an uncomfortable silence before Pete spoke trying to steer the conversation in another direction.

"Hey, how is Fleur? She sounds like a great kid."

Janine told him about how they came to be introduced to her and what a beautiful girl she was. "The crazy thing is she's bright, an amazing athlete and all she talks about is becoming a cop. Can you believe that? She pesters Don to distraction. But enough about us, how're you guys? How's Rick and Lucy?"

Pete told her how proud he was that Rick had taken after him and was a naturally gifted musician. He was already playing in his own band and starting to write songs. And then how Lucy loved riding and how he had got the stables up and running and had five racehorses, although without much success so far.

With the promise that she would try her best to get over they said goodbye and Pete put down the receiver. Judy gave him a hug and they stood for a moment and shed a few tears for someone who had been a major part of their lives.

Rick calling from his room brought them back to the present. He wanted Pete to help him with a song he was writing for his band and Judy watched as her husband proudly went up to listen to his son play his latest composition. Even though he was her son she had to admit he had definitely inherited the talent of his father, and wondered if it could possibly take him as far.

Janine had seemed quiet when Don came home and he asked her if there was a problem. She did her best to cover her feelings but, in the end, told him about Ray. He was shocked. They had been friends once, and he was sorry how it had all ended. As ex-cops they had had an affinity and working together to rescue Pete and then Janine from Benny Mulligan they had made a good team. He found it hard to believe Ray had changed so much once he tasted success as a singer and remembered the moment he sang at his and Janine's wedding party in Birmingham. But that was then, and he and Janine had made a new start to their life and now, with Fleur, they were a family.

They'd planned a housewarming party for that weekend, and this news was not going to spoil it.

On the day Janine and Fleur were up early. All the preparations were in hand by the time Don surfaced, leaving him to sort out the drinks, his favourite job. They'd decided to have it in the afternoon to make the most of the beautiful sunny weather, and living where they did it was just a case of walking across The Strand and you were on the beach.

There was an entertaining collection of guests who had all arrived bearing gifts, and Janine was pleased at how they all mingled together irrespective of who they were and what they did.

Vince Boyd and his 'secretary' had flown over from Nashville especially, and was deep in conversation with Vonda Statzler who it turned out had been a massive fan when she was younger the same as Janine. Manny Oberstein had turned up with his son Joel, who was now in charge of Westoria Records since his dad had retired although he was at great pains to tell Don he hadn't packed it in completely and was eager to talk to him about his new agency. Captain Lewis, Don's old boss at LAPD had been happy to attend and had brought Detective Anna Delaney with him which was interesting, as Don knew he was separated and seemed to be close to her but he wasn't sure just how close. Janine had noticed her arrive and thought how attractive she looked wearing a short summer dress and heels as opposed to her usual bulky uniform. It turned out that Anna had worked with Fleur's father when she first joined the force and had watched her grow up. She'd been concerned about her future after the terrible accident, but the way they were talking together and laughing she appeared to approve of the outcome.

Don was right about Captain Lewis and Anna, and this was a rare public outing for them preferring instead to keep their affair secret.

They had spent the morning in bed, but as always happened ended up talking about work. In particular the two cases Anna had been working on which due to unforeseen events seemed to have become closed. With the assassination of Mayor Claudia Inestes the Maltrocorp investigation had been suspended, especially as the funding which she announced had been withdrawn since the revelations in the letter sent to the LA Times immediately after her death. The persons responsible had still not been identified although in an interesting development the remains of a body found in the ravine below her old house in Laurel Canyon had turned out to be that of Claudia's former accountant, George Beckermann.

When she heard the news about Ray Law she had been angry. Her suspicions about him murdering Laura Weiss hinged on one piece of evidence, the missing shirt button. Her personal intuition told her it was his and although Janine denied it Anna knew it was. Now they were going to her party and she might have an opportunity to catch her off guard.

Don was pleased to see Marshall and Randy from Pete's band with their wives. Since the end of the last tour they had both gone off to do their own things and he was glad they could make it, and a wonderful surprise was when Dave and Henry arrived having flown in from Palm Springs. They had great news. There had been a breakthrough in the research into Dave's virus and he had already started the new treatment. It was early days but so far the signs were looking good.

Janine wished Pete could have been there as well. She hated to admit it but she missed him. Despite all their ups and downs he would always be someone special, and without him she wouldn't be here now. She'd had a letter from Judy updating her on FAM and how it was progressing and also that they were thinking of changing the name of The Lexxicon to Stratton's which was more in keeping with current trends and at the bottom almost as an afterthought she mentioned how Pete's health was a worry. She didn't go into detail but Janine remembered him telling her about his heart.

Anna Delaney interrupted her thoughts, saying hello and what a beautiful house it was. Janine thanked her and offered to give her a tour. They'd ended up on the rooftop patio and were looking across at the ocean when Anna spoke. "I know this is probably not the right time, but there's something really bugging me. Did you know more than you said about that shirt button?"

The question took Janine completely by surprise and she paused before answering.

"No Anna, as I said at the time I had sent all of my late husband's clothes to his management's office. I assume you looked there?"

Anna knew she was really pushing it but knowing she wouldn't get a better opportunity carried on. "Look Janine, we're off the record here. I know he did it, and I'm thinking you know he did it too."

Janine stood and stared at her. "What I do know is you're pretty close to outstaying your welcome." She turned her back on her and walked away. 'Damn! Doesn't she ever give it a rest,' she thought as she made her way back downstairs.

Don couldn't get over how different Dave looked. His whole persona seemed to have changed. Obviously now there was hope for a cure, things would begin to get better. But because he'd got to know him and experience all the trials and tribulations, he felt there was something else. He just couldn't put his finger on it. He was standing with Captain Lewis watching Dave and Henry talking animatedly with Vince Boyd, when the level of conversation dipped just as Vonda Statzler mentioned the shooting of Claudia Inestes. For a split-second Don saw a look on Dave's face as he turned that said it all. His old cop's radar had bleeped and he knew immediately who had been behind it. Not that he would say anything, after all he was retired and it was nothing to do with him anymore. But he knew.

Don and Janine were standing looking out across the ocean at the waves lapping softly on the sand. Fleur was in bed and they were having a nightcap before turning in themselves. It had been a fantastic day and surprisingly some exciting things could come out of it. Manny had asked Don to meet him to talk about his new agency; Dave Sanchez and Vince Boyd had discussed the possibility of writing and recording more songs; Captain Lewis had promised to invite Fleur down to headquarters during her holidays for work experience and he'd arranged to talk to Vonda about his divorce. It was then that it occurred to Janine. How it was fate that both her husbands had died with secrets. First Gerry and now Ray. Secrets which she knew, but would never tell.

CHAPTER THIRTY-FOUR

After his meeting with Ray, Pete had called Tommy Douglas and arranged to meet him at his stables. He'd decided to confront him about the rumours and knew it would be awkward, but it was something that had to be done.

Tommy was immediately aggressive towards the accusations. He denied having anything to do with the auctions and said he would find whoever was spreading the malicious gossip and deal with them. He tried to make out that Pete didn't know what he was talking about when it came to managing horses, and he should leave it to people with far more experience. What he didn't know was that Pete had asked another trainer, a young woman called Caren, to privately inspect his horses, and she had immediately pointed out cases of mouth ulcers, colic, and in the case of one of his mares the obvious need for blinkers. She had also told him that his vet's bills were extortionate.

When Pete told Tommy this he exploded with rage and said he left him no option but to resign, which unfortunately for Tommy was a bad move as Pete accepted his resignation with immediate effect and told him he would be paid a month's salary in lieu of notice. Tommy threatened him, saying he hadn't heard the last of it before storming out of the stables.

The new young trainer started the following day and immediately sacked the vet Tommy had employed. She had been to equestrian college and had knowledge of dealing with these basic maladies and set about getting the stables back up to scratch.

Pete hadn't discussed his suspicions about Tommy with Judy. They tended to let each other get on with their own business, and he knew she had enough on her plate with managing The Lexxicon. She'd recently decided to change the direction and the name after watching how the club scene had been evolving over the last couple of years. The core punters still came every week to watch the bands, but the trend for disco music was becoming much more popular and she knew she had to change to stand a chance of keeping at the top. The cost of the average band had increased but the amount of paying customers hadn't, whereas on disco nights the place was packed and she only had to pay a DJ with the rest pure profit. She could hear Gerry Fortuna arguing it wasn't what he would have done, but she had to move with the times. Even his old club The Hideout had recently become a disco called Sloopy's and The Lexxicon was now about to be relaunched as Stratton's. Bands would still play at the beginning of the week, but Thursday, Friday and Saturday would be DJs.

The incident with Tommy Douglas had shaken Pete and he felt unwell afterwards. It was obviously the stress of the argument and Tommy's threatening behaviour that had caused him to feel faint and slightly out of breath. He was sitting in the kitchen when Judy arrived home and she straight away noticed how pale he looked. He finally admitted what had happened and she called the doctor. He explained to Pete that he would have to start taking things a lot easier; cut down on the amount of alcohol he was drinking and stop smoking. Pete sat quietly taking in everything he was being told. What the doctor was saying was 'No More Rock and Roll' which to Pete was anathema. Spending the rest of his life living like a monk was not going to happen, but for the sake of peace and quiet he smiled and nodded at the appropriate times.

It had been a month since Tommy Douglas had left and Caren the new trainer was gradually turning things around. The horses were beginning to look a lot fitter, and she told Pete she was considering entering one of his best mares into a two-mile chase at Newmarket in a couple of weeks' time. She really fancied their chances, and full of optimism, Pete had filled in the necessary paperwork.

The day before the race they had watched as the mare went through her paces on the gallops and agreed she was looking better than ever. This could be the turning point, and a win would certainly improve Pete's standing as an owner. He left her and the jockey making their way back to the stables and decided to drop into the local pub for a drink on his way home. He'd just ordered a glass of red wine when Tommy Douglas walked in. The bar was virtually empty so there was no chance for Pete to avoid him, and he sat on a bar stool as his disgruntled ex-trainer ordered a large scotch.

"If I were you I'd be taking extra care."

Pete ignored him as best he could, but Tommy stayed where he was.

"Don't say you weren't warned."

Pete challenged him. "Is that a threat?"

Tommy looked around. They were still on their own and he leaned in close. "Take it however you want, but just remember this, around these parts no one fucks with Tommy Douglas." He drained his glass and walked out.

Tommy Douglas stopped at the phone box directly across the road on the village green. He made a couple of calls and left a few minutes later on his way to a rendezvous with two of his associates from the auction scam. They met up at a busy pub in the centre of Warwick and sat in the back room where they wouldn't be overheard.

Tommy got the drinks in and addressed the other two.

"OK here's the plan. We wait until dark then use the lane down the side of the stables. There's no security there. I told him to get some kind of alarm system installed but he was always moaning that everything was costing him a fortune. Well I'm gonna teach him a lesson that'll cost him more than money!"

They kept on drinking and by the time it was dark the three of them were too drunk to think straight, but Tommy was determined to make Pete pay for what he'd done. His two friends were starting to get worried that he was going to do something stupid, but knew they couldn't back down and reluctantly went along with him. He'd loaded the back of his car with half a dozen containers filled with petrol which sloshed around as he drove erratically towards Pete's house. They parked up at the back of the stables and watched as Pete and Judy came out with their son who was carrying a guitar case. That night, Pete's son Rick had a gig with his band and Pete had arranged for him and Judy to go and watch. It was in a pub a couple of miles away and Caren had agreed to babysit Lucy. She was staying with them until she managed to find her own place, and the arrangement suited her, especially as she had to be up early in the morning to travel to Newmarket. Caren and Lucy waved them off and closed the front door.

One of the men was starting to get cold feet and wanted to leave but

Tommy told him to shut up. He climbed out and walked around to the back of the car opening the boot. Pulling one of the petrol containers out he unsteadily made his way across the stable yard and started to pour the contents up the wall of one of the stalls. He hissed for the others to do the same and they did as he ordered. By now the horses were becoming restless and started to whinny and move around nervously. The two men started to back off but Tommy went back to the car and returned with another full container which he clumsily splashed across the end wall, and losing hold of it spilled the rest across himself. Ignoring the pleas of his two accomplices to leave he took out his cigarette lighter and flicked it creating a flame, but instead of setting light to the wall, the fumes coming from his clothes caught fire and with a loud 'whoosh' he became a human fireball.

He staggered around screaming and blindly fell onto one of the stall doors which immediately burst into flames. The horse inside reared up and kicked its hind legs breaking the door down with a loud crash. It jumped out landing on Tommy's burning body with all its weight, crushing his head with one of its hooves before galloping off into the darkness. By now the rest of the stalls were on fire and the other horses were frantically trying to escape. The two horrified men were running around opening doors to free the horses and didn't notice they had been joined by Caren and Pete's daughter Lucy. Caren quickly took stock of the situation and shouted at Lucy to run and phone the fire brigade and police while she went to try and round up the horses. Luckily they had all managed to escape and were running around together in the field, but Caren was concerned that she couldn't see Sparkle Lucy's pony.

After a few worried minutes whistling and calling her name she trotted across none the worse for the ordeal and Caren breathed a sigh of relief. She was calming them all down as the police and fire engines arrived and they soon had the blaze under control. The two accomplices had given themselves up and were now sitting in the back of the police car.

Pete and Judy were standing at the back of the room watching as Rick and his pals played their first set. The pub was full and although Pete thought the volume was a bit loud it was sounding great. He was smiling and loving how it was almost like watching a mirror image of himself, although even he had to admit Rick was much more advanced in his technique than he had been at that age. They were so engrossed in the show they didn't hear the fire engines or the police car racing past and it wasn't until the landlord came pushing through the crowd to tell him there was an urgent phone call for him, that they were aware there was anything wrong. Pete struggled to hear over the noise of the band but managed to understand the police officer as he explained there had been a fire at the stables. He said he thought most of the horses had managed to escape, and was about to tell him about the body when Pete dropped the phone.

Telling Judy he'd explain later, he drove back home at break-neck speed. As he raced into the drive he could see a stretcher being put into the back of an ambulance and jumped out of the car as it skidded to a stop. Pete could see Caren over at the ruined stables talking with the firemen and was about to join them when Lucy ran over to him. He was expecting her to be in tears, but she was remarkably calm and proudly told him how she had called the fire brigade and the police. She said they'd been worried about 'Sparkle' but she was fine. He was holding her hand when one of the police officers came over and said they should go inside to talk.

Pete took the policeman into the kitchen to be told about the 999 call from the house and attending to find the stables well alight. The officer went on to say they had discovered a body which had been badly burned, since identified as Tommy Douglas by two men currently in custody.

Pete was in shock. Even knowing that Tommy had threatened him earlier that day, he had never thought he was intending to do anything like this.

The police officer had gone back outside when Pete suddenly remembered Judy and Rick were still at the gig. Caren was busy making sure the horses were settled and the fire brigade was damping down the smouldering remains, which meant there was nobody to stay with Lucy while he went back to pick the others up so, making her promise to behave and do as she was told, they set off back to Rick's gig.

By the time they all arrived back home it was well past midnight and the police and fire brigade had left. Pete stood surveying the charred remains of the stables. Caren had managed to corral the horses and

'Sparkle' together and they were quietly standing in the corner of the field, hardly the ideal situation. He rang his friend Monty, apologising for the lateness of his call but Monty had already heard about the fire via the local grapevine and had been trying to contact Pete with the offer of some free stabling. This was a great relief and after getting everyone inside for a drink and in the case of Lucy and Rick bed, they made arrangements to transfer the horses over. Fortunately the transporter hadn't been damaged and they were just getting two of the horses loaded in when Monty arrived with his own lorry along with another friend who had a separate horse box and space in his stables, which meant they could rehouse them all in one go. Caren was happy to leave Sparkle on her own in the field and set off following the others.

Judy was concerned that all the excitement might affect Pete but he insisted on going although he didn't look well. Eventually he and Caren arrived back just as the sun was coming up, exhausted but relieved. They were about to go to bed when Pete remembered they were supposed to attend the race meeting at Newmarket. There was no way they could go, but the stewards had to be informed otherwise he'd incur a fine even though there were rather extenuating circumstances. His last task of a long and wearisome night was sending off a fax explaining what had happened.

CHAPTER THIRTY-FIVE

Work had started on rebuilding the new stables. It was going to take a while before it was finished and any of his horses could effectively compete again and Pete was beginning to wonder what to do with his time, when out of the blue he received a phone call from Janine in California.

She and Don had set up their own promotion company, and along with Manny Oberstein were starting to make waves on the West Coast. The first artist they had signed was Vince Boyd and he was recording a new album with Dave Sanchez writing and producing it. Pete was pleased to hear his old keyboard player was on the road to recovery, his partner Henry having been instrumental in funding successful research for a cure.

They were currently down in Nashville and according to Janine the tracks were sounding amazing but they had one major problem. The fans and the Country Music press were demanding another duet between Vince and Pete. Dave and Vince had written the song and all that was needed was for Pete to sing his part. She was explaining what a fantastic studio they were in and how the musicians were the best when Pete interrupted her.

"Hey listen, it sounds great, and I'd love to, but I'm just not well enough to fly over. My doctor has warned me I have to take things easy and what with the fire at the stables I couldn't do it. I'm really sorry."

Janine listened to what he said but wasn't going to give up that easily.

"OK I hear what you're saying but I'll talk to the guys and get back to you. There's things happening nowadays that you don't know about so leave it with me."

She hung up leaving Pete wondering what she had in mind.

What she actually had in mind was a revolutionary new way of recording using multi-track tape machines. They enabled the musicians to be able to record on more than one track at a time with up to twenty-four tracks available. Dave Sanchez had been experimenting in the studio, and they'd already discussed the possibility of recording Vince's vocal in Nashville and then taking the tape over to a studio near Pete in Birmingham where he could record his part. Dave would then mix the two together to make it sound like they were in the same room, and no one would know. It was putting the latest technology to the test, but with two great artists Janine thought it was worth a try.

She and Dave called Pete again the next day and told him their plan. He was sceptical at first but after a long conversation with Dave, who said he would send over a demo tape of the song for Pete to learn in advance and then fly over himself to be there at the recording, the deal was agreed. The prospect of working with his old friend again was too good to resist.

The song was called 'Never Say Goodbye' and Vince Boyd had already sung his vocals in the studio in Nashville. Now Dave was in Pete's house discussing the demo. It was a beautiful song and Pete had immediately fallen in love with it and couldn't wait to get in the studio to record his part. They were reminiscing about old times and Pete was amazed at how well Dave looked since he'd started on the revolutionary medication Henry had funded.

Dave explained how he would be forever in his debt and how strong their relationship was. He was enjoying living in Palm Springs but overjoyed to be working again, all down to Henry. He admitted he had no idea how he managed to earn his money. He told him how Henry would disappear for days on end, and then when he returned there would be a procession of extremely rich-looking people visiting the apartment to view the pictures he kept locked up in another room. But he left Henry to get on with it while he played the piano and wrote songs like 'Never Say Goodbye'. He sat down at Pete's piano and played it while Pete strummed on his acoustic and sang. It brought back so many memories and Pete silently cursed his illness thinking he'd give anything to be performing again.

The session was amazing and Pete's voice as good as ever, although at the end of the day he was really tired and happy to get home. Dave stayed on for an extra day and they messed around with a couple of ideas he'd wanted to play Pete. They briefly touched on the subject of Ray Law and how sad it was for him to go in such a tragic way, and

Dave mentioned he'd been at Janine's party that weekend and how recording the album with Vince had come about from meeting him there. He told Pete what a lovely girl Fleur was and how Janine and Don were a great couple. At the same time he was blown away by Rick, Pete's son. He'd played Dave a couple of his original songs and he was amazed at his talent. Unlike her dad and brother, Lucy was shy and had to be persuaded to show him her pony and how well she rode.

Dave left the next day with the multitrack tape and promised to send the finished song as soon as it was mixed.

The reaction back in Nashville was immense and everybody concerned was confident of a number one, which created another problem. How were they going to do a video when Pete couldn't come to them and Vince's schedule was so busy he couldn't go over to Pete like the last time? Dave was always looking at new ways to achieve things and had been talking with Randy Jones who had played bass with Pete's band and owned Whitland Studios. He now had one of the latest video companies and he and Dave had worked out a way that they could film Vince in Los Angeles and Pete in the UK, and by clever editing put them together on film as if they'd recorded it at the same time. Janine and Don had given them the go ahead and a week later Randy sat down to match the two films together. They had used a new technique which entailed filming both Pete and Vince in front of a sheet of green material. The green could then be replaced by any background they wanted, as if both Pete and Vince were in the same room. It was very complicated and took ages to match everything up, but by the time Randy and his team had finished it was impossible to spot the joins. With the song already at number one in the charts the video became the most watched on the new music channels and won all sorts of awards for technology as well as the song itself.

Pete was stunned as he watched the amazing film he and Vince featured in side-by-side, even though they'd never been in the same country together, never mind the same studio.

CHAPTER THIRTY-SIX

Just when he thought things couldn't be any more exciting, the builders called Pete to come over and look at the finished stables. They had done a great job, and learning from his mistakes, this time Pete had ensured they installed a modern hi-tech security system.

Everything was ready and the horses were returned to their new homes. Two of the old group had been sold on and replaced by two promising geldings who according to Caren were ready to race, so plans were made to enter one of them in a race at Warwick.

It was a fine, but chilly day and 'Out Of Bounds' was running in the second race on the card. Caren was optimistic it stood a good chance of being placed, and the large crowd of punters had got behind him with the bookies offering a cautious 2 to 1 odds. He'd looked good when he was saddled up in the parade ring and for once Pete felt confident. He'd looked around him in an attempt to speak with some of the other owners and trainers but noticed how everyone looked away and avoided making eye contact with him.

He was puzzled but ignored it, concentrating instead on Caren who certainly seemed to know what she was doing. The jockey had mounted up and ridden down to the start on the far side of the course. Pete's heart was pounding as the field assembled under the watchful eye of the starter. He seemed to keep them for ages before the tape went up and they were off. The race was two circuits of the course and Caren had instructed the jockey to hold him back for the first and then gradually give him his head for the second. As they came round for the first-time things seemed to be going fine with 'Out Of Bounds' comfortably in the middle of the field and looking relaxed. As instructed the jockey began to allow him more rein and he started to move through the field.

With two furlongs to go they were challenging for the lead. Pete couldn't help himself and along with the rest of the crowd started to shout encouragement as they entered the last furlong neck and neck with the favourite. Both jockeys were giving everything they had and as they hurtled towards the line the tension was mounting when suddenly 'Out

Of Bounds' began to slow allowing the favourite to stretch away and another horse to pass him before he reached the finishing line in third place.

It was a good result considering it was his first time out, but both Caren and Pete felt he could have done better. The journey home was in silence as they reflected on what could have been, but Caren had entered another one of their mares in a race up in Wetherby in two days' time so they put the result to the back of their minds and prepared for the next one.

Wetherby was cold and damp but there was a big crowd for the Bank Holiday meeting and their runner 'Judy's Choice' was looking fit and almost too eager. Once again Pete felt like he was being deliberately ignored by the other owners and trainers and decided to give his friend Monty a call to find out if he knew what it could be. His attention was brought back to the race as Caren warned the jockey that although the mare appeared full of energy in the parade ring and on her way down to the start, she was a really slow starter and had to be pushed all the way. The trick was to know how much, because if she hit the front too soon she could tire and the field would pass her by.

The starter had hardly got them in line before raising the tape and the field jumped off leaving 'Judy's Choice' at the back. As they came round for the first time Caren could see the jockey pushing her along in a group of runners just behind the two leaders. So long as he kept this up she thought they stood a chance of catching them, and slowly the gap between the leaders began to disappear with 'Judy's Choice' smoothly moving through on the inside and challenging for the lead. She was now on the shoulder of the leading horse with the winning post in sight when suddenly it was if she ran out of steam and disappeared back into the field, eventually finishing in sixth place.

Caren was beginning to doubt her abilities with the two failures and sat down with Pete in his kitchen. Over a cup of tea they discussed what had happened and what if anything they could do. She felt sure the horses should have won and had no explanation as to why they had slowed.

Unless it wasn't down to the horse!

To suspect a jockey of throwing a race was a serious accusation and they needed proof. Pete's previous experience with Tommy Douglas had made him a lot more cautious and aware of what went on behind the scenes. But race fixing. That was a completely different kettle of fish.

As they already had four more entries over the next few weeks at various racecourses around the country they decided to carry on as normal for the time being. Nothing changed however, as race after race Pete's horses never made a finish higher than third and on one occasion their mare finished so far behind the field she could have been going backwards, according to a distraught Caren. The more they sat and analysed the races the more their suspicions mounted that there was a vendetta against them. The horses were fit, but they all seemed unable to stay on to finish a race. Caren had even called an old teacher from the vet's college where she trained and asked him to come and check the horses over, but he could find nothing.

It wasn't until Pete and Judy had gone to dinner with Monty that something he said made Pete sit up and take notice. He was telling him how on a few occasions he'd suffered when the jockey's secret cabal had been in action. One of his best horses had been slowed down to finish third, because the syndicate had the top two already sorted. It was never proven, but he knew without a doubt that the jockey on his horse made sure it didn't win. He said it went on all the time, but without any concrete evidence they always got away with it. Pete explained what had been happening to his horses and how they just seemed to run out of steam, and he nodded his head knowingly. He went on to point out that he'd recently been to a dinner and heard some of his old friends discussing the death of Tommy Douglas and how a rumour had gone round that he'd been badly treated by the owner, a multimillionaire rock star. Pete was shocked but Monty explained that the racing fraternity was close knit who looked after their own, and if they suspected Pete of doing wrong by Tommy they'd make sure to get their own back, especially some of the jockeys. Things suddenly started to fall into place. The blatant way they ignored him in the parade ring, the suspicious way his horses never finished higher than third.

He didn't know how, but he would find a way to beat them.

The following week he had one of his horses running over in Ireland at the famous Laytown meeting which was unique, as it was run on the beach at a small seaside town north of Dublin. Pete and Judy had decided they would fly over with Rick and Lucy and have a few days holiday at the same time. On the day of the races the barriers were erected along the beach once the tide had gone out, and the large crowd gathered in a nearby field to watch. Pete had 'Firefly' entered in a seven-furlong race and both he and Caren were confident of a result. The atmosphere was electric as the runners lined up for the start and the crowd let out a huge roar as the starter set them off. 'Firefly' was boxed in slightly on the rails but the jockey skillfully manoeuvred her out and gave her her head as they hurtled down the beach. She quickly made up the ground and pulled level with the leaders as they neared the finish line. Pete and Judy were caught up in the moment shouting encouragement, with Rick and Lucy leaping up and down as the flying horses went past them in a blur of hooves and colourful silks. They knew 'Firefly' had been one of the three at the front but had no idea where she had finished until the announcer read out the result over the tannoy.

"First number seven, 'Firefly,' Second number…" They were screaming and shouting so loud they didn't hear the rest of the result, but they didn't care. They rushed over to the winner's enclosure where Caren was leading 'Firefly' in and patted her neck and back. Suddenly there was another announcement that there was an enquiry into the result due to an objection by one of the jockeys. Pete couldn't believe it. Once again it seemed he was being beaten by the jockeys, and there was an anxious wait while the stewards had a meeting to discuss the race.

Finally the announcer spoke again.

"After a meeting the stewards have decided there was no infringement and the objection is overruled. The result stands."

The cameras from the Irish News were there and approached Pete for an interview. Standing in front of the horse with his family around him he'd never felt so proud and gave Caren a big hug. The reporter had obviously done his homework and knew all about Pete, and it turned out he was a big fan. The piece went out on the News channel that night to the whole of Ireland, including a Mr. and Mrs. Burke sitting watching in their sitting room just down the road in a tiny village called Donone.

Joe recognised Pete from when he played at his daughter, Janine's wedding back in Birmingham and knew he had to contact him. It was the only way he could get a message to his daughter without the authorities knowing. He had a friend who was one of the stewards on the course and called him to ask if he knew where Pete and his family were staying. Half an hour later he had the address of their hotel. He jumped in his car and drove to the one-time stately home now converted into a luxury country hotel. He asked the receptionist if he could speak to Mr. Peterson and was shown into a small bar where Pete and his family were having a party.

He was embarrassed about intruding on their privacy and said he would come back in the morning, but Pete insisted he stay and have a drink. He vaguely remembered her father from Janine's wedding to Gerry when he had played at the reception with The Flames. Joe asked him if he could get a message to Janine. Her mother was in poor health and didn't have long to live, but they had been unable to contact her because of the restrictions still in place as a result of the bombing of Rudy's Nightclub. He explained how he and his wife along with two others involved had been secretly relocated in Ireland as part of a deal done by the UK and Irish governments. The main stipulation was they were not allowed to contact any of their relatives.

Pete listened intently and agreed straight away. He said for Joe to follow him and led him upstairs to their suite where he picked up the phone and dialled a number. Joe heard a young voice answer at the other end and Pete asked to speak to her mother.

He handed the phone to Joe.

"Hello?"

"Hello Janine, it's your Da."

There was silence then she cried out.

"Don, Don it's my dad. Hello. Oh Jesus, I can't believe it. Da is it really you? How're you, how's Mammy?"

Joe finally got to explain what had happened and how Janine's mother was seriously ill, and Janine listened as he told her how they'd followed what she was doing in America but hadn't been allowed to contact her.

Janine told him how she'd tried to get in touch but had been stopped from doing so. They were both so excited and talking at the same time when she said she had an idea. "Why don't I come over to see you and Mammy. Surely they can't stop me from doing that. I'll say I'm having a holiday in Ireland. Maybe I could even visit Ballykobh while I'm over and see some of my old school friends."

Her dad was speechless. He couldn't believe he was talking to his daughter after such a long time and that she was going to come over to see him and her mother.

"And I'll ask Jackie to come over too. We'll make it a family affair. I'll get Pete to give me the details of where he's staying and we can stay there."

Her dad thanked Pete for what he'd just done and drove back to his wife to tell her the news.

Janine put the phone down in Hermosa Beach and hugged Don and Fleur.

"Guys I'm going to Ireland to see my Mammy and Da and where I was born, and hopefully my sister too."

She explained to Don what had just happened and how she had decided to contact Jackie her sister and the pair of them could go over to see her parents. She told him how her dad had said her mother was seriously ill, and how they were still unable to contact anyone because of what the two governments had agreed.

Don was concerned that by going over she would risk getting into trouble, especially as she had already been told not to try to contact them before. But her mind was made up.

"Don't worry about me. We're there on holiday, so we can get them to come to the hotel for a meal and meet us. No one will know."

But Don wasn't convinced. "Those Special Branch guys can be pretty ruthless. I think you need to be really careful."

"So why don't you and Fleur come too? What perfect cover. We're on a family holiday seeing my homeland, and maybe Jackie can bring John and the kids. Perfect. I'll call her later and get everything set up. Let's see; we'll need flights and Pete's sending me the details of the hotel. It's supposed to be beautiful. An old stately home, you'll love it."

Don looked at Fleur and shrugged his shoulders.

"Looks like we're going to Ireland."

CHAPTER THIRTY-SEVEN

Janine called her sister, and after a bit of cajoling convinced her it was a great idea to bring her family over for a long weekend at the beautiful hotel in the Irish countryside where they could meet Don and Fleur. She'd deliberately omitted telling her she was arranging for their parents to be there too.

Her dad had contacted his friend the steward from the racecourse who agreed to stay in touch with Pete, who would in turn let him know when Janine was coming over. Her dad knew he was still being watched by the Garda, but was able to occasionally give them the slip. He'd heard from his friend that Janine was arriving the following week and would be staying at the same hotel as Pete had. She had arranged for a private room where they could meet, and all that remained was for Joe and his wife to go to the hotel for a special meal to celebrate their anniversary.

Janine, Don and Fleur flew in the day before and checked into their suite. Then early the next morning Janine's sister Jackie and John her husband arrived along with their two children. They all met up and had a great afternoon getting to know each other and relaxing around the indoor pool. Fleur was roughly the same age as Jackie's two children and they soon became best of friends. Don was the centre of attention with Jackie and John who had secretly never liked Ray Law.

That night the room had been prepared, and the two families arrived on time ready for their meal. Jackie was the first to notice the two extra places laid at the long dining table and was about to mention it to Janine when the door opened and their mother and father walked in. Jackie dropped her glass and Janine burst into tears as they both ran over and hugged their parents. It was obvious that their mother was very frail and they quickly sat her down as Janine introduced Don and Fleur. Her dad had brought his camera and was busy taking photos of everyone when the door was thrown open and two officers from the Garda walked in.

The room went silent as one of the men spoke.

"Who's the ex-cop from LAPD?"

Don stepped forward and announced it was him.

"We have a message from our Captain to say welcome to the Emerald Isle and we hope you all have a great night." He winked at Janine's father. "You go easy on that Guinness there Joe," he said and gave Janine's mother a kiss on the cheek.

They turned on their heels and walked out closing the door behind them as everyone breathed a huge sigh of relief.

The meal was served and after they'd all finished eating, Janine's dad Joe related exactly what had happened when Gerry's club, Rudi's, was bombed. He explained how they only ever wanted to get rid of the American drug dealers and that Frank, the man responsible for the bomb had assured them it would detonate at ten o'clock the next morning. They were all mortified when it went off that night, especially as one of their friends had been in the club with his wife. He said the scenes of devastation would live with him for the rest of his life.

Don stepped in just as the atmosphere was getting maudlin and announced there was a Ceilidh band performing in the hotel and they were about to start. Everyone made their way through to the main room where Janine and Jackie took turns dancing with their dad.

It had been a fantastic party and finally things were winding down. Joe decided it was time he got their mother back home, and after long hugs and kisses with tears flowing they made their way to the reception to get their coats. There, sitting in two armchairs by the roaring fire drinking coffee were the two Garda officers from before who stood up as they walked in.

The sergeant came over to them. "Now, we thought as we were close by we'd give you an escort home to make sure you got back safe." He gave Janine and Jackie a kiss apiece and shook hands with Don and John before linking arms with their mum and helping her out to Joe's car.

Sadly, it was the last time Janine and Jackie were to see her. A few weeks later she passed away peacefully in her sleep. Her final words to Joe concerned how happy she'd been to see her daughters and their families.

CHAPTER THIRTY-EIGHT

Dave Sanchez had returned home to the apartment in Palm Springs after his recording sessions in Nashville with Vince Boyd. He'd been back to the clinic for one of his treatments and was relieved to learn his condition was improving. Henry had disappeared on one of his trips leaving Dave to entertain himself playing the grand piano and experimenting with the new portable recording system he'd recently bought.

On the second day he was bored and sat wondering what to do. He'd been curious what was in the room that was always kept locked and after searching the apartment finally found the key in Henry's desk at the back of a drawer. With his heart beating fast he put the key in the lock and opened the door. The room had no windows so he switched on the light and almost fainted when he saw the contents. His knowledge of art was limited, but even he could recognise the works displayed on stands, leaning against the walls and standing on plinths. He had to be looking at the haul of countless art thefts he had read about and seen on the TV.

Now he understood why Henry's visitors were so secretive. Obviously he was selling priceless works of art to collectors who could never show them publicly; destined to remain hidden in vaults only for the pleasure of their corrupt owners. He remembered seeing a report about the theft of a Rembrandt valued at five million dollars, and there it was displayed on a carved wooden easel right in front of him. There was a Hockney, a Bosch, a Jackson Pollock propped up on the floor, sculptures he knew would be worth a fortune, and here they were all kept in a locked room in an apartment in Palm Springs.

Suddenly he started to panic. He had to get out of there. He switched off the light and locked the door again before quickly returning the key to the drawer where he'd found it.

What the hell was he going to do? Should he confront Henry? But if he did, Henry would know he'd been in the room. Maybe it would be best to say nothing. Perhaps he would eventually tell him.

Henry arrived home late the following night. Dave was already in bed when he heard him come into the apartment and after a few minutes finally come to bed. He pretended to be asleep and as Henry carefully slid in beside him trying not to wake him he decided to keep up the pretence.

The next morning, Henry was awake early and making breakfast when Dave walked into the kitchen. He gave Dave his cup of coffee and acted quite normally. Dave sat down at the table and found it difficult not to say anything about what he'd found, and what he now knew Henry was up to. He didn't know what to do or who to talk to. Claus was no good. Granted they had their own secret, but he couldn't trust him with something like this.

He finished his coffee and made an excuse to go out for a paper to give himself time to think. He was sitting on a bench in the park reading it when he noticed an article about the theft of a piece of modern art from a gallery in Chicago. It was a small sculpture worth half a million dollars and his blood ran cold. That must have been where Henry went. There was a photograph of the piece which he tore out, dropping the paper in a waste bin. He had to find out if it was in the locked room and would wait until Henry went out. He made his way back to the apartment and was about to sit down at the piano to play when Henry asked him if he could read the paper.

"What paper?"

"The paper you went out to buy. Didn't you get one?" Henry asked.

Dave was flummoxed. "Oh yeah, I read it and left it in the park, sorry. I didn't realise you wanted to read it."

Henry gave him a strange look before going back to what he was doing.

Dave sat down at the piano and started to play hoping he hadn't given himself away.

After lunch Henry announced he had to go out to meet one of his clients in Palm Springs. Dave was concentrating on recording a piano part and just waved as he left the apartment.

He waited for a while before going to Henry's desk and opening the drawer to find the key. It was in the same place as before but lying at the side of it was a gun. The situation was going from bad to worse, but he took the key and opened the door. He switched on the light and there right in front of him was the sculpture in the picture. He stood thinking what he should do when he heard a noise and panicking ran out of the room quickly locking it behind him and putting the key back in the desk. He walked out of the kitchen just as Henry came back into the apartment saying he'd forgotten some papers. Dave acted as naturally as he could but suddenly realised he hadn't turned off the light in the room. Or had he?

"Shit! Shit! Shit!" Dave thought he was going to faint.

Henry had gone into his office to look for the papers and luckily hadn't noticed the look of panic on Dave's face. He found what he was after and went out again. Dave had almost passed out with fear but pulled himself together and once again took the key and opened the door. To his relief he had turned off the light, but he knew he couldn't let that situation happen again.

He decided, against his better judgement, to speak to Don. He had always been trustworthy when it came to any problems with the guys in the band, and had in particular helped Dave with the Maltrocorp situation. And he had a feeling Don knew he had been involved in the death of Claudia Inestes but hadn't said anything.

He picked up the phone and called him.

CHAPTER THIRTY-NINE

Pete was talking to Caren in the stables one day when his friend Monty turned up.

He congratulated them both on their recent exciting win over in Ireland, explained how it had made the UK news and said he'd been thinking about Pete's problem, and that he might have a possible solution.

The three of them sat down in Pete's kitchen and he began to outline his plan. It would involve bending the rules a little, but as Pete had been on the receiving end of such harsh treatment he didn't think it was worth worrying about. He explained how they could play the jockeys at their own game, and with a bit of luck earn themselves a tidy profit.

The first part involved a bit of old-fashioned disguise. Caren would make sure 'Firefly' couldn't be recognized by painting over the distinctive white markings on her face using a special dye which she would apply the day before the race.

The second part needed Monty to enter 'Firefly' under a new name with him listed as the owner. This wasn't a problem as he was still officially registered even though he'd retired. He would say, if questioned, that he had just bought the horse and was running it to try it out in a decent field.

The third part entailed booking one of the top jockeys to ride her. The jockey they chose would accept the offer because he was an old friend of Monty, and regularly used to ride for him. Whilst a successful rider, he was not the brightest, and would hopefully not have the intelligence to suspect he was part of a sting. Monty knew he would be involved in the usual set up to hold the horse back for a midfield finish. However, what he didn't know was that 'Firefly' would easily outrun the field despite his best attempts to stop her.

The final and most tricky part of the scam was placing bets spread around the bookies that didn't make them suspicious. The jockeys involved would have made sure the usual suspects were notified and would be setting the odds in their favour on the day, unaware that they were going to be played at their own game.

The meeting they chose was at Newmarket and Pete had entered two of his other horses in the early races on the card. Caren had taken 'Firefly' over to Monty's stables the day before as she would be travelling with them separately. Now called 'Queen's Command,' Caren had done a great job with the change of appearance, although her only concern was if it rained. The dye she'd used wasn't completely waterproof which could be a problem. However, her worries were unfounded when the following day dawned with a bright blue sky and a clear forecast as the two teams set off.

It was as if 'Firefly' knew what was going on. She seemed to adopt a completely different persona when she arrived at the course. Usually bright and frisky, she was lethargic and quiet, not drawing any attention to herself. In fact she was so quiet Caren was worried if she had a problem, but Monty reassured her everything was fine and to concentrate on Pete's entries.

As in previous outings their two horses ran well only finishing fourth and seventh, but for once they weren't concerned. They went through the motions of unsaddling and making sure they were fine, before Pete strolled over to the parade ring. The runners and riders were getting ready for the race before Firefly's, and he spotted their jockey who was standing waiting for his ride to be led over. Pete had noticed the betting for the next race had 'Queen's Command' at long odds, which meant so far no one suspected anything. He spotted Monty and together they walked over to the jockey and immediately the penny dropped but it was too late for him to do anything as the horse he was riding was ready and he mounted to ride away to the start.

Pete and Monty walked back to the stand to watch the race in which their jockey came in third, and once again made their way across to the parade ring as the runners for the next race were led in. 'Queen's Command' looked immaculate and a lot livelier than before, and was now being handled by Caren. They stood admiring her when an announcement came over the public address system.

"Attention please. There is a jockey change in the next race. Due to injury the rider on 'Queen's Command' will now be…" Pete didn't hear the name as he ran across to the changing rooms, arriving just in time to see their man being escorted out by a paramedic. Before Pete had a chance to speak the jockey shrugged his shoulders and with a smirk climbed into the back of a waiting ambulance.

By the time he got back to Monty the runners had all left, and were on their way down to the start. Their replacement jockey had been one of the young reserves kept on standby, and Pete felt like they'd been beaten again, but Monty was smiling. He told him he knew the young lad who was the replacement. He had trained at his stables when he first started riding, and he'd given him instructions on exactly what to do. As they were at the starting tapes the odds were still long which meant they hadn't been rumbled, and if their plan succeeded they stood to make a lot of money as well as getting one over on the jockeys.

They quickly headed over to the stands where they watched as the race began. It was run over two circuits and the jockey did as he was told, holding 'Queen's Command' back in the middle of the field as they passed the finish line for the first time. Watching through his binoculars Pete followed them round to the far side of the course, where 'Queen's Command' was now smoothly gliding up into second place just behind the favourite.

They were neck and neck as they came round the final bend and Pete's heart was beating fast. The favourite was being ridden by one of the top jockeys they knew was part of the syndicate, and from the aggressive way he was riding he wasn't about to be beaten by an unknown. He was using his whip to keep slightly ahead and Pete was beginning to think it was going to be the same old story, when suddenly their rider just loosened his grip and gave 'Queen's Command' her head. She lunged past the other horse leaving her chasing shadows as she passed the winning post three lengths clear.

The roar from the crowd was deafening as Caren led the jubilant jockey and his sweating mount into the winner's enclosure.

Pete and Monty were laughing as the jockey on the favourite walked into the second-place stall and dismounted with a scowl.

He was about to walk away when Pete called after him. "I think that's one for me."

They turned back as Caren was patting the winner on her head and laughing as she noticed the dye on her hands where she had held her.

The obligatory celebration photographs all showed Pete, Monty, the jockey and Caren smiling, with 'Queen's Command' conveniently turning her head away on every shot.

The champagne flowed that night as they totted up their winnings. It probably wouldn't even dent the syndicate's purse, but it had taught them a lesson that they weren't infallible. It had also shown Pete he could never win against such insurmountable odds, and maybe the time was right to bow out on a high. He would keep 'Sparkle,' Lucy's pony, who everyone loved, and Monty had offered to help him sell the rest of his horses including 'Firefly' which he thought would command a good price. So, without too many regrets he decided the time was right to get out of 'The Sport of Kings'.

CHAPTER FORTY

Don and Dave sat out on the roof terrace at the house in Hermosa Beach where Don had set up his office.

Don was shocked at Dave's revelation and thought back to the quiet, well-dressed man he'd met at the mayor's inauguration. Dave had described how he'd discovered all the pieces of art hidden in the locked room in Henry's apartment. Then told him how after reading about the recent theft of the sculpture in Chicago he'd seen in the room after Henry had returned from his recent trip away.

Dave was concerned that the man he was living with was linked with danger. The clients he'd met on the odd occasion seemed genuine, but always had an element of menace about them and finding the gun in Henry's drawer had really scared him.

Don listened sympathetically. He was in a tricky situation. What Dave had told him in confidence could help solve outstanding cases of art theft, but without a warrant the police could never prove anything. He got the impression there was something else Dave wanted to talk about, but was reluctant to open up completely. He knew if he spoke to his old friend Captain Lewis he would be bound to involve Anna Delaney, and things could get out of hand. And at the root of the problem was Dave's relationship with Henry.

He wondered what Janine would say. She was out shopping with Fleur and he decided he would wait until later over a drink or two to ask her opinion.

Back in the UK, Pete had thought a lot after Dave's last visit. Just the easy way they had worked together had made him realise he could never give up music. It was in his blood and irrespective of his health and the warnings from his doctor, he was going to give it one more go. Thanks to Monty, he'd sold all his horses, and was standing looking at the empty stables when he had an idea.

He contacted the company who'd rebuilt them after the fire, and asked if they could come back and make him a small recording studio. He remembered when Gerry first bought the house and told him of his idea, and now finally he was going to do it.

Judy wasn't too happy that Pete was defying his doctor, but knew she'd never win. In fact she'd reluctantly agreed to take him to Stratton's, as The Lexxicon was now called, to get up and jam with the occasional band he knew.

Once or twice, even though he was at school the next day, Pete had taken Rick with him, and stood and watched as his son rocked with some of the best players around.

Slowly but surely music was becoming Pete's life again.

Dave was having a good day. In fact, it was turning into a great day. Pete Peterson had called him first thing to say he had just commissioned a new recording studio to be built in his old stables, and he would be ready to start writing again as soon as it was finished. Pete had asked him to send him details of his setup to make sure the equipment he installed was compatible, enabling them to work on the same songs even though they were on opposite sides of the Atlantic. He'd then gone for his regular appointment at the clinic where the doctor told him the last blood test he'd had was showing a marked improvement, and they were starting to believe they might have found a cure for his virus.

When he got back to the apartment Henry had left him a note, saying he'd had to go to LA and would be back late so not to wait up. It annoyed Dave that he hadn't told him, because he'd arranged to meet Janine at Whitland Studios and they could have gone together. Instead he had to drive the two hour journey on his own.

Whatof course he didn't know was that Henry had received a call while Dave was at the clinic telling him a priceless Reubens miniature would be at a gallery in LA that night. His contact assured him it was a simple matter of entering through a back door and disabling the alarm system. There would only be one security guard on duty, and he had been paid to be elsewhere. Henry had received an outrageous offer for the tiny portrait of Charles the First from one of his most valuable clients, and knew he had to get it. He'd quickly put together his kit in the black leather hold-all he kept in the locked room, and hesitated before picking up his pistol as he replaced the key. Being armed wasn't his usual style, but something in the back of his mind told him he should take the gun, although hopefully he wouldn't need it. He'd never had to use it before, but then there was always a first time.

The small gallery was situated on Rodeo Drive next to the Cartier store, and had a colourful display of paintings in the front window. Henry had driven past slowly and noted the narrow alley that ran along the back which would be his way in. The gallery was closed, as it was preparing for the new exhibition which would include the Reubens.

He found a space nearby and parked his car. Taking his hold-all from the trunk he made his way to the rear. The alley was deserted as he took out his small bunch of lock picks, and within a matter of seconds he'd opened the back door. It was then just a case of disabling the alarm by inputting the code he'd been given. The control box inside the door was beeping as he typed in the code. 1 0 8 5 7 9 ...the beeping continued. He typed the numbers again. 1 0 8 5 7 9. It still continued but the beeps were getting longer and he started to panic knowing he had seconds before the alarm went off. He checked the piece of paper he'd written the code on. 1 0 8 6 7 9...6 7 9! He typed it in again 1 0 8 6 7 9 and the beeping stopped. He was sweating. How could he have mistaken the 6 for a 5? He was getting careless.

Using his torch he made his way across the gallery floor to where the miniature was supposed to be hung, except it wasn't there. His contact had assured him that's where it would be displayed, but all he saw was an empty space. He was aware he had already been in the gallery too long, and although the guard had been taken care of there was the possibility he would be returning soon. He was wondering what to do next when the decision was made for him. The lights in the gallery suddenly came on, and standing in the middle of the floor pointing a gun at him was the security guard. He'd been set up.

Henry didn't give the man time to speak and dived behind a screen pulling his gun from his bag. The guard fired a shot but it went high and wide. Henry made a run for the back door firing at where he thought the man was, but he'd anticipated Henry's move and ducked behind a pillar and as Henry carried on the guard stepped out and fired again.

This time Henry was hit in his side and fell to the floor motionless.

The guard then made a stupid mistake. He assumed Henry was dead and walked towards the prone body with his gun at his side. To his astonishment Henry rolled over and shot him straight through the heart.

Henry, now in serious pain from the wound which was bleeding badly, struggled to get back to his feet. In the distance he could hear police sirens and knew he had to get out quickly. He managed to open the back door, and made his way down the alley towards where he'd parked his car. He was losing a lot of blood, and by the time he opened the driver's door he was beginning to feel weak. He had a first aid kit in his hold-all, but then cursed when he realised he'd left it in the gallery.

Rodeo Drive was now full of police cars all heading past him towards the gallery, so as carefully as he could he slowly drove off in the opposite direction. He was about to pull around the corner into Santa Monica Boulevard when a policemen ran out into the road, pointing to the trail of blood leading to where his car had been parked. In his mirror he spotted two officers jumping back into their car and, with a squeal of tyres, setting off to give chase.

Henry pushed his foot down hard on the accelerator and skidded round into the flow of traffic. Swerving between slower moving cars he managed to put some distance between him and his pursuers, but he knew he wouldn't be able to keep it up. He saw a diner on his right set back from the road, and turned off sharply slamming his brakes on and slewing into the car park, while at the same time throwing open his door. He almost fell out, but managed to stumble to his feet and in through the door waving his gun in front of him.

The juke box was playing an old Dolly Parton song, and there were a few customers sitting at tables turning round to see what the commotion was. He fired a shot into the air and told them to get out. All except the waitress who was standing in the aisle. He pointed his gun at her and told her to stay where she was, and that she wouldn't get hurt if she did as she was told.

The customers were running out into the car park as the chasing police car raced in, and skidded to a stop behind Henry's car. They all pointed to the man inside standing inside next to the waitress holding a gun. Not wanting to make the situation any worse than it already was, the two policemen called headquarters for backup, reporting an armed hostage situation.

Captain Lewis took the message at headquarters and put out an APB with the details. Detective Anna Delaney and her partner Sergeant Joe Budd immediately responded radioing they were in the vicinity and set off with their siren wailing.

They arrived minutes later to find a television van already pulling in just outside the cordon the officers were in the process of setting up. Amazed at how news travelled so fast in LA, Anna knew she had to work quickly before things started to get out of hand. The TV reporter was getting ready to record his piece to camera as she reached the two officers who had been first on the scene. They pointed out the car with its door still wide open and a trail of blood leading into the diner and she asked if a trace had been run on the plate.

One of the officers replied it was registered to a Henry Walton from Palm Springs. She wrote the information down and was about to speak to her partner Joe when she realised she recognised the name. She flicked through her notebook and although she couldn't find anything, the name still rang a bell. She called her boss, Captain Lewis, and asked him if he recognised the name but he felt the same as her. It rang a bell but he couldn't place it; he said he'd call her back.

Thinking about possible connections, thee Captain remembered taking Anna to a party at Janine and Don's house in Hermosa Beach. Don was an old, trusted friend and he called him.

"Henry Walton, Henry Walton? Yes, he's Dave Sanchez's partner. They were at the party together. He's a fine art dealer if I remember rightly. Why?"

"He's holding a hostage at gunpoint in a diner on Santa Monica Boulevard. Something to do with an art theft gone wrong."

"Shit!" Don exclaimed. "Dave told me about this the other day. Said he's got a room full of stolen art worth millions. I promised him I wouldn't say anything, but it looks like it's a bit late now."

"Anna's already there. I'll tell her."

Don thought a minute. "Hey listen, Dave's at Whitland Studios with Janine. It's only just down the road. Maybe he could talk to him. It's gotta be worth a try."

Dave and Janine had just watched the news flash on the TV in the studios and hadn't taken much notice. The sound was down and the details running along the bottom of the screen were sketchy so when Randy, the owner, called Janine to the phone, and she went over to take the call, her face swiftly went from smiling to horror as Don told her what was happening.

She put the phone down and grabbed Dave saying there was an emergency and to get in the car. She raced out of the car park doing her best to explain everything Don had told her as she drove.

Moments later they came to a mass of traffic caused by the incident, but Janine managed to drive around most of it and eventually parked a block away. She and Dave jumped out and ran as fast as they could towards the diner. A policeman held up his hand and stopped them as they got closer, but Dave quickly explained who he was and after a call to Anna they were allowed through.

Dave could see Henry through the window and wanted to rush to him, but Anna held him back. He looked around; there were officers with guns everywhere surrounding the diner.

"We have to do this carefully," Anna explained. "He's been shot and will be very stressed. Any wrong move and he could panic." She said she was unhappy about letting him go in on his own, but Dave argued and said he was sure he could talk to him.

"Okay, we've got to get that girl out safely, so whatever you do, tell him if he lets her go it'll be better for him," Anna said as he pulled on the bullet-proof vest she insisted he wear.

Dave was noticeably nervous as he cautiously made his way to the door. Henry had seen him coming and pointed the gun towards the waitress as Dave walked in.

"Stay where you are. Don't come any closer," Henry said looking pale. "Why did you have to come? This is none of your business."

Dave was desperately trying to remain calm, but he could see Henry was bleeding badly. "Of course it's my business. Did you think I didn't know what you were doing?"

"I did it for you."

"But why? Surely we had everything we wanted."

"I only used to do the odd small job. It was fun and I made good money, but when you needed treatment I had to do more to pay for it."

Dave made a move towards him but he pointed his gun to make him stop.

"The police said you should let the girl go."

Henry thought for a moment then turned to the waitress. "Get out now, go on!"

The girl ran out of the door towards a waiting policeman who grabbed her, pulling her to safety.

Dave pleaded with him. "You need to go to hospital. You're losing too much blood."

Henry shook his head. "It's too late for that now." He looked at Dave with sorrow in his eyes. "I'm sorry. I had planned for us to be together much longer." He coughed and slowly collapsed onto the floor. Dave ran over to him as Anna Delaney and two armed policemen burst through the door, but by the time they reached him he was already dead.

Dave slowly turned and walked out of the door where Janine threw her arms around him and they stood and cried together.

Henry's funeral was a quiet affair. Dave had made arrangements for him to be cremated in Palm Springs and apart from himself, Janine and Don, there were no other mourners. The aftermath of the failed robbery at the gallery, and the hostage siege at the diner had led to Henry's apartment being searched by a team of detectives from the international art theft department. They were astonished at the haul of priceless pieces hidden in his room. The value ran into the tens of millions, and luckily they had been recovered before disappearing into the private collections of Henry's shady customers never to be seen again.

Searching his desk, the detectives also found what appeared to be Henry's little black book, which apparently contained the names of all his clients.

There had been some interesting revelations, including one name that surprised everyone. None more so than Janine when Don told her. Vonda Statzler would appear to have been one of Henry's customers. Janine thought back to the first time she'd visited her office, and the impressive array of modern art displayed on the walls. She smiled as she wondered how Vonda was going to talk her way out of that situation.

The three of them were sitting in a café on North Palm Canyon Drive after the ceremony, drinking coffee, when Dave made a startling revelation to his two friends.

"I was responsible for the death of Claudia Inestes. It was my idea."

Don and Janine sat quietly and listened as he told them the whole story. How, from when he found out that she was behind Maltrocorp he had planned to kill her at the mayoral inauguration, but couldn't go through with it because they were there with Pete and Henry. He explained how his friend Claus had constructed a device, which would have triggered a canister of poisonous gas when he played a specific note on the piano and pressed a pedal at the same time. He described how he felt when she came over to the piano and kissed his cheek, unaware she had just narrowly escaped death.

But he knew he could never allow Claudia to get away with it; especially when she had the nerve to announce she would be giving public money to the company of which she was the major shareholder. That was the last straw as far as he was concerned. Once again he contacted Claus and found out he was a trained sniper. It had been easy to find the address of her ranch in Santa Clarita and observe her daily routine. Once they had parked the truck across the drive, all Claus had to do was wait for the driver to stop. And when he did, Claudia had made it even easier by lowering her window to ask what was happening.

When Dave finished Don nodded his head. "I knew from the look on your face at our party. It was only for a fraction of a second, but it said it all. Anyway you've no need to worry. I'm a retired cop now, so what you've just told us will stay with us."

Janine who had been listening, spoke up. "All the same I'd be very careful if you're in the company of Detective Anna Delaney at any point. That woman is a damn nuisance. She was still pestering me about Ray at the party, even though she knew he'd just died."

Don changed the subject. "Janine tells me you and Pete have started writing again. That's got to be good news."

Dave visibly cheered up. "Yeah, he's in the process of getting one of his stables converted to a small recording studio and as soon as it's ready we're gonna be putting some ideas down."

"I've already told Joel, Manny's son about it and he can't wait to hear what you two come up with," Janine said.

"I've not heard him sound so positive in a long while," Dave told them.

"What does Judy have to say about it?" Janine asked.

"Well I think she's realised that music is Pete's life, and there's nothing she says or does that's gonna stop him. Plus his kid, Rick is an awesome talent. You should keep an eye on him, he's gonna be as big as his dad."

CHAPTER FORTY-ONE

Captain Lewis had kept his promise and Fleur was sitting in his office along with Detective Anna Delaney. He'd invited her to spend her holiday at Police Headquarters and she'd astounded them with her knowledge and ability. Anna had taken her out on patrol with her partner Sergeant Joe Budd, and they'd been impressed with how she could remember details of things she'd seen and recall them so easily. Anna thought that if she maintained her enthusiasm she would easily make detective one day.

Fleur was loving every moment and Janine and Don had never seen her so happy. Janine was still unsure about her becoming a cop but Don had no problems with it, and quietly encouraged her as much as he could.

One evening they were eating dinner and Fleur was telling them about her day and what she'd been doing. "I mean it was awesome. Detective Anna took me down to the range and let me fire her gun."

Janine dropped her fork and looked annoyed. "She did what!" she said angrily.

"How did you do?" Don asked, trying to calm down Janine.

"I scored ninety five out of a hundred. Pretty good huh?"

Don was shocked and raised his eyebrows. "Ninety five, are you sure?"

"Yeah, honest. You can ask Captain Lewis. He had the same look on his face when Anna told him."

Janine was still annoyed but asked Don what it all meant.

"Well if that's so, she's in the category of expert marksman. Even I could only score eighty-nine on a good day!"

"I know. Captain Lewis told me," Fleur said grinning.

"Well I still don't like you having anything to do with guns."

"Hey look, it's gonna be a fact of life if she does join the force, so she might as well get used to it now." Don said. "And it's done under strict supervision, am I right?"

Fleur nodded. "I had to wear ear defenders too."

"So what else happened today?" Janine asked changing the subject.

"Oh it was great, I went on a robbery investigation. We went to this office in Santa Monica and I recognised the woman whose paintings had been stolen. She came to our party.

Janine stopped her.

"Hang on a minute. Which woman?"

"She was called Vonda Statzler. Her office had been broken into and a load of paintings stolen, and Anna and Joe went to investigate it and they took me with them."

Janine looked at Don.

"How strange. Vonda's name crops up in Henry's little black book and then shortly after her paintings get stolen. I must give her a call."

"Her office was a mess. Although she didn't seem too upset," Fleur said.

"What did Anna say?"

"Oh, she just asked her what was missing and examined the lock which had been smashed, and said they'd look into it. Funny though. It was if she didn't believe what the woman told her."

Janine called Vonda the following morning.

"Hey Janine how's things? Your girl was down here yesterday. I expect she told you what happened."

"Yeah that's why I'm calling. Is everything alright? Are you OK?"

"The place is a mess but other than that I'm fine. Say, your girl is one smart kid. Tell her if she wants a job in law I'll have her any day. How about we grab a drink sometime? It'd be good to have a catch-up."

"You know what, I was thinking the same thing. What's your diary like this week?"

They agreed to meet the next afternoon and Don raised his eyebrows as she replaced the receiver.

"Are you sure about that? Don't go getting involved, especially where Detective Anna Delaney is involved. And Fleur's not going to be too impressed if your name pops up in the enquiry."

"Don't worry, I'm just intrigued how she's going to wriggle her way out of it."

They adjourned to Rico's bar as soon as Janine arrived, and he immediately set up two Martinis.

"So come on, I'm dying to know how on earth did your name end up in Henry Walton's little black book?"

Vonda took a sip of her Martini. "It's not as bad as it seems really. I bought some paintings off him years ago. All above board I hasten to add. That was before he got into the naughty stuff. I mean I knew what he was up to but never had any further dealings with him." She took another sip of her drink and looked at Janine with a wry grin. "At least that's what I told the cops, and that's what I'm sticking to."

"So what about the paintings you had in your office."

"Now see, that's kind of interesting, because they were all copies. The good stuff is at home locked away."

"So why break in and steal a load of fakes?"

"That's what I've been wondering about. Somebody must have thought it worth the effort. Hey, that detective who came round yesterday is a real hustler. I remember you and her having a bit of a difference of opinion at your party."

"Yeah she's a pushy bitch. Thing is, remember what I told you that time, about my ex-husband? Well she knows; at least she thinks she knows. That's what she was questioning me about at the party. I mean I know he was a bastard, but I don't want him remembered as a murderer."

"Well don't worry, your secret's safe with me." They clinked glasses.

Detective Anna Delaney and her partner Sergeant Joe Budd were sitting at Anna's desk in police headquarters. They'd asked Fleur to join them, and were sharing ideas about their recent visit to Vonda Statzler's office. Anna was puzzled as to why the victim of the robbery hadn't seemed too upset, even though her collection of paintings had been stolen.

Fleur was sitting quietly when she raised her hand to speak, which made Anna and Joe laugh. "What? Oh I'm sorry it's force of habit from school. Anyway I was thinking, perhaps they were fakes or something which is why she wasn't too worried. Maybe it wasn't about the paintings at all."

Anna was thoughtful. "She's a pretty tough attorney by all accounts. It might be worth finding out what cases she's working on at the moment."

Joe suddenly spoke. "I remember reading a book once about this magician who committed crimes, and he used misdirection to make you think he was doing one thing when in fact he was doing something else completely."

"Well it's definitely worth another trip to Miss Statzler's to ask some more questions," Anna said pulling on her coat. "Let's go. You coming Fleur?"

Fleur didn't need a second invitation.

They arrived at Vonda's office just as she and Janine were coming out of Rico's bar a little worse for wear. Luckily Vonda spotted them and they edged back into the bar until the cops left.

"Phew, that could have been embarrassing," Janine said slurring slightly. "Good job Fleur didn't see me like this. I'd have never heard the end of it."

They agreed to meet up again soon, and Janine fell into a taxi.

She was relatively sober by the time Fleur arrived home later that evening and listened as she told them all about her day and their visit to

Vonda's office. She was particularly interested in what she said about how Anna hadn't been convinced by Vonda's story and how Fleur had thought the paintings might be a diversion. She had to admit Vonda was right, Fleur was one smart kid.

Vonda had called her investigator Tony, and they were sitting in her office looking at the spaces on the walls where the paintings had been. The rest of the mess had been cleared up, and she was smoking a cigarette with her feet up on the desk.

She'd hoped Tony might have an idea about what had happened and why, but he was as much in the dark as she was.

He asked her about the current case she was working on, which was a high-profile divorce involving a well-known actor's wife who'd been caught playing around with a football player from the Los Angeles Rams. They'd been photographed in rather compromising positions at his mansion, while her husband was away shooting a film in Europe. Whoever had taken the photos had sent copies to the husband who was suing for divorce. However, the wife, who Vonda was representing was countersuing. She was accusing the husband of having a gay relationship with one of his co-stars in the film, causing her to seek fulfilment elsewhere, and it had started to get messy. The husband in question, Jason Landorr was a heart throb with millions of female admirers, and if these accusations became public knowledge it would almost certainly ruin his career. His wife, Kathy Landorr, an actress herself, was threatening to go on Alan Brookstein's show, and give a 'tell-all' interview revealing her husband's secret. She had told Vonda she had a video as proof which she was prepared to show during the interview.

Tony was suspicious that the burglary was somehow linked to this case, and whoever had raided the office could have thought Vonda was in possession of the video. In truth Vonda doubted there actually was a video, as she had yet to see it; and she suspected Kathy was grandstanding in an attempt to get as much money out of her husband as possible. Her own career had stalled, and marrying him was an act of desperation. She had become a joke within the industry with most directors avoiding her due to her cocaine habit, although her sexual demands were legendary. Many a director had attempted to seduce Kathy Blake, as she was, and left the following morning with the tattered remains of his tail between his legs. Had he still been alive, Ray Law would have testified to that.

The discussion prompted Vonda to call Kathy and ask her to come in to the office with the video, but she'd cried off, claiming she was ill. This made Vonda even more suspicious. She was just pondering her next move when there was a call from Janine.

"Hey Janine, I don't hear from you for ages, then two calls in two days. What's up?"

Janine had been reading the gossip column in the LA Times and spotted a story about rumours of a spat between Jason Landorr and his wife Kathy. She instantly recognised Kathy as the actress who Pete had been having a high-profile relationship with until their dramatic row in the VIP lounge at LAX. She explained how Kathy had manipulated the situation with Pete to get on the Johnny Carlton show in attempt to boost her flagging career.

Vonda was listening and writing down notes as Janine talked. It would appear her client was a serial loser moving from one meal ticket to the next. She wondered if the footballer, Mitchell Morris Jr. was aware he was being used just like the others. It also occurred to her that Tony could be right. Jason Landorr was renowned for protecting his assets, and if he thought there was a video in existence which could jeopardise his career he would stop at nothing to get his hands on it.

She thanked Janine for the information and called Tony.

Kathy Landorr had no intention of going to Vonda Statzler's office. She was on her way to see her current lover at his mansion to drink Cristal champagne and have sex with the help of some Grade A cocaine she'd just had delivered. The sham of a marriage to her faggot of a husband Jason was over. In reality it never really was a marriage. He needed a female on his arm to ward off the persistent rumours about his sexuality, and she desperately needed credibility. Her stock was at an all-time low after being evicted from her house in Malibu. Luckily she'd been in the right place at the right time when she met Jason Landorr at an awards ceremony, and was photographed getting cosy with him at the party afterwards. One thing led to another and she was suddenly Mrs. Jason Landorr. The press went crazy and she was back in the limelight again. The trouble was, once the nuptials were over the real Jason Landorr soon revealed himself as a selfish, highly opinionated gay, who surrounded himself with a constant supply of sycophants who attended to his every whim. Kathy soon tired of this, and even though she'd signed a pre-nuptial non-disclosure agreement, she started to look around for someone to share her sexual appetite with. Enter Mitchell Morris Jr.; blond, good looking, a star half-back she met at a charity event in aid of the homeless. They found themselves seated next to each other during the dinner, and when Kathy made him laugh by asking about his tight end, his offer to show it to her was enthusiastically accepted.

Mitchell was a powerfully built, six foot four athlete who according to his official biography didn't drink alcohol, smoke cigarettes and heaven forbid indulge in drugs of any kind. So when Kathy took a wrap of cocaine from her handbag and chopped out a long line for herself on his black marble topped coffee table, she knew she was in for a long night when he asked her for the same.

Opening a champagne bottle and grabbing two flutes, he took her hand and led her outside to his bubbling hot tub on the terrace. She stepped out of her evening dress and slid into the warm water as he followed her in. They sat drinking the chilled champagne when she took a deep breath and lowered her head under the water, taking him in her mouth. She worked on him for what seemed an age before breaking the surface gasping for air and was about to carry on when he lifted her up and lowered her down on him making her squeal. She wrapped her arms around his neck as he slowly screwed her deeply with a relentless rhythm until she cried out, experiencing a shuddering orgasm. She was breathlessly holding onto him, when she realised he was still hard and couldn't believe his stamina as he started again. She was concentrating so much on his pleasure, when he finally began to get excited she found herself coming again, and their screams of ecstasy shattered the stillness of the night.

Eventually they climbed out of the tub and kissed still dripping wet, wrapped large fluffy towels around themselves and padded back to the lounge; unaware of the long-range lens trained on them from the bushes at the edge of his garden, capturing their every move.

CHAPTER FORTY-TWO

In the Warwickshire countryside, one of Kathy's ex-lovers, Pete Peterson, was sitting in his newly finished recording studio. He had received a package of tapes from Dave Sanchez over in Palm Springs with his song ideas and now he was recording his guitar parts alongside Dave's keyboards. It was a new way of working for him, but he was enjoying the freedom to experiment without the pressure of being in a big studio costing lots of money.

He had also started writing with his son Rick, who being from the younger generation, had mastered the recording technique instantly without having to constantly refer to the instruction manual like his dad. This really miffed Pete, but he accepted it and admired the way his son was rapidly becoming an amazing musician. He could see so much of himself in him, but he was streets ahead of Pete when he was that age.

At the same time he'd noticed what a gifted rider his daughter Lucy was becoming. She and Judy had been attending all the local shows and gymkhanas quietly racking up an impressive collection of cups and rosettes. His old trainer Caren, who now worked for his friend Monty had encouraged her, and Lucy spent every weekend learning under her watchful eye, resulting in her becoming recognised as one of the most talented upcoming youngsters in the country. By default Judy had become her manager, driver and biggest fan taking her to all the events, congratulating her when she won and commiserating when she didn't.

Pete and Dave had already written half an album's worth of songs and their creativity was in full flow once again. Over in Los Angeles Janine and Don had heard some of the rough mixes and were excited. It was early days, but she could sense the beginnings of a major comeback album. She knew Pete's health issues would always be a problem, but in her dreams she could see one last show at the LA Memorial Coliseum. She didn't know how she was going to do it, but knew she was going to give it one hell of a go.

Jason Landorr was sitting in his trailer on the set of his latest movie when he received the large brown envelope containing the photographs. He spread them out on the table examining each of the prints closely. He smiled at his assistant. "Well I'll give him one thing, he's certainly a big boy!"

They both raised their eyebrows and laughed.

"Send the guy his money and tell him he did a good job. And put a thousand-dollar bonus in. I always appreciate good workmanship."

He collected the prints up and returned them to the envelope. Part one of his plan to get rid of his money-grabbing bitch of a wife was taken care of. Now all he had to do was make sure this supposed video was destroyed, and he knew just the man to do it.

Dawson worked part time for attorney Melissa Thomson-Howes, but also undertook private commissions, especially if the price was right. His main job was as a private detective, but he could lend his hand to most things if necessary. He preferred to stay on the right side of the law, although he was always prepared to make an exception. When Jason Landorr called he had a feeling it would be one of those times.

He'd had experiences with Vonda Statzler before, the most recent being when Melissa had represented the husband of one of her clients. That had ended in defeat, but he wasn't one to bear grudges. However, this particular task was more challenging. Jason had told him about a video tape that his wife was planning to use against him. He assumed it would be in Vonda's office as she was representing the wife and wanted Dawson to find and destroy it.

He'd told him to make it look like an ordinary burglary so there was no suspicion of him being involved. Dawson knew Vonda collected paintings, so if they were stolen it would cover up the disappearance of the tape. He'd sat in his car outside her office waiting for her to leave, and after watching her lock up and drive away he broke in and made a thorough search for the tape. Unfortunately apart from a couple of rock concerts there was no video. He made sure to mess the place up before taking the dreadful paintings she had on the walls. Dawson was no art expert but he thought they looked like they'd been painted by a five-year-old kid. He'd stashed them in the trunk of his car and driven off to report back to his client.

Jason Landorr was livid when Dawson called to say he couldn't find the tape. "There is no way I'll let her go on a TV chat show and show that video. I'll see her dead before I allow that to happen" he'd said.

Dawson hadn't liked how the tone of the conversation had changed. Burglary was one thing but he drew the line at murder.

Kathy Landorr was on her way to Mitchell Morris Jr's mansion looking forward to another session of outrageous sex. She had always thought she could screw, but this guy was an animal. Powered by regular lines of coke the last time she was there, he'd had her just about anywhere and everywhere they could find in his mansion, and she was going back for more when her attorney had called, bugging her to see the video she'd told her about, but she wasn't prepared to reveal her prized possession just yet.

She'd received a package containing a poor-quality video from 'a friend' and although partially blurred, one of the two male participants in the hard-core sex scene was definitely her husband Jason Landorr. After watching it through and realising its value she had stored it in a safe-deposit box until it was needed; hopefully when the TV company signed the contract for her appearance on the Alan Brookstein Show.

Her taxi pulled into the drive of the football player's mansion where she was confronted by a scrum of reporters and photographers. For Kathy this was just like the old times being hounded by the paparazzi, and she preened in front of the cameras offering "No comment" to the questions being shouted at her.

The front door opened and she was pulled inside by a furious Mitchell.

"What the hell do you think you're doing?" he yelled at her, his face red with anger.

"Don't worry, babe. I can handle them," Kathy replied calmly.

"Don't worry! Have you any idea what this is going to do to my reputation?" He was still shouting.

Kathy looked at him and gave him a peck on the cheek as she slipped her coat off. "Funny. I don't recall you being bothered about your reputation when you fucked my brains out the other night after snorting half my stash, babe!"

Mitchell stood staring at her as she poured herself a glass of champagne and flopped down on one of his white suede sofas.

"And anyway, a bit of publicity never did anyone any harm. I suggest you pour yourself a glass of Cristal, sit down and relax. Once they realise they're not getting any more they'll all scuttle off to whatever hole they crawled out from, and we can continue where we left off. I had a delivery of some rather special blow this morning which I think you're going to enjoy."

"Oh yeah, these arrived earlier, with a note saying copies had been sent to The Rams and the press." Mitchell handed her an envelope.

Kathy took the prints out and flicked through them.

"Damn! This is Jason's doing. Look I'm sorry, I didn't mean for you to be involved. But you were just so hot at that dinner and when you offered to show me your tight end..."

There was a silence then they both laughed.

"Maybe you're right. It's about time I dropped that 'whiter than white' shit and became the 'real' me," he said downing a glass of champagne in one.

She reached out her hand and he scooped her off the sofa carrying her up the sweeping staircase towards his bedroom.

"Now, what was that about continuing from where we left off."

She felt like Vivien Leigh in *Gone With The Wind* as she wrapped her arms around his neck.

It was dark outside and they were lying naked in his bed. The effects of the last lines of cocaine had worn off and they were both asleep when Kathy rolled over and partially waking up thought she smelled something burning. She lay for a few seconds before realising there definitely was a strong smell. She sat up and shook Mitchell to rouse him. He slowly came to his senses and suddenly became aware of what she was saying to him.

"Fire! Mitchell; there's a fire. Wake up!"

He jumped out of bed and ran to the door and was about to pull it open but stopped. He remembered seeing a film where someone had opened a door and the flames had created a fireball sucking up all the oxygen. He ran instead to his bathroom and quickly threw a towel in the bath soaking it with water, then jammed it along the bottom of the door. He told Kathy to follow him on to the balcony.

As they stood outside they could see all around them his mansion was ablaze. He climbed over the rail and got hold of the wooden trellis which supported an old Wisteria. It was a long drop to the terrace down below but it seemed sturdy enough and he reached out for Kathy's hand to help her. There was a loud 'whomp' as the bedroom door collapsed and the flames burst into the room just as she climbed over the edge. He almost lost her grip, but managed to hold on and pull her to him. With her legs wrapped around his waist he slowly climbed down. They could hear the sound of sirens in the distance as they stood looking at his mansion being reduced to a smouldering shell.

Vonda and Tony were sitting in Rico's watching the news report of the fire, when Rico called over there was a phone call for Tony. He stood listening as his contact from the LAPD told him 'off the record' they had a witness who'd seen a car driving away from Vonda's office on the night of the burglary. The plates were registered to a friend of his...Dawson.

Tony thanked him and put the phone down telling Vonda he had to run an errand. He drove across town to a bar he knew Dawson used, and found him sitting in a booth on his own. He sat down next to him and pushed a gun into his side. "Hey Dawson, I think you and I need to talk." He dug the gun hard into his ribs and Dawson flinched as Tony stood up and beckoned for him to follow.

Outside Dawson held up his hands. "Look Tony, I'm sorry. Jason Landorr wanted the tape and told me to make it look like a normal robbery. But I mean, those paintings...my kid could have done better. I had nothing to do with the fire though, I swear. You should know me better than that. I don't do murder, no way!"

Tony did believe him. He was right, they both bent the rules a little now and then, but neither had ever committed murder. "So you got any idea who did it?"

"No, but I tell you, Jason was one pissed guy when I told him I didn't find the video. Said there was no way he'd let Kathy do that TV show, and he'd see her dead before he allowed it to happen."

After the blaze at Mitchell's, Kathy had gone into hiding; Vonda had booked her into a motel under an assumed name. The Fire Department had carried out an investigation and their report confirmed the fire had been started deliberately. In the meantime the producers of The Alan Brookstein Show had been in touch with Vonda to agree the terms for Kathy to appear. Suddenly it was a massive scoop. The press was buzzing with the news that the truth about Jason Landorr was finally going to be revealed, live on TV.

In his trailer on the set in Europe, Jason Landorr was beside himself with anger. He threw the phone across the room after his agent back in LA told him Kathy had been booked to appear on Alan Brookstein's show. His personal assistant rushed in to find out what the problem was and found Jason shaking with rage.

"Get me that idiot who was supposed to sort her out."

The assistant found the phone on the floor and dialled a number. When a voice answered he passed the receiver to Jason.

"Now listen to what I say you incompetent prick. You have one more chance to redeem yourself. Screw this up and I'll find you, and believe me you don't want me to have to find you! I want my wife dealt with. I don't care how, just so long as she doesn't appear on that TV show. You got that?"

The voice at the other end said he understood and Jason passed the phone back to his assistant.

Putting aside their differences, Tony and Dawson had joined forces and were taking turns to watch Kathy. She was going crazy cooped up in the motel room, but Vonda had managed to pacify her by telling her how much she'd negotiated for her fee to appear on the show. She'd also managed to smuggle Mitchell in for a night, which had kept her suitably occupied and put a smile on her face. It was still there when Vonda had picked her up to fetch the tape from her safety deposit box.

So far Vonda had doubted there actually was a tape, but when Kathy walked out of the bank and handed it over she finally breathed a sigh of relief. She passed it to Tony who drove to the TV station, where he gave it to the technician who immediately made a copy. The show was scheduled for broadcasting later that night and preparations were already underway.

Dawson had accompanied Vonda and Kathy back to her office and they went through the contract, making sure she understood everything that had been agreed. Tony had called to say they had reviewed the video, and although it would have to be heavily censored there was enough footage they could legally use; enough to substantiate Kathy's claims. He said he'd checked the security arrangements at the studios and everything seemed to be fine, but that he and Dawson would be there anyway.

The man Jason Landorr had spoken to on the phone had entered the studios earlier that morning dressed as a cleaner, using a false ID. He'd managed to blend in, making sure he always looked busy whenever anyone gave him more than a fleeting glance. As the time for the recording approached people around him became engrossed in their duties, and he'd slipped out of his cleaner's outfit and into that of a security guard using another fake ID. He'd spent his time roaming the corridors checking exits and doing his best to become anonymous.

An hour before showtime Dawson drove up with Vonda and Kathy. Tony met them at the door and they were whisked through reception straight into the Green Room, where Alan Brookstein was waiting. He stood as they entered and came over to give Kathy a hug and kiss.

Kathy introduced Vonda, and they all relaxed as Alan poured them a glass of champagne and told Kathy what he wanted to ask her, and how they would introduce the video.

Vonda sipped her drink and sat watching, admiring the way Kathy was so calm, and how nothing seemed to phase her; then remembered she'd done all this so many times before. Although it had to be said, not quite as intense as tonight.

The make-up lady came in and apologised for interrupting, but needed Kathy to come with her.

As they went out, Tony, who was standing in the doorway noticed a security guard who he hadn't seen earlier. He watched as the guard followed them down to the make-up room, and out of curiosity went to check. He called to the man to stop and the immediate response was dramatic. The man turned, pulling a gun and firing a shot which caught Tony in the arm.

Alerted by the noise Dawson ran down the corridor from the opposite direction, just as the gunman pushed Kathy and the make-up woman into the room. He fired another shot at Dawson forcing him to dive for cover and ducked in behind them. Tony was leaning on the wall checking his arm as the other security guards arrived, and he quickly told them what had happened.

Inside the make-up room the man waved his gun and told the two women to sit down, while he turned and looked back down the corridor to check what was happening. He could hear the real guards approaching and fired another warning shot in their direction which made them stop. He turned to see if there was another way out but there wasn't. He was trapped.

He told Kathy to stand up and come over to him, but was distracted by more noise from the corridor. Instead of doing as she was told, she grabbed the nearest thing she could find; a fire extinguisher hanging on the wall, and blasted him with the contents. Taken by surprise, the gunman put his hands up in front of his face and stumbled backwards out of the room; giving Dawson the opportunity to pounce and wrestle him to the ground. Tony appeared seconds later followed by the other security guards, and the attacker was swiftly overpowered.

At the front of the building, unaware of the drama unfolding backstage, the audience for the show was filing into reception. The sound of police sirens filled the air, and suddenly two LAPD officers ran through the entrance with their guns drawn. One of the guards shouted to them, and led the way to the office where the gunman had been taken.

Tony's injury was luckily just a flesh wound, and he and Dawson were standing over him as the door burst open and Kathy ran in. She slapped the face of her attacker and started screaming at him demanding to know who had told him to do it. He was refusing to speak until she hit him with her fist, and he mumbled a name. She stood back and demanded he speak louder or she would hit him again, and knowing he was beaten the man gave the name of her husband. Jason Landorr.

The two police officers arrived just as he said the name and were about to take him away when Tony stopped them.

"Did you set the fire?" The man nodded. "On whose orders?"

"Jason Landorr's."

He turned to the officers and noticed Alan Brookstein standing in the doorway. "Looks like you got one hell of a story here." He flinched as Kathy gave him and Dawson a hug.

There was a voice from behind them in the corridor.

"Five minutes Alan, are you ready?"

"Oh yes I'm ready. The question is, is Hollywood ready?"

Showtime, and Alan Brookstein had walked on set to a raucous reception. He was all smiles, and when the intro music finished he went into his opening script; then he introduced his guest Kathy Landorr.

There were a few boos amongst the applause as she sat down in an easy chair opposite Alan. She crossed her legs nonchalantly and sipped a glass of water from the table beside her. The cameras moved in for a close-up, and considering what had just happened she looked remarkably relaxed.

Alan started by asking her about her early career, and even mentioned her affair with Pete Peterson of which she said she had fond memories.

There was a perceptible change in the atmosphere when he mentioned her husband Jason Landorr. He sensed her bristle slightly, and using his journalistic expertise knew the time was right to push her. The audience had picked up on the vibe too.

"So how long after you were married did you realise something was wrong?"

"About five minutes."

Alan Brookstein looked at her, shocked by the answer.

She laughed. "Actually it was less than that. Look I knew he was gay before I married him; he needed a female on his arm to deny all the rumours and I needed…" she paused. "Well, I was in all kinds of financial trouble, and it was the perfect solution. And he said no matter what happened I'd be taken care of, so I thought, 'What the hell, let's do it.' Trouble is I didn't bargain on all the baggage. His demanding this, that and the other, and trust me there was plenty of the other. But not with me!"

The audience laughed, but Alan wasn't finished yet. "So let's come to the video. Tell me about that."

Kathy paused and took another drink deliberately drawing out the moment.

"Look, I couldn't do it anymore. The pretence at award ceremonies. Posing for photos. It was all fake and I wanted out, but he said no. I didn't think I was being unreasonable, but he started threatening me with lawyers and then it got out of hand."

"What do you mean by out of hand?"

"I received this video in the post from 'an admirer', and once I'd watched it I thought, here's my way out. When I told him he went crazy and refused to discuss it. The next thing he goes off to film in Europe, and someone burgles my attorney's office looking for the tape. Except it's not there. And OK so I'll admit, I had a scene with someone. Nothing wrong with that, two consenting adults, but suddenly he's setting fire to the guy's place trying to kill me."

"And do you have proof of this?"

"Yeah, the arsonist just tried to kill me backstage, and admitted setting fire to Mitchell's place on Jason Landorr's instructions."

There were shouts coming from the audience. Some females were shouting "Liar" but Kathy ignored them.

"I know it must be a shock for you fans, but believe me it's true."

The shouts were getting louder and Alan allowed them to carry on for a while before raising his hands to quieten them.

"OK so we've heard what Kathy's had to say, and now let's take a look at the video. This was brought in this morning; our lawyers looked at it and advised us to censor certain sections but here it is, and I'll leave you to make up your own minds. The screen at the back of the set was suddenly filled with the slightly blurred images of two men having sex.

Then one of them spoke. "Oh God Jay, that is so good."

"You like that? Tell me you like that!" It was unmistakably Jason Landorr's voice.

There was a scream from the audience. Nooooooo!"

The same voice spoke again more aggressively. "You like it when Jason Landorr ***** you. Yeah?" The expletive had been bleeped.

There was pandemonium in the audience as women were standing up shouting. The screen went blank and Alan Brookstein appealed for quiet. Finally he spoke. "Well I don't know about you, but I think that's pretty conclusive. Obviously we're going to contact Mr. Landorr's representatives and give him the opportunity to come on the show."

Kathy was sitting quite still. She hadn't looked at the screen while the film played, but motioned to the host she'd like to speak. She looked out at the audience.

"Believe me, I didn't want to do this. He could have settled it amicably. But he tried to kill me. Twice! So I'm not going to apologise because he deserves everything that happens to him."

She stood up and walked off the set, some of the women in the audience still shouting after her, although the majority stood and applauded.

The following morning Vonda had just arrived in her office as the phone started to ring. She was wearing a David Bowie Ziggy Stardust T-shirt and jeans and lighting a cigarette she picked up the receiver. She listened for a couple of minutes without saying a word and put the phone down.

"Holy Shit!"

She picked up the receiver again and dialled a number. Kathy picked up on the fifth ring sounding slightly out of breath.

"Is Mitchell there with you?" Vonda asked.

"Yeah why?"

"You might want to prepare yourself for what I'm about to say."

"For fuck's sake Vonda what's up?"

"Jason Landorr was found dead in his trailer last night. He'd hung himself. He'd been sent a copy of the show. The tape was still in the player."

"Oh God!"

"So I have a few questions for you. Did Jason have any dependents?"

"He had a sister, but she died a few years ago."

"Did he leave a will?"

"Not that I'm aware."

"We'll have to do a thorough search."

"So what does this mean?"

"Well if he left no will, and you're his sole beneficiary, looks like you could be a very rich lady."

Vonda pulled the receiver away from her ear as Kathy screamed.

CHAPTER FORTY-THREE

The detective was sitting at her desk when the phone rang. "Delaney."

An English voice asked. "Is that Detective Anna Delaney of the Los Angeles Police Department?"

"Sure is. Who wants to know?"

"Oh, hello. My name is George Thompson, although people usually call me Ginger. Anyway I'm sorry to bother you, but I'm a forensic scientist based in Birmingham in the UK and a strange thing has just happened. I've been analysing a routine blood sample, and the results flagged up a link to one of your cases."

Anna intrigued asked, "Really, which one?"

"Hang on I have it here. Ah yes, the murder of a Laura Weiss. Was that your case?"

"Yes it was."

"I'm sorry it's taken so long to contact you, but we're still a bit in the dark ages over here with DNA tests and the like, but anyway as I say I seem to have a match to the blood sample you found on a wall."

Anna was trying not to sound excited.

"That's great, er, Ginger. Can you tell me who the match is?"

"Ah yes now this is where it gets strange. You see it's an old colleague of mine. Ray Law."

Anna almost dropped the phone, but asked him if he could repeat what he'd just said.

"Yes. Ray Law. He was a DCI here in Birmingham before he left and moved to California. But he was involved in a hit and run accident over here and sadly died. Does this make any sense?"

"Er, yes. Yes it does. It might just be the missing link I've been looking for. Do you think you could send me your results?"

"Yes of course. I'll have my assistant fax them over."

"Thank you Ginger, you've been a great help."

She put the phone down and punched the air as she stood up and walked over to the Captain's office.

He looked up as she knocked and came in. "You like the cat who got the cream. What's up?"

She could hardly contain herself but managed to sit down and explain what had just happened.

Instead of being as happy as Anna, he looked perturbed. Over her shoulder he could see his old friend Don Rosario and Janine walking into the office with their daughter Fleur. "I think it's great news that you could have finally solved the case, but look behind you. Are you sure you want to be the one to destroy his memory?"

She looked around and went to answer him, but he stopped her.

"For once I think we could use a little discretion and keep this between us, don't you?"

"But he murdered her. And not only that, tried to destroy the evidence."

"I know, I know. But he was one of ours, and I just think maybe it would be better to leave it as it is. You know the truth, and I've a feeling deep down so does Janine. So why can't we keep it like that."

Fleur saw the two of them in the office and waved with a big smile on her face.

Anna turned back to him. "OK. You know what? Maybe I didn't get that call after all." She stood up and opened the door and said hello to Don and Janine, and beckoned for Fleur to follow her. "C'mon kid, let's go find Joe, we got a robbery to check out."

Chief forensic scientist Ginger Thompson was sitting in his office at

Lloyd House, West Midlands Police Headquarters, when there was a knock on the door, and DCI Matt Burgess walked in.

"Sorry to bother you Ginger but I just heard about your conversation with LAPD."

"Ah yes, that was a tricky call to make especially when it's one of our own, but sadly had to be done. However, there was something that I've since found out that maybe him dying like that was a blessing in disguise."

Matt Burgess looked at him questioningly. "Oh?"

"Yes, the tests on his organs came back showing he had advanced cirrhosis of the liver. He would have only lasted at the most a couple of years. Which is strange, as I checked on the medical he had when he joined the force and everything was quite normal."

"From what I heard he was hitting the bottle pretty hard, especially since he came back from LA. I went to see him when he played at The Lexxicon but never got to meet him. It's such a shame how it ended like that. He was a really good singer you know."

"Well this time I'm keeping the information between the two of us."

"Who did you speak to at the LAPD?"

Ginger explained he'd called the detective whose name was on the original evidence log, a Detective Anna Delaney. She hadn't given anything away during their short conversation, but he thought she sounded pretty pleased.

"I felt really bad that it had taken so long. But the fact his organs and blood sample had been kept in storage meant I could revisit the examination, even though his body had been cremated. You went to the funeral didn't you?"

Matt looked forlorn. "Yes, it was sad really. We were good mates when he was here, and when he came back for Bobby McGregor's trial. Trouble with Ray was his dick ruled his brain!"

Matt thought back to the night he took Ray to The King's Head for a pint and turned his back to speak to a friend. The next thing he saw was

Ray leaving with the venerable Ms. Julia Davies and that was that. And the time when he'd told Matt, in confidence, he'd been warned by his boss George Williams to be careful with Janine Fortuna. 'And he ended up marrying her. Lucky Sod!'

"It was supposed to be a quiet service, but word got out, and loads of women turned up all claiming they knew him and how he'd told them they could be in his film. Which was a joke, because there never was a film. Typical Ray. He was a sucker for a pretty face! Nice to see Pete Peterson there though. He even performed one of Ray's songs. It was called 'The Love Game' and he'd slowed it down and played it on acoustic guitar. I don't think there was a dry eye in the church."

Janine and Don were sitting in Captain Lewis' office.

He'd asked them to come in to talk about their daughter, Fleur. He waited until she left with Anna and her partner Joe.

"You know Don I gotta tell you, she's the brightest kid I've seen in years. Intelligent, quick, tough and shoots like a goddam marksman. I know you haven't decided yet what you want her to do, but trust me she'll make a first-class cop."

Janine had expressed her doubts to Don on numerous occasions, but had to admit her daughter was never happier than when she was on her way to police headquarters. She had struck up a strong friendship with Anna, and even though Janine had a problem with the detective and her attitude, she couldn't help but notice the chemistry between them.

Unbeknownst to Janine, Don and his old boss had been regularly talking about Fleur, and the Captain had said how she was a really popular character around the building. Never afraid to ask questions, and often surprising people with her knowledge and understanding despite her age. But it was her ability to look at situations from another angle that was so intriguing. He told Don he would make sure she was fast-tracked to junior detective if she joined the force and passed all her exams. All they had to do now was convince Janine. So it was a shock to Don, when on their way home she turned to him and said she didn't have a problem if that's what Fleur wanted to do. It made sense since her original father was a cop and now her new dad, Don had been a cop, and who was she to stand in her way. They decided to tell her their decision as soon as Anna dropped her home.

Their beautiful daughter squealed with delight when they told her their decision and hugged and kissed them. There were tears of happiness when she finally went to bed, although standing on the roof top patio looking out over the ocean Janine couldn't help hoping she'd made the right decision.

CHAPTER FORTY-FOUR

Pete Peterson had been having similar thoughts to Janine about his two children. Rick was becoming an accomplished musician, especially now he had access to the recording studio Pete had built in the old stable block, and although he was doing well at school, his only ambition was to be a musician like his dad. And who was Pete to say he couldn't.

He felt sorry for his daughter Lucy that she didn't get the same attention as her brother, but Lucy didn't seem to mind. She loved riding, and was becoming well known in her own right; there was talk she could get into the English show jumping team. She wasn't gifted academically but made up for it with her equestrian talent.

But Pete's health was still a cause for concern, and he constantly infuriated his doctor by missing his check-ups and insisting he wasn't going to give up his drinking. He had promised to reduce the amount of red wine he was consuming though.

The writing with Dave Sanchez was going well, and although slow at times they were gradually compiling a collection of songs good enough for a new album. Dave was completely cured of the mystery virus thanks to the treatment he'd had; paid for by the ill-gotten gains of his late partner Henry Walton. He'd moved back to LA after Henry died. He no longer feared reprisals from the Maltrocorp situation especially as the mayor Claudia Inestes was also dead. He now rented a small apartment in Venice Beach, not far from Pete's first place. It was in a block where the late Jim Morrison had lived, and he was happily getting back in the swing of things.

He regularly communicated with Janine and Don playing them whichever latest song he and Pete had just finished. They'd already secured a deal with Westoria Records and Manny Oberstein's son Joel, who now ran the company after his father retired, was patiently waiting for the finished tracks of the so far untitled album.

Meanwhile Manny was working with Don and Janine in their promotion company. They had secretly been discussing a plan that Janine had suggested, which if it came to fruition could make them all very rich.

The only problem was it relied on one person, and that person was seriously ill. Pete Peterson.

Janine wanted to do one last concert with Pete as a farewell to his fans. Her dream was for him to play one of the biggest shows Los Angeles had ever seen. At the Memorial Coliseum. She'd already spoken to a film company, who wanted to broadcast the show live on network television as well as filming it for DVD. It would also be released as a double album packaged with the studio recording. She'd tentatively mentioned it to Dave who thought it was a great idea, but had yet to work out how to approach Pete. He certainly seemed to be enjoying working again, but so far only in the studio. She was going to have to pick the right time. She knew if she could sit down with him he would do it. But then she would have to convince Judy, who was fiercely protective of him and acutely aware of how ill he really was. The only way to do it was to fly over and meet them both face to face.

It struck her that it was years since the last time she was in the UK. Visiting Pete in London and then the disastrous Birmingham trip to surprise Ray. And what a surprise it was. Who'd have thought everything would have turned out like it had? Thankfully time was a great healer, and now with a wonderful family of her own she finally felt like things were right. Her promotion company with Don and Manny Oberstein was becoming really successful, and her daughter Fleur was now a junior detective in the LAPD having aced her entry exams. True to his word, Captain Lewis had overseen her progress, and she had become the youngest junior detective in the force's history. Her dad was so proud of her, and knew had her real parents still been alive they would have felt the same way.

Janine had discussed her visit to Pete with Don and Manny, and all were in agreement she should do everything possible to get his agreement; and as she sat in the upstairs lounge of the British Airways 747 sipping her champagne she felt confident. Don and Manny had encouraged her to fly Concorde, but that would have meant flying to New York before catching the supersonic jet, because it was banned from flying overland. And anyway she was quite happy relaxing in her First Class seat, catching up on new films she hadn't had chance to watch at home. Judy had insisted on meeting her at Heathrow, and she was sure she would be getting a grilling from her before she met Pete. She was looking forward to returning to the house that her and Gerry had once owned, and meeting Pete's family, who like Fleur were growing up so fast. Dave Sanchez had already told her all about Pete's talented son Rick, and then there was Lucy his daughter, the budding equestrian star. She was so proud of Judy and how she'd dealt with everything. It couldn't have been easy reading about the father of your child and his many public relationships whilst he was in America, and you were on your own back in the UK. But to her credit she'd dealt with it all, including managing the top club in Birmingham as well as creating one of the most highly rated agencies in the country.

Janine had managed to get some sleep on the flight, so felt pretty good as they made their way to Judy's Mercedes. It was a top of the range saloon and as they swept out of the multi-storey car park she felt herself relaxing back into the soft leather seat.

"I'm not sure whether you've had a wasted journey," Judy said as they pulled on to the motorway. "Pete's GP is pretty adamant that he should be taking things easy. And I'm not too keen on it myself if I have to be honest."

Janine had known it wasn't going to be easy, but already sensed she would have to use all her powers of persuasion if she was going to swing this. She was about to tell Judy her plan, but decided to feign tiredness until she could get her and Pete together. She actually fell asleep and woke up only as Judy turned into the drive up to the house. She brushed a tear from her eye as she remembered the first time Gerry had taken her to see it, and how proud he'd been with his suit of armour in the hall. Pete had met them at the door and welcomed her in, and surprise, surprise, there it was, still in exactly the same place at the bottom of the sweeping staircase. Rick and Lucy were also in the hall waiting to meet her, and after all the hugs and kisses they went into the huge lounge which had a roaring fire in the inglenook fireplace. Remarkably it was not much different from the last time Janine had been there. The decor had changed, but the layout was exactly the same and she felt immediately at home.

The first thing she noticed was how thin Pete had got. He never was overweight, but now he was almost skeletal. Dave Sanchez hadn't mentioned this weight loss, and it came as a shock to Janine who suddenly thought that this whole idea might not be as easy as she imagined. But in himself Pete seemed fine. He sat in an armchair with a glass of red wine, and enthused about how well the writing was going with Dave. He promised to show Janine his new studio later just as Judy walked in and announced dinner was ready. She and Lucy had prepared a beef stew with fresh local vegetables which Janine had to admit smelled wonderful, considering she hadn't eaten anything since last night on the flight. It was every bit as good as it promised, and she gratefully accepted a second helping. She noticed Pete only ate a small portion, washing it down with another glass of wine.

After the meal Pete grabbed her hand and took her out to see his new recording studio along with Rick. She remembered how the stables had originally looked, but now they were completely different since the fire. Pete opened the door to his state-of-the-art setup and ushered her in. Rick sat down at the desk and was instantly in control. She watched as father and son worked in perfect unison, and was enveloped by the sound of Pete back to his best. The hairs on her neck stood up and she found herself smiling as one after another she listened to great new songs.

She could tell by the look on his face that Pete Peterson was back, and better than ever. It was a more mature sound which perfectly reflected where he was with his life.

He looked her in the eye. "So the question is what happens next? I know you well enough that you haven't flown all the way over here to compliment me on the new songs. You have a plan, I can tell. So let's hear it."

Janine stood up and wished she could have a cigarette, but Pete had given up smoking and it would have been wrong. "OK. We've already got the offer of a release on the album from Westoria, but I want to do something that will set you up financially for the rest of your life."

Pete looked intrigued. "Go on."

"The biggest concert LA as ever seen at the Memorial Coliseum filmed and broadcast live. Released as a double album and DVD. I've already spoken to everyone concerned and they're ready to give the green light. It's all down to you."

Pete sat back and let out a long breath. He looked at Rick who was sitting listening intently.

"Well I'll tell you the first problem. Judy. She's gonna say I'm not well enough to do even one gig, never mind fly to the States."

Janine was about to say something but he stopped her. "But that's not insurmountable. What d'you say Rick?"

Rick looked at his dad and then at Janine. "She can be pretty stubborn at times. But it sounds really cool."

Pete carried on. "There's a couple of things I would have to insist on though."

Janine waited for him to continue.

"Firstly I'd want my old band. Dave, Marshall and Randy. And also my boy here. He needs to be there with me."

Janine nodded her head. "I don't see any of that as a problem."

"And secondly I'd want the rest of the family there too."

Janine leaned over and kissed his cheek. "You know this is going to be the biggest ever. But what about Judy?"

"Leave Judy to me."

"Have you got a title for the album yet ?"

"I didn't have, but I've just thought of it; 'One Last Encore'."

CHAPTER FORTY-FIVE

Don had noticed Fleur wasn't herself recently and broached the subject over dinner. Janine was still in the UK with Pete, and the two of them were sharing a pizza. Fleur had got home late and was unusually quiet. "How's things going?" he asked.

She shrugged her shoulders as she picked at a slice of pepperoni.

He persevered, sensing there was something she was bottling up. "Any new cases?"

She shook her head and took a drink of her Coke.

Don decided to continue to push her. "Look, if there's something on your mind you should get it out into the open; maybe I can help?"

She sat without speaking for a while then finally she said, "It's some of the older guys at headquarters. They're always making fun of me. They call me 'The Rookie' and seem to like winding me up all the time."

"Just ignore them. There's always jealousy especially when they see a young girl doing well."

"Yeah, well they wouldn't have done it if my dad were alive!"

The minute she said it she saw the crestfallen look on Don's face, and knew she'd made a huge mistake. Desperate to try and salvage the situation she jumped up and ran round the table, throwing her arms around him. "I'm so sorry, I didn't mean that to come out like it did. You know I love you and Janine and I wouldn't want anyone else in the world to be my parents."

Don hugged her back. Her outburst had hurt him, but in the back of his mind he knew what she'd had to endure. "I know honey, and we both realise how difficult it's been for you at times, but remember we'll always be here for you. You are part of our lives now and nothing will ever stop us loving you as our own."

They were interrupted by the phone ringing, and Don's face as he answered it told Fleur it was Janine. In his usual casual manner Don said everything was fine and he and Fleur were having dinner. He didn't mention her problems or what had just happened, and finished by saying they were looking forward to her return. He gave Fleur a big smile, and said Janine was tying up a few loose ends and would be back within a week. "She sends her love and hopes everything's going great."

Janine had called home from her bedroom in Pete's mansion. She looked around her and remembered back to when she'd first moved in with Gerry and how it had felt designing the rooms, and was happy that it would always be a memory. She was tired but elated after finally persuading Judy that everything would be taken care of during Pete's trip to Los Angeles, and they'd shaken hands on the deal. It was now down to Janine to sort out the logistics of putting on one of the biggest shows LA had ever seen. The studio album was almost complete and the new material sounded amazing. She knew that once Pete was back with the band the concert would make history.

Fleur was on her way home after finishing late at police headquarters. She'd accepted a lift in one of the cruisers, but the two officers had picked up an urgent request for assistance, so she'd got them to drop her off at a drugstore where she could pick up a coke before calling a cab. The area wasn't the best they could have chosen, with a predominantly Hispanic population, but as long as she didn't hang around too long she knew she'd be fine. She went into the old shop which was on the corner of a block of rundown premises mostly boarded up. She acknowledged the old Mexican who was serving behind the checkout and wandered to the back of the store to where the fridges, full of cans and bottles were humming.

She had just picked out a cold cola when she heard the front door open and raised voices. Standing perfectly still she listened, as two young males with Mexican accents shouted at the old man to give them the money from the cash register. She silently crept forward and peeped around the row of shelves. She could see one of the youths had a gun pointed at the old man who was refusing to open the till. She knew she should call for backup, but noticed how the one holding the gun was getting more agitated.

As she watched, the old man raised a baseball bat he had found from somewhere and swung it at his attacker. The robber stepped back to avoid the old man's swing and calmly shot him. Fleur knew she had to react and her training suddenly kicked in. Forgetting about backup, she drew her gun and stepped out into the aisle facing the gunman.

"LAPD! PUT DOWN YOUR WEAPON!"

She held her gun in front of her pointing it at him. The young man turned towards her. He could see she was nervous.

"Eh chica! You got big cojones. What you gonna do, shoot me?" He and his accomplice laughed.

Fleur didn't move and repeated her request.

"I SAID PUT DOWN YOUR WEAPON!"

The gunman looked at his friend and in the same movement swung back round and fired at Fleur. But she'd been one step ahead of him and had shifted her stance offering him a narrower target and his shot missed her.

Without hesitating she squeezed the trigger and fired, hitting him in the chest and knocking him backwards. He fell onto a display of tinned beans which collapsed sending cans rolling everywhere. Fleur continued to point her gun at the other robber while calling for assistance. Within minutes she could hear a siren, and the two officers who had earlier dropped her off ran into the shop with their guns drawn. Recognising their colleague, they listened to her account of what had just happened and called an ambulance for the shopkeeper. He was still conscious, but said nothing as he was taken out on a stretcher.

The gunman was pronounced dead by the paramedics, but they had to call the police surgeon to make it official. As the officers were taking the other robber out, he suddenly started shouting that the woman police officer had killed his friend in cold blood. He said he saw everything and that she just walked out from behind the shelf and shot him dead. Fleur insisted she had identified herself and told him to drop his weapon, but he fired at her first. She was visibly shaken, and one of the officers took over and arranged for another car to pick her up and take her back to headquarters where she could make her statement.

Captain Lewis was waiting when she arrived and led her into his office. He was calm and assured her everything would be OK, but police protocol was that there would have to be an investigation and she would be temporarily suspended. He called Anna Delaney to come in and take charge of the case.

Eventually after giving her statement Don arrived to take her home, and allowed her to shed her tears on his shoulder as they walked back to the car. It was difficult trying to convince her that it was one of the oldest tricks in the book; to accuse the police officer of being the aggressor, and that Anna was the best person to be in charge.

Detective Anna Delaney had sat down in the interrogation room opposite the Mexican youth who was called Carlos. His legal representative was next to him looking stern, but she didn't look at either of them. Instead she spread her papers out on the table between them, and leaned back in her chair clicking her pen. The youth was still high on whatever stimulants he and his dead partner had been taking, and fidgeted on his chair before starting to talk loudly and fast.

"She did it! She killed him! Police bitch! Didn't give him no chance, just pulled the trigger. Killed Jose!"

Anna sat calmly listening to him, waiting until he stopped. "Did you and Jose often go out and rob drugstores?" The solicitor made to interrupt her but she raised her hand to stop him. "I'll rephrase that. Did you know Jose was carrying a loaded gun?"

"Yeah man, he always got a piece. We Tarantulas. Just in case the Maños are around."

Anna noticed the small tattoo of a spider on his neck. "And had Jose ever used it before?"

"No man, it was like, for safety."

"And so when Jose threatened the shopkeeper with it and asked him to open his till, that was just for safety, yes?"

"The old man, he swung a baseball bat at us."

"And that warranted Jose to shoot him?"

"No man, he only meant to scare him. Just so he'd hand over the money."

Anna leaned back again and stared at the large brown stain in the corner of the ceiling.

"Then, according to your statement, Junior Detective Rosario just appeared and shot your friend Jose without warning and in cold blood?" She leaned forward again.

"Yeah she just shot him right in front of me. I saw it all."

"And Jose didn't fire at her first?"

"No man, it all happened so fast."

Anna tidied her pen and papers and stood up.

"That's all for now." She walked out and closed the door behind her. She went into the observation room where her boyfriend Captain Lewis was watching.

"I need to go and speak to the old man. He's been released from hospital. It was just a flesh wound."

Janine had arrived back early the next morning, and on the way home from the airport Don had explained what had happened. Fleur was sitting quietly on the balcony when they walked in and immediately ran over to Janine bursting into tears. When she had eventually calmed down they all sat around the table and Don took charge. He went through the process that would take place, and emphasised that Fleur had nothing to worry about. Anna Delaney was a good detective, and despite her and Janine not seeing eye to eye on certain things he was sure she would sort it out.

Janine then went on to tell them how her visit to Pete had gone and that he'd agreed in principle to perform. It was now up to her, Don and Manny to put together the plan for one of the biggest concerts Los Angeles had ever witnessed, and they had a year to do it.

Detective Anna Delaney and her newly promoted partner Detective Joe Budd pulled up outside the drugstore where the shooting had occurred. The police crime scene investigators were there, and after signing in they went through to the back where the old shopkeeper was sitting with his wife and daughter. The daughter spoke English and was able to translate for her father. Anna suspected straight away something was wrong when she asked him to describe what had happened. His reply was translated by his daughter. "He says he can't remember what happened."

Anna remained calm but addressed the daughter. "Has he had a visit from anyone?"

The daughter asked him and he replied forcibly. "He says no one has been. He just can't remember."

"Does he have CCTV in the shop?"

"He says it doesn't work."

Anna thanked them and went back out into the shop and found the head CSI. She stood in front of the till and turned to her right to face the back of the store.

"Fleur said he fired at her and missed. See if you can find a slug in the back wall over there," she said pointing towards the rear of the shop.

Minutes later they had the bullet. It would be taken back to hopefully be matched with the one they'd already found which had wounded the shopkeeper. They were just leaving the store when the old man's daughter came running out.

"Two men came to visit my father this morning. I don't know what they said, but he's been really scared ever since."

"Could you describe them?" Anna asked her.

"Not really, but one of them had a big spider tattooed on his neck."

Anna looked at Joe Budd.

"Thank you for your help."

They drove back to headquarters and a visit to Ballistics.

The officer in charge of the Ballistics department was sitting at his microscope when Anna and Joe entered. His laboratory was a windowless room hidden away in the bowels of the LAPD headquarters just big enough for the three of them. Under normal circumstances their case would take its place in the queue, which would sometimes be a week before he could attend to it but, as it was one of their own officers involved, he had fast-tracked it, and was examining the unique striations on the two bullets from the drugstore. He sat up with a triumphant smile and invited Anna to look through the twin eyepieces. She could clearly see two bullets side by side with exactly the same markings, undoubtedly making them a match and proving they had been fired from the same gun.

Anna breathed a sigh of relief. Fleur had been telling the truth when she said the gunman had fired at her first. Now all she had to do was break his partner.

She was just about to go home later that day when her phone rang. It was the Ballistics department again, asking if she could come down to see something which might be of interest to her. Wondering what could be so important, she made her way back down to the laboratory where the same officer was waiting for her. He explained after she had left he did a bit more checking of the bullets with recent outstanding cases, and found that the same gun had been used on another robbery and a drive-by killing.

Anna gave him a hug making him blush and almost sprinted up the stairs back to her office. Suddenly the case had become far more interesting.

Captain Lewis had been happy to call Fleur asking her to come to his office for a meeting. Anna Delaney was sitting with him when Fleur walked in, and she explained what they had discovered.

The good news was her suspension had been lifted, although Captain Lewis wanted her to remain in the office until they had a result on the holdups and drive-by shooting. Anna was going to question Carlos again, and they were happy for Fleur to watch from the observation room.

Carlos was slouched in his chair when Anna walked into the interrogation room. His legal representative was sitting next to him as Anna sat down and placed the papers she was carrying on the table. "Good morning Carlos, I trust you slept well," she said.

"Listen, when you gonna let me go? I told you what happened. She shot my friend in cold blood. When you gonna charge her with murder?"

Anna was relaxed as she shuffled the papers and picked out one of the sheets. "Are you still sticking to your statement that my colleague fired without warning, and your friend Jose didn't shoot at her first?"

"Yeah, that's right. She just shot him dead."

She slid the sheet across the table towards him. "So how come we found a bullet from Jose's gun in the wall behind where Junior Detective Rosario was standing?"

Carlos was quiet and looked at his attorney who was busy reading the paper.

"And more bad news for you Carlos. The gun belonging to Jose was used in another robbery and a drive-by shooting. So it looks like you're looking at a long stretch inside for aiding and abetting."

She stood up ready to leave when Carlos shouted for her to stop. "Look these robberies weren't my idea. It was Jose. He wanted to show he was a big guy in the Tarantulas. He made me go with him."

Anna returned and sat down again. "OK so let's go back over everything you've said. Did junior detective Rosario shout a warning to Jose?"

Carlos nodded.

"I need you to say yes or no for the record," Anna said.

"Yes."

"And did Jose fire at junior detective Rosario first?

"Yes."

In the observation room Fleur breathed a loud sigh of relief as she watched with Captain Lewis. Back in the room Anna wasn't finished.

"Who ordered the drive-by shooting?"

"It was one of the Tarantulas. They wanted to send a message to the Maños and Jose volunteered."

Anna stood up again and walked over to the door.

Carlos shouted after her. "Hey what about me? I helped you here, what do I get in return?"

Anna stopped and turned round to look at him. "Once we release your statement to the press I'm sure your friends, the Tarantulas, will take care of your reward."

She opened the door and walked out leaving Carlos realising he'd probably just signed his own death warrant.

Fleur was holding back her tears, and gave Anna a hug when she walked into the observation room.

"Thank you so much," she said as Anna looked slightly embarrassed.

"It's not me you have to thank, it's the guy down in Ballistics who spotted the match with the shooting."

Captain Lewis who had been standing watching gave his secret girlfriend a squeeze, and Fleur smiled at the small show of affection. Janine might not be her biggest admirer, but Detective Anna Delaney had just saved Fleur's police career from stalling before it had chance to get started, and for that she would be eternally grateful.

CHAPTER FORTY-SIX

After Janine left to fly back to Los Angeles, Pete and Judy sat down and had a long conversation about what he'd agreed to. Judy expressed her apprehension about his health, and whether he would be able to deal with the stress of travelling and then performing on such a massive scale. But Pete was adamant he could deal with it, and reassured her he was fine and couldn't wait to get started.

What he hadn't told her was the increasing pains he was suffering on a regular basis. He knew he couldn't go to the doctor because that would only involve more tests, and every possibility of him being advised not to travel. So he resigned himself to suffering in silence. The new album was sounding great and the recording was finished. All that remained was Dave Sanchez mixing and mastering it over in LA, and Pete had the greatest faith in his ability. Performing it live was another kettle of fish and would be a challenge, but Janine had assured him that his original band were ready and waiting, and along with Rick he knew it would sound amazing. It was a long time since he had last performed on any kind of stage never mind a huge concert. Granted he'd played his guitar at a few parties and he'd been practising a lot in his studio, but it was the stamina required that concerned him the most. Maybe Judy had a point; maybe he couldn't do it again on such a big scale. He sat in his studio holding his precious Gibson Les Paul Gold Top and suddenly shook his head.

'For fuck's sake listen to me. Since when did Pete Peterson become a quitter! I'm gonna play this concert, whatever it takes babe!' He laughed to himself at the phrase Gerry Fortuna was so fond of using. 'Yeah, whatever it takes babe! Are you ready LA? Cos' Pete Peterson is coming for you."

Since getting back home Janine had got straight on the case with Don and Manny. To overcome the problem of his flying to LA they had decided to hire a personal jet to fly him from Birmingham Airport direct to LAX. The whole family could travel together and they wouldn't have to worry about scheduled flight times. Also she'd used Manny's connections and reserved the Presidential Suite in the Beverly Hills Hotel for the weeks before and after the concert, so Pete could rehearse with the band in Whitland Studios. The figures she'd calculated for the prospective earnings from ticket sales, broadcasting revenue and record and DVD sales were incredible. The advance sales on the album, once news leaked out of the plans for the concert, had already made it a Platinum disc. Now all Pete had to do was keep it together and pull it off one last time. Easier said than done, but she knew he could do it, if not for himself then for his family.

It wasn't going quite to plan back in the UK. Pete's son Rick found his dad collapsed in the recording studio one night, and although they'd managed to keep it from Judy, he was anxious whether Pete would be able to make it. For his part, Pete had promised him he would remember to take his tablets from now on, and things had gradually improved, but it was still a worry.

One thing that Pete had omitted to tell Dave Sanchez when they were recording the new songs, was that most of the guitars on the tracks had been played by Rick. Pete was so impressed by his son's ability he had allowed him to play on the new material, and Dave hadn't noticed. At least that was what Pete thought. Unbeknown to him, Dave had realised what was happening, and not wanting to upset the flow had kept quiet, marvelling at Rick's playing. So when he found out Pete had insisted on Rick playing with him, Dave knew it would be fantastic. Plus he had a very special surprise up his sleeve for when they all came over.

Don and Janine had been relieved when the investigation into Fleur had been dropped, but they were concerned that she didn't seem to have any interest in the opposite sex. Don knew what it was like working in the LAPD, and how easily it could take over your life. It had happened to him, and he didn't want the same thing with Fleur. Both he and Janine had encouraged her to go out with as many young guys as possible, but she didn't seem bothered. Her excuse was the guys her age were boring and spent their spare time playing computer games. She was still young and had plenty of time, but Don didn't want her missing any opportunities. She was growing into a very attractive young woman, and as much as he felt protective towards her, he knew she could handle herself as she had shown in the incident in the drugstore. At least the teasing had stopped in the office since they realised she was capable of shooting to kill. In fact she had been recommended for a citation for bravery which she had initially dismissed, but Don had insisted she accept. As he pointed out 'things like that don't come along every day', and what she had done deserved recognition. So she had reluctantly agreed, and had been presented with her award in front of the whole headquarters. Don and Janine had been invited to attend, and were proudly photographed with the recipient.

Lucy had met Lorenzo Di Bonturo on her last trip to Europe representing Great Britain in the World Championships. He was the star rider of the American team, as well as being extremely attractive. He had made it quite obvious he was interested in Lucy but the security at the event was tight, and they had only managed a fleeting moment to say hello and exchange contact numbers. Since returning to the States he had sent her a string of messages, and now finally she was going to be not only in his country, but in Los Angeles where he lived.

She had done some research, and found out his family were extremely rich. His great grandfather had owned what was regarded as the best pasta factory in Sicily, and when his grandson, Enzo's father, had moved to LA in the 70s, he had gradually built up the family business, and was now a multi-millionaire supplying pasta to all the top restaurants in the country. This had enabled Enzo to live the life of a playboy, and riding had become his passion. He was extremely good at it. Up until now Lucy had managed to keep him a secret from the rest of the family, but when she reached California she was determined to meet up with him again. Hopefully this time for more than merely a polite greeting.

The week before the flight Pete had reluctantly agreed to visit his doctor for a check-up, and after being subjected to a strenuous full body examination he sat nervously in his surgery waiting for the results. For once his GP had relatively good news. The fact he had been taking his medication on a regular basis and cut down on his alcohol intake, meant a slight but measurable improvement. Providing Pete promised to keep it up he was happy for him to make the trip. He emphasised however that under no circumstances should Pete be subjected to constant stress.

Judy's thoughts as they drove away were how was Pete going to be able to play such a huge concert without being subjected to stress? She decided not to bring down his mood by saying anything.

Rick was trying to control both his nerves and excitement about the trip. He was nervous because he didn't want to let his dad down, especially as Pete had made such a big deal about him playing with the band. But at the same time he was excited because it was the chance of a lifetime, and there was no way he was going to mess up. He'd spent every spare minute playing along to the new material, as well as some of Pete's greatest hits which he knew would be included in the set. Pete on the other hand had been taking things easy since the relatively good news from the doctor. He'd spent time in his studio singing along to the songs, and was happy with how his voice sounded considering the length of time since he last sang in anger. He secretly wasn't worried at all about Rick. He knew his son was good enough, and in fact recognised he was already world class. For that reason he couldn't wait to get started.

And finally the day arrived for the trip. The four of them had spent the previous day packing, unpacking and packing again. Now Judy sat in the minibus with everything safely in the back. Pete's Gibson Les Paul and Rick's Fender Telecaster were the last to go in.

The Gulfstream G200 sat on the tarmac at Birmingham Airport as they were driven out to board. Immigration and customs had been effortless, and Pete thought back to the first time at Heathrow when he met Vince Boyd and the actor Charles Morse. And how Janine had been starstruck. It was amazing how things had changed on his journey. And here he was again about to set off on probably his last trip to America.

The private jet was unbelievable. Huge leather armchairs and a steward to take care of their every needs. It was roughly an eleven-hour flight but Pete was happy to just lie back and sleep until they arrived. He loved the excitement on the faces of Rick and Lucy and how Judy took everything in her stride. She could be facing another huge challenge soon he thought. She reached out and held his hand tightly as the jet accelerated down the runway and lifted off into the grey skies over the Midlands. Soon they would be in the sunshine, and he reclined his seat closing his eyes.

The flight was completely uneventful with not a hint of any turbulence, and as they approached LAX Pete awoke to see the sun glinting off the waves of the Pacific. Their journey through US Immigration was trouble free, and this time, because the guitars had travelled with them on the jet, there was no repeat of the first time Pete had landed on US soil. He smiled at the memory, although he couldn't recall the woman's name.

Janine and Don were waiting in Arrivals, and after huge hugs all round they guided them to the enormous people carrier waiting outside.

Janine had arranged a small welcome party for when they arrived at the hotel. She was well aware of the time difference, and the fact that their bodies thought it should be eight o'clock in the evening although it was only midday LA time. She knew they would be tired, but the trick was to stay up and go to bed local time which would hopefully stabilise their body clocks.

Waiting in the bar was Pete's band - Dave, Marshall and Randy - and with them Vince Boyd. Judy had first met the guys when Pete played Birmingham and the band were stunned to see the tiny baby she'd brought to the dressing room at The Lexxicon was now a tall handsome young man, and along with his attractive sister they made a wonderful family.

Eventually the flight caught up with them and one by one they slipped away to bed, leaving Janine, Don and Vince at the bar. It was good to see Vince again, and he reminded Janine of the last time they'd met in the bar, and how he'd rescued her from a very frisky Charles Morse. She thought about how she'd never actually spoken to Charles since that night, and hoped their strange friendship hadn't been broken by it. She determined to get an invitation to the concert sent to his agent.

Lucy was wide awake, lying on her bed watching a dreadful American chat show. She'd tried everything but couldn't sleep, so she decided to call Lorenzo. It was a long shot, but he used to send messages to her at all times of day and night, so she thought she'd take a chance. The phone rang twice and it was picked up but no one spoke.

She whispered into the mouthpiece. "Hello? Lorenzo?"

"Who's that?" It was him.

"It's me, Lucy."

"Lucy? Hey babe is it really you? Where are you?"

"I'm in LA. At the Beverly Hills Hotel."

He whistled. "Hey that's real posh. How come you're there?"

"I'm here with my family. Don't you remember? I told you, my dad's playing a concert at the Memorial Coliseum."

"Hey yeah, that's really cool."

"So I was kind of hoping we could meet up seeing as I'm here?"

"Yeah, sure. Say how about we go riding? You could come out to the ranch."

Lucy thought for a minute. She was going to have to come up with an excuse to get away but she'd heard Janine invite her mum over to Hermosa Beach while her dad and Rick were rehearsing.

"That would be cool. How about tomorrow?"

"I'll pick you up at the hotel," Lorenzo said.

"No. Hang on; I'll have to meet you. I'll say I've been invited by the American team and we're going to go riding. My mum doesn't know about you yet."

He laughed. "Hey no problem. So how about you meet me on Sunset? There's a coffee place called *The Mean Bean*. I'll meet you in there at eleven. And don't worry about riding gear we've got loads out here."

She put the phone down and shivered with excitement. 'Lorenzo Di Bonturo, all to myself. Wait until the others in the team back home hear about that!'

CHAPTER FORTY-SEVEN

Pete and Rick had arrived at Whitland Studios refreshed and ready. Randy had set up the studio for them with a cabinet and amp and a twin combo. Marshall had put his kit in the night before and Dave Sanchez was just finishing wiring his keyboards when they walked in. It took a matter of moments before they were playing the groove for one of the new songs on 'One Last Encore' and Pete sat back as Rick strummed the chords. There were admiring smiles all round as the band eased through the arrangement, although Pete wasn't about to tell the others that it was his son who'd played the guitar in the first place. One after another they effortlessly played the tunes, and by the time they decided to take a break they had completed half the set already.

As they were about to leave the studio to get a drink, Dave called Rick and Pete over to where he was set up and pointed to a battered guitar case. "I've got a present for you, Rick. Open it."

Rick bent down and opened the case to reveal an old white Fender Stratocaster which had obviously seen some use. He picked it up and plugged it into his amp and played a couple of riffs. Pete was standing back watching with a puzzled look on his face. He looked at Dave. "Is that what I think it is?"

Dave gave him a knowing smile. "I found it under a load of stuff at the back of Henry's secret room and took it out before the cops arrived."

By now Marshall and Randy had joined them. Randy suddenly let out a shout. "Fuck! It's Hendrix's Star Spangled Banner Strat! But they said it had disappeared."

Dave nodded. "Yeah into Henry's secret room. So what do you think Rick? D'you like it?"

Rick was lost for words. "It's incredible." He went to take it off.

"It's yours," Dave said. "Better someone like you play it than it end up in a glass case in some millionaire's house. Enjoy it man; it suits you."

Lucy was sitting in the coffee shop when Lorenzo walked in. He was wearing a short-sleeved white linen shirt and a pair of tight denim jeans, and with his sun-streaked hair looked like one of the stars you'd see in Hollywood. He spotted her straight away and came over to her table, leaning over to kiss her on the mouth. She felt herself tingle as he took her hand and led her to his truck parked outside.

She had decided to wear something light and had chosen a pair of white jeans with a cotton top covered in large pink flowers with matching pink lipstick and a pair of white Converse trainers. She slung her cream leather purse over her shoulder as he gallantly opened the door for her and she climbed in. He was older than her and a lot more experienced according to the rumours about him, but Lucy wasn't a naïve little girl. She'd had plenty of moments at horse shows in the back of the transporter, and was well prepared.

They drove out to his parent's ranch in the Santa Clarita hills. Enzo, as he liked to be called, had given Lucy a running commentary as they drove. Slowing down he pointed to a driveway and mentioned the assassination of the mayor, Claudia Inestes, who had been a close friend of his father's.

They reached the Di Bonturo ranch which comprised a large single storey traditional farmhouse covered in bright red Virginia Creeper, and a block of stables similar in size to the ones that had burned down back home. Enzo took her to the tack room where there were plenty of boots, hats and jackets of all sizes. He left her choosing which to wear, and brought out two beautiful chestnut mares ready saddled for them to ride. Lucy appeared wearing a pair of black riding boots and a grey protective hat. Not the sexiest of attires, but it would have to do. Enzo had pulled on a pair of designer riding boots and his black helmet emblazoned with the Stars and Stripes. He looked every inch the superstar rider he was, as he helped Lucy to mount up.

They set off and rode across country for about an hour, ending up on a ridge overlooking the valley. It was a spectacular view and as they both dismounted Enzo pulled Lucy towards him and kissed her again. This time a little stronger and she could feel his excitement as he held her close. Her heart started to beat faster. She knew she should play hard to get, but she'd done that in the past and it had ended up a disaster. Instead she took his hand and led him over to a patch of grass, pulling him down and kissing him as they lay together. She was feeling herself reacting to him and slowly opened his shirt, leaning down to kiss his chest.

He started to moan softly, as she undid the belt on his jeans and slipped her fingers inside. Her heart was beating fast and she felt herself getting more excited. She was holding his erection and began to slowly rub it as she eased it out of his briefs. They were both breathing heavily as she pulled him towards her when he suddenly let out a groan. She realised what had happened and let go with a cry of disgust. Lorenzo Di Bonturo the famed American lothario had just blown his lot in her hand and was currently sitting with his head bowed. He looked up at her with tears in his eyes.

"Please don't say anything about this. I'm so sorry. I've kind of got this problem and I don't know what to do. I desperately want to have sex, but every time I get to a certain point the same thing happens."

She reached out and touched his arm. "Look, I'm sorry for making that noise. It was just such a surprise. I mean you were doing so well up to that point." She gave him a cheeky grin. "Maybe all you need is a little more practice." She leaned over and kissed him, at the same time pushing him back and starting to stroke him again. "Now let's see, where were we."

Afterwards they lay together holding each other. Lucy stroked his cheek. She could still feel him inside her. "You see. All it takes is a little practice."

He held her tight and kissed her. "Oh my god Lucy, you are incredible. I've never felt like that before in my life."

Lucy smiled and thought to herself. 'Mmmm. This could be the beginning of a beautiful friendship.'

CHAPTER FORTY-EIGHT

The day of the concert had dawned fine and sunny. The threatened rain had not materialised and the expectant seventy-five thousand sell-out crowd waited excitedly to take their seats in the iconic venue clutching their commemorative T-shirts, programmes and neckerchiefs. The sound check had gone perfectly and Janine, Don and Manny Oberstein stood side stage and smiled at each other while reflecting on the months of work it had taken to get to where they were at this moment. Now all the negotiating and flattering of the retired legend seemed worthwhile as they'd watched the man himself, Pete Peterson walk up to the microphone. He'd looked totally relaxed and with the tan he'd developed since arriving in LA, quite well, belying the real truth of his chronic ill-health due to the years of alcohol and substance abuse whilst touring the world promoting his multi-platinum selling albums.

His demand that he would only perform if he was accompanied by his son and his original band had turned out to be a master stroke. Word had spread like wildfire that something unique was going to happen and tickets for the show were changing hands for hundreds of dollars outside the stadium.

The rehearsals had been amazing and Dave Sanchez almost wished they could have recorded them as well, but now the time was here. He couldn't remember being so excited about a gig before in his life and, looking around at the others, the feeling seemed mutual.

The backstage area was buzzing. Pete's daughter Lucy had arrived with a handsome young man who she introduced to everyone as Enzo. They seemed to be quite attached and wandered off holding hands. Manny Oberstein and his son were there with various members of Westoria Records. Vince Boyd had arrived without his boyfriend much to Dave's surprise, and also, to Janine's astonishment, Charles Morse had turned up too. He had been very gracious when he met her giving her an embarrassed peck on the cheek. Fleur had phoned to say she was on her way. She'd been held up with something at headquarters but would definitely make it for the show.

Over the week they'd been in LA, Pete's wife Judy had finally relaxed when she saw how much he was enjoying himself, but now her worried look bothered Janine. She'd gone to his dressing room to make sure everything was alright, but without his shirt on Pete was noticeably frail, and already appeared exhausted from just the sound check. He looked up and smiled as she stood in the doorway.

"Hey, don't worry. It's only Rock and Roll! Whatever it takes babe," he said as he swallowed a handful of pills washed down with a large glass of red wine.

Janine saw Judy shaking her head sitting behind him. She was about to say something, but before she had chance Don saved the awkward situation by walking in with the set list for Pete. Just like in the old days when he'd been Pete's tour manager, the two still had a brotherly bond.

It was rapidly approaching showtime, and the tension was apparent as the band stood together waiting for the cue for them to go onstage. Then something magical happened. Pete walked out of his dressing room dressed in his hallmark black leather trousers and gleaming white shirt, and went up to Rick his son, hugged him and whispered something in his ear which made him smile. He had a special handshake for Marshall Thompson and Randy Jones, and a long embrace for Dave Sanchez. They all seemed to visibly relax and one by one walked onstage to a deafening roar from the largest crowd ever experienced at the grand old venue. Finally, the biggest welcome was reserved for when Pete strode out and stood centre-stage with his arms spread wide, acknowledging the tumultuous acclaim. His beaming smile hid the sudden sharp pain he felt, but ever the professional he picked up his guitar and slowly walked towards the microphone.

"Hello Los Angeles. It's been a while!"

The band came in bang on cue with the intro to 'In Flames', and the crowd erupted. One after another they played the hits, interspersed with tracks from the new album 'One Last Encore'. Pete cleverly orchestrated the proceedings taking the occasional solo, and then letting Rick loose playing the white Hendrix Stratocaster on the others. At one point in the show he allowed the momentum to pause. It was a poignant moment as he went over to each member, and as he individually introduced them gave each a heartfelt hug. He'd started with drummer

Marshall Thomas, then bassist Randy Jones and had given a long intro to his fellow songwriter and friend Dave Sanchez, all receiving huge ovations. The biggest acclaim was reserved for when he introduced his son Rick.

Janine, standing side stage with Judy, was finding it difficult to hold back the tears. In all the time she'd know him, she'd never seen Pete so prescient. What did he know that no one else knew? As he turned to give the cue for the next number he looked across, making eye contact with her and winked, then visibly cringed as he spun round to face the crowd. At that moment Janine knew there was something very wrong. She glanced at Judy who seemed to have had the same thought, but there was nothing either of them could do.

She looked round for Don and spotted him standing with Fleur across the other side of the stage. She couldn't help notice her daughter had the strangest look on her face. One of sheer rapture, and she was gazing unashamedly at Rick, Pete's son. 'Oh God! Not another Peterson!' she thought. But her attention was brought back to Pete.

Fortunately the band had reached the last number of the set because he was looking really tired. But with a burst of energy from somewhere, he finished the song. He called the others together at the front of the stage where they linked arms to take a bow. The crowd was going mad, and the band did a couple more bows before finally leaving the stage. Pete was barely able to reach his dressing room and collapsed as he came through the door. Judy had been prepared for just such an eventuality and immediately called for the paramedics on duty in the stadium. They were there in seconds, and after a brief examination carefully lifted Pete onto a stretcher fastening an oxygen mask across his mouth and nose. There was confusion in the backstage area as the crowd was shouting for more. The noise was getting louder and louder. The three members of the band, Dave, Randy and Marshall were standing together not knowing what to do. Rick was at his dad's side in the dressing room. Pete indicated for them to lift the mask off his face and said something to him.

Rick turned to the others. "He said to play 'Never Say Goodbye.'"

Marshall, Randy and Dave understood. It was the song he'd recorded with Vince Boyd which they'd rehearsed in case they needed an extra song. They started to walk back out on stage to huge cheers but Pete grasped Rick's hand and whispered to him.

"That was my Last Encore, but this is your opening number. I love you son. Don't let me down!"

EPILOGUE

Rick left the dressing room and stood outside on his own for a few moments with his eyes closed. Then he took a deep breath and walked on stage, picked up his dad's guitar and approached the microphone where Pete had been. He waited for the noise to die down and finally spoke.

"My dad's not too good, but he wanted you to hear this."

He then played the most emotional guitar solo that anyone in the stadium had ever heard, and with a voice reminiscent of his father when he was younger, he sang the first lines of the song...

"WHEN I LEAVE YOU,
DON'T EVER SAY GOODBYE,
ONLY HASTA LLEUGO,
UNTIL WE MEET AGAIN

Pete lay on the stretcher and listened. As Rick finished his solo he squeezed Judy's hand, whispered 'I Love You' and closed his eyes. She knew he'd gone and let out a loud sob which was drowned by the sound on stage and unheard by anyone else.

She looked around her. They were completely alone. One of the world's greatest superstars had just died and no one knew. Maybe it was for the best. Pete had obviously known what was going to happen and made sure Rick would be seen and recognised as his successor. She looked again at him and suddenly realised he had a smile on his face. He was at peace and his plans had all worked perfectly.

Janine was unaware of what had just happened backstage, but as Rick stood in front of her, she half closed her eyes and recalled watching a young Pete Peterson at The Hideout all those years ago. The same stance, swagger and talent in bucketloads. She looked across at Fleur and saw the look that used to be on all the admiring young girls. 'Sex On Legs!' they used to say. And right in front of her, baring his soul, was the next generation.

Don was standing by her side and when she caught his eye he was laughing, because he knew exactly what was going through her mind.

'Do I really want to do this again?'

'DAMN RIGHT I DO!'

The Pete Peterson Tapes continue with Book 4

'We All Love The Winner'

ACKNOWLEDGMENTS

Thank you so much for reading One Last Encore. Originally this was going to be the last book in the trilogy, but with the immense talent of Rick Peterson how could I possibly stop now?

I can't express how much fun I've had writing these stories and I hope you've enjoyed them as much.

I'd like to thank my publisher Andrew Sparke and his team at APS Books for their faith in my books.

Also my reading team of Steve and Tracey Adams and my lovely daughter Beth.

I also want to belatedly thank my old musical pal Dougie James who advised me about 'The Sport of Kings' and its pitfalls. RIP mate x

And finally to my best friend Cissy Stone for her never ending support and encouragement.

Des Tong

For more information check out:

https://andrewsparke.com/des-tong/

Facebook www.Facebook.com/destong and

X (Twitter) @TongAuthor

And if you have time, go to www.youtube.com/destongtv where you will find my Life Stories series, promo music videos I have created, and everything else I'm involved in.

FICTION FROM APS BOOKS
(www.andrewsparke.com)

Davey J Ashfield: Footsteps On The Teign
Davey J Ashfield Contracting With The Devil
Davey J Ashfield: A Turkey And One More Easter Egg
Des Tong: Whatever It Takes Babe
Des Tong In Flames
Fenella Bass: Hornbeams
Fenella Bass:: Shadows
Fenella Bass: Darkness
HR Beasley: Nothing Left To Hide
Lee Benson: So You Want To Own An Art Gallery
Lee Benson: Where's Your Art gallery Now?
Lee Benson: Now You're The Artist…Deal With It
Lee Benson: No Naked Walls
TF Byrne Damage Limitation
Nargis Darby: A Different Shade Of Love
J.W.Darcy Looking For Luca
J.W.Darcy: Ladybird Ladybird
J.W.Darcy: Legacy Of Lies
J.W.Darcy: Love Lust & Needful Things
Paul Dickinson: Franzi The Hero
Jane Evans: The Third Bridge
Simon Falshaw: The Stone
Peter Georgiadis: Not Cast In Stone
Peter Georgiadis: The Mute Swan's Song
Peter Georgiadis: Edilstein
Peter Georgiadis: A Murderous Journey
Milton Godfrey: The Danger Lies In Fear
Chris Grayling: A Week Is…A Long Time
Jean Harvey: Pandemic
Michel Henri: Mister Penny Whistle
Michel Henri: The Death Of The Duchess Of Grasmere
Michel Henri: Abducted By Faerie
Laurie Hornsby: Postcards From The Seaside
Hugh Lupus An Extra Knot (Parts I-VI)
Hugh Lupus: Mr. Donaldson's Company
Lorna MacDonald-Bradley: Dealga

Alison Manning: World Without Endless Sheep
Colin Mardell: Keep Her Safe
Colin Mardell: Bring Them Home
Ian Meacheam: An Inspector Called
Ian Meacheam: Time And The Consequences
Ian Meacheam: Broad Lines Narrow Margins
Ian Meacheam & Mark Peckett: Seven Stages
Alex O'Connor: Time For The Polka Dot
Mark Peckett: Joffie's Mark
Peter Raposo: dUst
Peter Raposo: the illusion of movement
Peter Raposo: cast away your dreams of darkness
Peter Raposo: Second Life
Peter Raposo: Pussy Foot
Peter Raposo: This Is Not The End
Peter Raposo: Talk About Proust
Peter Raposo: All Women Are Mortal
Peter Raposo: The Sinking City
Tony Rowland: Traitor Lodger German Spy
Tony Saunders: Publish and Be Dead
Andrew Sparke: Abuse Cocaine & Soft Furnishings
Andrew Sparke: Copper Trance & Motorways
Phil Thompson: Momentary Lapses In Concentration
Paul C. Walsh: A Place Between The Mountains
Paul C. Walsh: Hallowed Turf
Rebecca Warren: The Art Of Loss
Martin White: Life Unfinished
AJ Woolfenden: Mystique: A Bitten Past
Various: Brumology
Various: Unshriven

Printed in Great Britain
by Amazon

OTHER GARFIELD

Garfield Pocket Books
(over six million copies sold)

Pocket Books		Price	ISBN
Am I Bothered?		£3.99	978-1-84161-379-6
Don't Ask!		£3.99	978-1-84161-247-8
Feed Me!		£3.99	978-1-84161-242-3
Going for Gold		£3.99	978-1-84161-364-2
Gooooal!		£3.99	978-1-84161-329-1
Gotcha!		£3.50	978-1-84161-226-3
I Am What I Am!		£3.99	978-1-84161-243-0
I Don't Do Windows!	(new)	£3.99	978-1-84161-374-1
Kowabunga		£3.99	978-1-84161-246-1
Numero Uno		£3.99	978-1-84161-297-3
S.W.A.L.K.		£3.50	978-1-84161-225-6
Talk to the Paw		£3.99	978-1-84161-317-8
Time to Delegate		£3.99	978-1-84161-296-6
Wan2tlk?		£3.99	978-1-84161-264-5
Wassup?		£3.99	978-1-84161-355-0
Your Point Is?	(new)	£3.99	978-1-84161-370-3